SHADOW OF DECEIT: A CHRISTIAN ROMANTIC SUSPENSE

SHADOW LAKE SURVIVAL

SUSAN SLEEMAN

Published by Edge of Your Seat Books, Inc.

Contact the publisher at contact@edgeofyourseatbooks.com

Copyright © 2023 by Susan Sleeman

Cover design by Kelly A. Martin of KAM Design

This book is a work of fiction. Characters, names, places, and incidents in this novel are either products of the imagination or are used fictitiously. Any resemblance to real people, either living or dead, to events, businesses, or locales is entirely coincidental.

1

He'd come for her. Full throttle. The proof in Mia Blackburn's hand as he looked on—a threat in neat rows of shiny magazine letters glued to stark white paper.

Evergreen Resort will never be yours. Leave town now or you will pay.

She looked up at her father as his continued hatred burned in her hand, exactly like she feared would happen if she ever returned home.

Her mouth went dry, and her throat tightened. She desperately wanted to fire an accusation his way, but couldn't form any words.

"What is it you want, Mia?" He picked a speck of lint from his navy suit coat and flicked it into the air.

Wow. Nothing had changed. He'd flicked her upcoming answer away as easily as the fuzz. Right here in Shadow Lake's small post office with old brass mailboxes and worn tile floors.

Not unusual for him. He'd been acting this way since she'd turned thirteen.

Sure, she hadn't seen him for ten years, but she was used

to his behavior—expected it even. Then why did it sting so badly?

Tears dampened her eyes.

No. Don't you dare.

No way she would cry. She willed back the tears and located the armor she'd forged over the years. She slipped inside the steel plating and drew a deep breath.

"I never thought you'd want me to leave town bad enough to resort to threats." She thrust the page out, her hand shaking. "And why bother sending hate mail when you could threaten me in person?"

He grabbed the paper and stared at it. "This isn't something I would do."

She continued to watch him. "Interesting response. Not a definitive no. Just not something you would do?"

He shoved the paper back into her hand, his expression blank and unreadable. Moments ticked by. Painful. She was ready to squirm out from under his microscopic intensity, but willed herself to remain still.

He heaved a sigh. "As usual, you've made it very clear what you think of me. I won't respond to your accusation." He spun and exited the building, the small bell above the door tinkling in a cheerful chime, belying the lingering tension.

Through the window, she continued to track his progress as he strode down the street in the morning sunshine to his Mercedes. Why had she even stopped to get the mail first thing on arrival in town? If she hadn't come here, she wouldn't have run into her father.

He climbed into his shiny car and drove off. Her anger dissipated a fraction, and a hint of reason returned. She could breathe again, if only to inhale the lingering musky scent of the cologne he'd worn for as long as she could remember.

She let out a long breath. Dragged in another. She didn't want to be like this. Tense. Anxious. Fearful. Less than an hour in town and she'd returned to the motherless thirteen-year-old girl who cried herself to sleep every night, hoping for comfort from her remaining parent and getting none.

She thought she'd dealt with this pain. Put it behind her. Obviously not. But maybe she was wrong. Maybe he really hadn't done this. Maybe someone else wanted her to leave Shadow Lake to stop her from fulfilling the terms of her uncle's unusual will.

She had to live at Evergreen Resort for one full year to inherit the property, sleeping on site every night of that year. The only exemption her Uncle Wally, Evergreen's owner, had given her was that she could leave the property if her life was in danger.

Wally's lawyer said her uncle was concerned about natural disasters or a fire or something like that. But his intent was for her to make every effort to reside on the property unless it was completely uninhabitable. Then and only then could she leave, and the property would immediately revert to her.

An escape and yet not one. Even if the main lodge became uninhabitable there were cabins she could live in. She doubted he ever thought about someone trying to scare her away. But someone was doing just that. She didn't care about owning the land or even the money if she sold it, but she did care about honoring the wishes of the man who'd been more of a father to her for the past ten years than her biological father. She would honor him no matter what came her way.

The clang of the bells over the door sounded. Had her father returned?

She spun.

Oh no. Not her father, but equally as stressful. Maybe worse.

"Ryan." She whispered her ex-boyfriend's name like a desperate plea for help as he held the door for several townspeople coming in to collect their mail.

A jolt of awareness shot through her.

Don't look over here. Please don't!

He strolled into the space and she couldn't look away.

Gone was the boy, in his place a man dressed in worn jeans, rugged boots, and an army-green T-shirt that revealed his built chest. Sun-streaked blond hair was cut shorter, emphasizing his skin bronzed from the summer sun. His warm expression and greetings offered to the others spoke to his love of this small town and its people.

She needed to stop staring and escape the post office before he spotted her. She grabbed her mail from the counter and inched along the wall.

As if feeling her movements, he turned in her direction. Of course he did. As a wilderness guide and tracker, he had strong situational awareness, and she wouldn't get anything past him.

Recognition widened his piercing blue eyes.

"Mia, wow. Is that really you?" he called with genuine fondness as if they'd parted as best friends.

How could he seem so glad to see her? They'd been in love, but she'd left him to get away from her father. He should be angry with her. Or at the very least not want to talk to her.

He headed her way, taking long, powerful strides over the worn tile floor. He gave her a thorough once over, and the appreciative response sent her heart firing fast. The heated emotion in his expression hadn't changed since they'd dated. Not one bit.

And she hated to admit it—but she liked it.

"I almost didn't recognize you with the new look." He lifted a strand of her shoulder-length hair she'd straightened and dyed nearly black from her natural obnoxious red.

His touch sent Mia jerking back. She'd known she would see him. It was a given. He directed a wilderness counseling program for teens, and they leased cabins at her uncle's resort. She'd pictured this moment many times. So very many times. Had prepared great dialogue even.

So where was her voice today? Why wouldn't the words she'd imagined come to mind?

"I remember that look." His trademark crooked grin spread slowly across his face. "Got it every time I messed up."

Come on, Mia. Where are your quick, witty comebacks?

"You okay?" he asked.

"I'm fine." Fine? She wasn't fine. Not in any way. This was all too much. Way too much. First the threat. Then her father. Now Ryan.

All within the first hour of arriving back home when she'd hoped to fly under the radar.

"I'm sorry to hear about Wally," he said, filling her awkward silence. "I remember as a kid how I would count down the days until he left Atlanta to come up here for the summer. He was the best neighbor ever." His soft smile pulled the corner of his mouth higher. "And all the kids loved his camp. Takes a special person to give so much time and money to help underprivileged kids like he did. I'm gonna miss him."

"Me too," she managed to say.

Great. She sounded like a terrified mouse. Maybe it was better that she was tongue-tied or she might bring up their past in front of the others now openly watching them.

Small towns had big ears in public places. The last thing she needed was gossip about her served as the entrée on dinner tables all around town tonight. She'd had enough of that in high school. Enough to last a lifetime. Her fault. Totally. She'd sparked the local gossip often by rebelling against her father's rigid control, skipping school, and partying the night away.

Her best option was to cut this short. "If you'll excuse me, I really need to get to Evergreen and unpack."

In search of car keys, she used her hip to shift her purse dangling from her shoulder as she transferred the mail and letter to her other hand. She fumbled. The mail slipped, crashing to the floor.

Ryan squatted and reached for the alarming letter.

He didn't need to see the warning.

She lunged toward the page, but his hand whispered softly over hers and snatched up the paper to scan the message.

Exactly what she didn't want to happen. She wouldn't rip it from his hand and make it seem even more important. Instead, she slid the avalanche of envelopes into a stack.

"What's this?" Deep crevices of concern burrowed into his face. "You can't seriously be thinking about going there after receiving this threat?" He shook the paper. "We have to report this to my brother. Russ is the county sheriff now. And you need to stay somewhere safe until he figures out who sent the letter."

She couldn't let anyone know that her father had likely sent such a threatening letter. Not even Russ.

"We don't need Russ involved in this. Someone is just playing a practical joke." Not believing her own words, she couldn't look at Ryan and grabbed the threat from his hand. And she couldn't handle him being so kind to her after she'd hurt him so badly. She already felt guilty enough and didn't deserve his kindness and concern.

She bolted past him and into the crisp August morning.

"Mia, wait," he called after her. "You could be in danger."

She kept going, picking up her pace. His concern warmed her heart in way she hadn't felt since last seeing him. But she didn't need him trying to take care of her or his brother digging into her life. She'd been self-sufficient for years, and she didn't need any help. She'd be fine.

And talking to him? That was more dangerous at the moment than anything. She'd hurt him once. Badly. She wasn't going to hang around there and do it again. He deserved far better.

~

Ryan charged out to the sidewalk while Mia raced away from him as if he had a contagious disease. The high heels on her designer boots clicked on the concrete, and her suede coat swished on her hips. Not surprising that she'd bolted like one of the skittish horses they used for long trail rides with troubled teens.

She'd bailed on him once before. Cut him to the core. But he wanted to reconcile with her if she would consider it. Deep down anyway. It was the Christian thing to do for sure.

Then why did he also want to run in the other direction?

Because her eyes had seared into him, that's why. They weren't filled with the same defiance like when she'd taken off on him after high school. Not today. A vulnerability tugged at his need to help a woman in distress. Any woman, but especially her. And now? Now she was running away from him again. Horse galloping speed running away. Head-strong bolt. Not thinking—like she was prone to do.

Act fast. Strike back. Run. But she could be heading into danger.

He couldn't let that happen.

He rushed after the sound of her skyscraper heels

7

echoing down the street and into the sweet, tantalizing fragrance lingering behind.

Had his tomboy taken to wearing perfume?

She'd definitely given up the ratty jeans and slogan T-shirts she used to wear. Today, dark blue jeans emphasized her long legs. Perfect on the current Mia, who'd traded her fiery red curls for sleek black hair gleaming in the brilliant sunlight.

Her hand shook as she pointed the key fob at the door of a sweet red Mustang convertible.

Not at all a practical car for the rural roads in the area. She would know that, so why rent a convertible? Or had she moved back permanently and brought her car from Atlanta?

She glanced at him as she climbed into the vehicle at record speed.

She might not want anything to do with him, but he wouldn't let her get hurt just to spite him. He breathed deep to control rising emotions and stopped next to the driver's door. She ignored him and lowered the roof.

"Mia, please." He planted his hands on the door frame. "I get that we parted on bad terms, but don't do something foolish to get away from me."

She sat, rigid and unresponsive, hand on key, resting on the steering wheel.

He leaned into her space. "Give me a minute. After we talk, if you still want to go, I'll back off."

Her head slowly rose, and a gleaming strand of hair blew into her face. It would take some time for him to adjust to her new look. Not that he didn't like it. Layered hair curved softly around her face, giving her a sophisticated appearance that was all too appealing.

He reached out to tuck the stray strand behind her ear.

She beat him to it and fixed a tired gaze on his face. She

tapped her jeweled watch with a nail painted baby blue. "You have exactly one minute."

The distress in her tone almost stopped his words. Almost. "It's crazy to go to Evergreen alone. You never know what the person who sent the threat intends to do."

"I'm pretty sure it's from my father. He does such over-the-top things. Uncle Wally's will says I have to live at Evergreen for a year to inherit it. If I leave town the resort goes to my brother, David."

"David gets Evergreen if you leave?" Ryan took a few moments to process her announcement. "The lakefront location makes the property worth a chunk of change. Seems like David would be the logical person to want you to leave for the money a sale would bring."

She sighed and closed her eyes for a moment before locking them on him. "I'm not certain about my father. David *is* a possibility, but I doubt it. Uncle Wally told me David's doing well for himself."

"Yeah, that's what it looks like, but he's older than you and probably thinks Evergreen should be his." *And he didn't run away from here.* "Or at least the two of you should share it."

She blinked her long lashes. "I might've been gone for a long time, and don't know him anymore, but he always took Dad's side. And my father? Well..." She shook her head. "He always believed David was more deserving of everything. Why not this? And why not do his best to be sure David got the place." Her voice trembled.

Oh, man. She'd been through so much and had put up a huge wall to fend off any additional hurt when she had a heart of gold underneath. Ryan had gotten through the tough exterior in high school and wanted to hold her. To comfort her the way he'd done after one of her father's many rampages. But she'd ended things with him. Rejected him, and his touch wouldn't likely be welcomed.

He looked over her head and searched for words to keep her from rushing to the resort. But what could he say to make her see the danger she could be in when she didn't care about anything he had to say?

Maybe he could paint a dire picture. "You may be right about the letter coming from your dad, but are you willing to risk your life on it?"

She recoiled as if he'd slapped her. "I appreciate your concern. I really do, but I doubt anyone is waiting to pounce on me at the resort. Now I have to go."

She revved the engine, and he reluctantly stepped back. She flung her arm over the seat to reverse onto the street. He had no idea why she'd reacted in such a strong way, but he did know he'd failed her. Maybe seriously failed when her life depended on his help.

Back when they'd been a couple, he hadn't lived by his faith. Her either. He didn't know how she stood on it these days, but Ryan had God to turn to. The One who never disappointed anyone and offered the perfect solution to everything.

Ryan focused on the impressive stand of Douglas firs in the distance and lifted his face.

Please keep Mia safe and let her see my sincere desire to reconcile our past.

At the screech of tires, he snapped his head back to catch Mia's car shooting down the street. His gut tightened. Sure it did. She'd bolted on him again. How could it not be tight? But despite that, the familiar sight brought a brief smile. Mia might dress all prissy and girly now, but she remembered how to handle a car like a NASCAR driver.

Oh, yeah, she'd always been a little spitfire. Rebelling against her father. Getting into trouble left and right.

Calming down some the year they were together. Taking up again the last few days she'd remained in town after they'd split up, maybe as a way to show everyone she didn't need him.

And she *didn't* need him. Not now, anyway.

Instincts and the desire to do the right thing with Mia told him to jump in his truck and follow her. He wouldn't. Not with the threatening message. For that he should go see his brother. Get law enforcement involved.

Ryan could talk with her later—iron out the past. But not if the person behind the letter made good on his threat and ended her life.

2

At the end of Evergreen's driveway, Mia disconnected her call with the 911 operator and leaned her elbows on the steering wheel of her car, hands covering her mouth. Dense smoke clung to the resort's sign and surrounding treetops like cotton candy on a stick. The air was thick with fumes, not the sort of pleasant scents drifting from a campfire, but serious gusts of blackness settling into the open car and irritating her lungs.

Ahead, the barn flared in oranges and reds as if a meteor had streaked from the sky and plunged into the building. Heart beating erratically, she let the advice of the 911 operator settle in. Move to a safe location. Wait for the fire department to arrive.

That's what she should do, but what if Ryan still kept horses in the barn? If they were trapped, she couldn't sit there and do nothing. She had to try to rescue them.

She raised the car's roof then scrambled out. Intense heat slammed her face—forcing her back a few feet. She listened for cries of distress as she ran the length of the barn and circled the backside.

Embers shot into the air. Explosions—bullet-like pings

—struck the walls. The heat and caustic air seared her lungs. She raced around the other side. Howling screams from the consuming fire eased, and the heat receded a bit, allowing her to inch closer to the acrid smoke seeping through cracks in the walls.

A noise sounded from inside. A whimper. Quiet. Muffled.

Her imagination or a person?

Panting from exertion and the thickened air, she stopped and leaned closer to a window.

There it was again. A terrified mewl. A kitten or maybe a small child.

She grabbed a large rock. Shattered the window.

Blistering heat whooshed out. She lurched back and ripped off her jacket to hold it in front of her face.

"Is someone there?" she called, and swiped thick sweat from her forehead.

"Help!" The voice was tiny and high, fragile like a porcelain doll.

Who in the world?

Jacket over her fingers, Mia cleared the largest shards of glass and plunged her head through the opening. Her eyes instantly watered, her nose stung.

"Where are you?" she yelled through drying lips and squinted against the bitter smoke.

A petite tear-stained face peeked from a cave of hay bales. Mia guessed the innocent child to be around six or seven and terrified.

Oh, man. This is bad. Really bad.

Shadow Lake's all-volunteer fire department wouldn't arrive for some time. She couldn't wait. The child needed help now. Mia had to act.

"Don't be afraid." Mia lowered her jacket and offered a comforting smile. The abrasive air fought to take her down, and she drew in labored breaths as she scanned the space.

This end of the barn was quickly filling with smoke. She glanced to the left where a pickup truck had succumbed to searing flames. If anyone was in the truck there was no hope, but the child was another story.

"Come here, honey." Mia curled her index finger for the little girl. "I'll get you out of here and everything will be all right."

The child blinked in rapid succession then wailed like the fire siren Mia wished she would hear screaming up the drive. The girl darted back into her hiding spot, and her sobs ratcheted up.

"No! No! Don't hide!" Fear coursed through Mia.

Now what?

She had no other choice. None. She would have to go in and carry the girl to the window. The flames were advancing fast. She had to move quickly.

Mia cleared the remaining glass with her jacket-covered hand and slithered over the windowsill. Missed shards ripped into her stomach. Pain stabbed her side. Too bad. A child was counting on her. Sticky blood soaked her shirt as she inched forward and pushed aside hay bales. The child burrowed deeper into the haven like a baby animal threatened by a predator.

Mia leaned in and forced a calm tone to her voice. "Hi, my name's Mia. What's yours?"

"J-J-Jessie Maddox." Her voice was raspy and high.

Mia startled at the mention of the Maddox name. Was this child related to Ryan? Maybe his daughter even?

Jessie coughed hard enough to launch an entire country from her throat.

Not a time to think about Ryan.

Mia held out her hand. "Take my hand."

Jessie flung her arms around Mia's neck. The pungent smell of smoke clung to her soft blond hair, and her little body trembled. Mia draped her jacket over their heads and turned to the window.

The roof over the truck collapsed. A blazing support beam crashing down and blocking their escape. Sparks shot toward the rafters. The flaming wood ignited dry hay.

Jessie clutched Mia tighter, a deep wracking cough shaking them both. They couldn't reach the window, and the back door sported huge chains.

No. No. No.

Mia's leg muscles threatened to collapse under her.

Think of something. Now. Before the flames take hold and the smoke kills you both.

She scanned the only wall not engulfed in flames. There! In the door. Wally had installed a pet door for his dog. The opening wasn't big enough for Mia, but Jessie could fit through.

"I have a way out for you. Hang on tight." Carrying Jessie, Mia climbed from the bales and rushed to the back door. Her lungs were seared from smoke and exertion, and her eyes continued to water, reducing her vision. She dug deep for strength and set the child down to rip off the pet door's pliable flap. "Okay, Jessie. Climb through."

Jessie didn't move.

"Honey, please." Mia managed to get out through parched lips. "You'll be safe on the other side."

"My Uncle Ryan's a fireman. He'll come for me."

"He's probably on his way here to help us but it could take time. I need you to go out to meet him." She gave Jessie a quick hug and then maneuvered her little body through the opening.

Turning sideways, Mia wedged her head, one shoulder, and arm through the opening. She gulped outside air, and her lips cracked from the effort. Although tainted, the air was less dense—easier to breathe.

Jessie stood beside the door as if concrete encased her feet.

"Jessie." Mia tugged on the girl's ankle. "Go to the porch and wait until someone comes."

She nodded but didn't move.

"Go, now!" Mia shouted, though it pained her to yell at this physically and emotionally exhausted child.

Jessie snapped from her daze. "I'll bring Uncle Ryan to help when he gets here."

Mia nodded her approval and watched until the plodding little feet moved out of sight. Mia wanted to be rescued more than anything, even if that meant Ryan did the rescuing.

On the off chance she missed an escape route, she pulled her body back inside and looked around. Thirty feet to the wall of flames. Thirty feet of hay and dry timber waiting for fire to consume and destroy. Sizzling flames obliterated the path to the window and the front door. A miracle or the doggie door were her only ways out.

Please, I can't handle this. Coming back here is all I can manage. This is too much.

Really? She was calling out to God?

Hah! He hadn't answered her prayers for years. Starting with when He allowed her mother to die. Now Wally.

She was on her own again. The way God seemed to like it. Well, she wouldn't lie down and die.

Drawing her legs up, she crammed her upper body through the opening. The frame tore at the gash on her side. She bit her lip to control the pain as she squirmed and twisted.

Right, left, up, down, she pushed.

Nothing. No movement in the door.

She tried to ease back to find a tool to widen the opening, but she couldn't move. Not a fraction of an inch.

"Face it, Mia, you're stuck." Looking up at the smoke-filled sky, she relaxed her muscles to conserve her energy for another try.

The irony of her situation struck her as funny. She laughed in tiny giggles, hinting at a major meltdown.

She'd summoned all her courage to return to Shadow Lake and face the people who'd hurt her the most, only to die in a fire in her first hour in town.

~

Ryan stood on the porch of Evergreen's main lodge with his niece Jessie. His two-way pager continued to emit details of the fire from the holder on his hip. No need to listen. He had a clear view of the blaze and had all the information he needed. Mia was stuck and needed rescuing. End of story.

"Stay right here." He forced himself to ignore his niece's tears and pointed to EMT Lisa Watson. "Watson will stay with you, and I'll be right back."

He grabbed his pry bar and charged down the wide steps. Praying the rest of his all-volunteer crew arrived soon, he rushed toward the barn. Surging flames consumed the left half of the building, cracking and spitting glowing embers.

Life-sucking flames.

This was bad. Really bad.

Was he too late? Could it be a repeat of that horrible day three years ago?

Stop, Don't think about that now. Today you're on time. You will save her.

He charged at the roaring inferno. He had on his SCBA tank and mask to breathe clean air as he dodged raining debris like an Olympic hurdler—one weighed down by the heavy turnout gear.

If he hadn't been nearby when his pager went off, no one would be here to rescue Mia, and he would have another tragedy on his hands.

He careened around the corner.

Whoa! There she was. Mia. His Mia. No. Not his anymore.

She protruded from the doggie door, her upper body crumpled to the ground, but she was breathing.

Alive.

He should be able to pry her free before the flames reached her, but the smoke she'd already inhaled could still claim her life.

His steps faltered as uncertainty settled over him like the thick smoke billowing from the barn. This was too close for comfort.

God, don't let this end the way it did with Cara.

"Are you okay?" Ryan called to Mia.

She craned her neck at him, and her eyes fluttered open. Tears glistened, most likely smoke-induced. No sign of recognition.

She didn't know it was him. Probably a good thing.

"Did you find Jessie?" Her tone was frantic. "Is she okay?"

Yeah, this was Mia all right. Always concerned for others in distress. "She's fine. She's with the EMTs, and I called her dad."

"Good, I wanted to—" A harsh cough tore her words away. The spasm intensified, racking her body.

This wasn't good. He only had his pry bar.

He slammed it into the door and prayed it was tool enough to do the job. There was no one else to help, and there was no time to get another tool as the blaze flared to life around them.

Mia's heart threatened to explode as the heat surged toward her legs.

"Keep your head down," the firefighter yelled through his mask.

Ryan? Could it be him?

"I'm prying the door frame free. Should have you out in no time."

He shoved the big bar into the wood and rippling shocks traveled toward the ground. Waves of pain reverberated into her injured side. She held her lip fast between clamped teeth.

Heat advanced her way. She couldn't see the flames, but they were coming.

Angry. Seeking. Terrifying.

She drew her legs up as far as she could.

The firefighter jammed the pry bar in again. Could he free her in time?

Panic set in, and she couldn't breathe.

He repeated the thrust of his arms.

One. Two. Three. All the way to seven.

The wood gave way and the door frame split in two. The metal tool clunked to the ground, and her face plunged toward the dirt.

"Got you," he said, clutching her under the arms before she face-planted as he ripped the door free. "Can you stand?"

Could her legs hold her? That was the real question. She took an assessment. "My legs are numb."

"Then I'll have to carry you." He didn't wait for her

agreement but in one swift motion, slipped his hands under her legs and lifted her.

Sirens screamed in the background. *Finally.*

He gently settled her against his broad chest. His jacket scratched roughly against her skin.

Didn't matter. Not one bit. She was out of the blazing barn. Snuggled safely against his chest.

The wall he'd freed her from groaned and shuttered as if heaving a last breath. She looked over his shoulder as flames climbed the wall not five feet from where she'd been trapped.

"That wall's going to come down on us if we don't move faster." He picked up speed and crossed the grass with sure footing.

She caught sight of the nametag on his chest. Ryan Maddox.

It *was* Ryan. He drew her even closer.

Umm, nice. She was safe. Truly safe. At least for now. It'd been so long since she'd felt protected like this. Not since she'd left him to go live with Wally in Atlanta.

She concentrated on drawing the improving air into her aching lungs. He stopped by a vintage pickup parked far away from the danger.

Squatting, he settled her against a rusted wheel well. "There you go. Are you hurt?"

"Thank you. If you hadn't come along, I—" Her voice broke on a ragged cough, and she couldn't speak. She turned her face from the flames that would be searing into her flesh if Ryan hadn't arrived.

A screaming red truck bounced down the driveway. Several personal vehicles followed.

"Are you injured?" Ryan flipped up his visor and fixed warm blue eyes on her.

Oh, man. She'd hurt this man big time and now she owed him her life.

Keep your mind on the fire. Sort this out later.

"I'm okay." Mostly, she was. She'd worry about her side later. "How's Jessie doing?"

"She's with the EMTs and should be fine. Thanks to you."

"I didn't do anything anyone else wouldn't do. I was just in the right place at the right time."

"Not true. Many people wouldn't go into a burning building for any reason."

"How could they not after seeing a terrified child?" She shook her head, but dizziness assaulted her, and she stopped.

He eyed her until she wanted to squirm away from the intensity. "I know we didn't part on the best of terms, but we have to forget that for now and talk about the fire. We have to consider that someone started it to scare you away. Or even kill you."

"You're jumping to conclusions." Conclusions she'd reached but wouldn't speak aloud. "The fire could've started on its own."

"Possibly." He crooked his thumb at the barn. "Won't take long until we know for sure. Until then, I want you to stay away from Evergreen."

She coughed and leaned her head against the truck. "Would you mind if we didn't talk about this right now? I'm just thankful you came along when you did, and I'm happy to be alive."

"Okay, but we'll talk later." He laid a gentle hand on her cheek. "You're letting our breakup cloud the issue, and you're acting reckless."

She let his hand linger like a caress. The tender warmth

21

felt right. Like old times, before the breakup. When she thought they'd be together forever. When she believed in the pure love of a man. When she could afford to take chances.

That had changed.

She wiggled away from his touch. "I appreciate you rescuing me. I really do, and I'll forever be grateful, but you don't have to worry about me."

He lifted his helmet and ran a hand over his sweaty hair. "Forget we know each other. Listen to what my experience as a former deputy is saying. This isn't something you mess with. We should call Russ and tell him about the letter."

"You were a deputy?" Wally had never mentioned it. Not surprising. She'd told him she didn't want to hear about Ryan. It hurt too much to see the life she might've had if only she'd stayed.

Ryan nodded. "Got my master's in public administration and discovered I don't like being inside all day. My brothers made law enforcement look intriguing. I thought being a deputy would give me enough of the great Oregon outdoors."

He paused, a faraway look on his face.

"And?" she asked, and hated that she needed to know more.

"I was wrong. Tried it for four years, but when the executive director for Wilderness Ways resigned, I stepped in. I'm finally where I want to be. Doing that and working with the family business." He ran a finger around the collar of his turnout jacket. "So trust me when I say, we need to report this to Russ."

She didn't know what business he was referring to. She knew his parents closed their resort next door. Maybe that was what he was talking about. In any event, it wasn't important now.

Not when her return home without any drama with the

locals was at stake. "I don't want anyone to hear about the threat. I need time to process the news. Then I'll handle it my way."

"But this is too—"

"Please. No." Her raised voice brought on another round of coughing, sending shards of pain through her side. "I don't want everyone in town gossiping about me on my first day back. If you still care about me at all, you'll keep this to yourself." She locked her gaze on his. "Promise me you won't tell Russ. Or anyone."

"Fine." He released a frustrated breath. "I'll go along with you, but you should reconsider and tell him yourself."

"I'll think about it." And she would. Likely nonstop.

"She okay, Maddox?" A firefighter with Chief lettered on his helmet hustled toward them. She recognized him as one of her father's golfing buddies.

Ryan stood but didn't look away. "I sure hope so."

His double meaning didn't escape her, but she forced back the emotions.

The chief locked his inquisitive gaze on her. "You and Jessie the only ones in the barn, Mia?"

"As far as I know," Mia said, blocking out Ryan and paying full attention to the chief. "There's a truck in there, but it was completely engulfed in flames by the time I got into the barn. I don't know if anyone was in it, but at least Jessie escaped unharmed."

The chief faced Ryan. "Maddox, you go help Updike investigate that truck. Watson can take care of Mia."

"On it." Ryan let his eyes linger long enough to tug Mia's emotions back to life, then he took off.

As much as she tried, she couldn't help but watch him as he battled his way into the south end of the building. Fear for his safety crept over her. He was risking his life to check the truck for survivors. Something brave firefighters did every day.

But her heart didn't clutch for those firefighters.

What was up with that anyway? Did she have residual feelings for him or had his kind, compassionate behavior caught her off-guard, much like their past interactions had?

A female EMT came forward and squatted next to Mia, ending Ryan's captivating pull.

Good. Now Mia could get her mind off him and on to determining how to follow up on the fire. She would do what she always did in a time of crisis.

Regroup, organize, and control her steps. Keep her feelings at bay. Not let them get in her way. Especially with Ryan. With him threatening her emotional stability, she would need to formulate an extra-detailed course of action to keep him from derailing her plans.

She had to find the person who wanted her gone.

If not gone, dead.

3

Sitting on the lodge's steps, Mia steeled herself against the blustery gust of wind kicking up from the north and sliding crisply over her. Not that she minded the cooling air after the heat of the fire, but she didn't like the gusts of smoke. Nor did she like the way the resort employees stood behind barriers watching her.

Didn't seem to bother EMT Lisa Watson as she strapped a blood pressure cuff on Mia's arm. Lisa was in the same graduating class as Mia, but thankfully her former classmate didn't feel a need to reminisce.

Mia tried to relax and turned her head toward Jessie, who was sitting in the back of the ambulance. Lisa's partner ministered to the pipsqueak of a girl who asked non-stop questions about the procedures. Her tone was lighthearted, and she cracked up when the EMT tickled her, but a haunted glaze dulled the sheen of her eyes.

As a counselor, Mia knew kids had the ability to recover faster from trauma than adults. Children could also appear to be fine but suffer tremendous emotional scars.

She'd heard Ryan tell Lisa that he called Jessie's dad.

Jessie had to belong to the middle Maddox brother, Russ, or their oldest brother, Reid.

Didn't matter to her. As long as she wasn't Ryan's child. Not that Mia should even be feeling this way, but she was. So what if Ryan had married and had a child? Mia had left him. He had every right to move on and be happy. That's all she wanted for him was to be happy and live his best life.

Once she knew who Jessie's parents were, Mia would make a point of sharing the signs to watch for that indicated a residual problem so the sweet young thing didn't suffer long-term trauma from the fire.

"Do you know when Jessie's parents will get here?" Mia asked.

Lisa removed the cuff. "Jessie's mother died a year ago, but Reid is on his way."

Oh, no. Poor little girl. So young to lose a mother. Mia would talk to Reid about Jessie then. Last Mia had heard, Reid was an FBI agent in Portland. But if they were here on a weekday, maybe he'd changed jobs. Or they could be on vacation.

"He lives at the resort next door," Lisa said, answering that question. "But he's with clients on a wilderness hike. He'll get here as soon as he can."

"Clients?" Mia had no idea what Lisa was talking about.

"After Reid's wife died, he moved back here to be near family." Lisa wrapped the cord around the folded cuff. "The brothers took over their parents' property and started a company called Shadow Lake Survival. Cool business. They teach survival skills to city folks for big bucks. Reid runs it. Ryan works there when he's not on duty with Wilderness Ways, and Russ fills in if he's needed."

Interesting, but not a surprise. Their dad had led wilderness treks in the past, and the boys picked up the skills. And Ryan would love being in the outdoors even more.

Lisa planted her stethoscope on Mia's chest and frowned. "I hope Jessie's lungs sound better than yours."

Mia looked at the child. She seemed ready to crumple to the ground. Mia knew that haunting look. She now shared something with Jessie besides the fire. They were both living through the devastation of losing a mother. Mia had suffered from the loss for years but it had to be harder on the little girl.

Lisa pulled her stethoscope free and tsked. "We need to get you to the hospital."

No. Not the hospital. Her father was a doctor and could be there.

Mia sat up and tried to control her emotions. No way she wanted to come across as a crazy woman. "I'd rather not go unless it's absolutely necessary."

"Trust me. It's necessary." Lisa's somber tone left no room for argument. She summoned her partner on a radio and then strapped an oxygen mask over Mia's mouth.

Mia inhaled the cool oxygen and tried to relax even as pain ripped into her side from the transfer to the gurney and bouncing on the stretcher as they loaded her into the ambulance. Jessie sat on a bench seat below a wall of equipment. Mia offered a smile, maybe not visible through the mask, but Mia would do everything she could to help the child and a smile was about all she could offer at the moment.

Jessie's face mirrored Mia's emotions, and she slid off the bench to kneel near Mia's head.

"Don't tell anyone I was in the barn," Jessie whispered in Mia's ear.

Mia lifted her mask. "You weren't supposed to be in there?"

"No." Jessie clasped her hands together. "Since my mom

died, everybody says I shouldn't be alone so much. But I like to be alone to read."

Mia knew Jessie's pain. The constant ache never left her heart the first year after her mom died in the car accident. Not to mention living the next four years with a father who blamed her for causing the crash that took her mother's life.

Jessie tugged on Mia's arm. "Will you promise not to tell?"

Mia wanted to give this poor motherless child anything she asked for, but she couldn't. "I don't need to tell anyone, Jessie. They already know you were in the barn, or you wouldn't be in here with me."

"I could say I came in to save you."

Ah, right. Mia had seen this often in her counseling sessions with troubled teens. Jessie was hiding something. Her pained expression said there was much more at stake here than her father learning she'd been somewhere she wasn't supposed to be.

Mia clasped Jessie's tiny hands. "What's this really about?"

She jerked her hands free, and her eyes took on a defiant tightness. "I'm sorry about the barn, okay? I didn't do anything bad. I didn't start the fire. I was just reading. Wally used to let me read in there whenever I wanted to."

"I don't think the fire was your fault. It must have been an accident. Maybe electrical."

"Uh-uh. A man started it."

"What?" Mia's word screeched out.

Jessie jerked back.

"It's okay." Mia softened her tone. "You can tell me."

"A really big man drove a truck into the barn. He got out and poured something stinky on the hay. Then he threw matches on it. He said, 'This ought to scare her.' He laughed and left the truck behind. He was so scary. Big and no hair and mean looking." Her voice had continued to rise. "Do you think the man meant me? To scare *me*?"

Couldn't be Mia's dad for sure. He had plenty of hair. But one thing Mia knew for certain—whoever this guy was didn't mean Jessie. He meant Mia. Exactly as the letter warned her.

But who was he? Had her father hired him? Or perhaps the letter wasn't from her father after all?

"Jessie," Ryan called from the open doors. "Are you sure that's what you saw?"

"Uncle Ryan." Jessie hopped up and moved slowly toward her uncle. "Honest, it's what I saw. You're not mad that I was in the barn?" She peered at Ryan until his face broke in a warm smile, and he held out his arms. She bolted from the seat and charged into him.

Mia sat up and connected with Ryan's troubled expression as he peered over the child's shoulder. He pulled Jessie tighter and stared at Mia with the implication of Jessie's words stamped on his face.

The fire was no accident.

Still dressed in his turnouts, Ryan sat on the bench running the length of the ambulance. The combined odors of alcohol and cleaning disinfectant overpowered the smoke on their clothing. The space was tight, but Jessie had begged him to ride with her. He would do anything to distract her from her residual terror, so he persuaded Watson to accommodate the four of them.

Mia lay across from him, and Jessie rested on his lap, oxygen mask strapped to her face, reclining with her head crooked in his arm. He stroked her sooty hair as he bounced on the seat from the rhythmic beat of the tires spinning over rough pavement. After losing her mom to a battle with cancer, Jessie's emotional state had been tenuous before the fire. Now, she verged on breaking down. Reid better arrive at the hospital soon.

Then there was Mia.

He covertly checked her out. She'd closed her expressive eyes and drew oxygen through the mask, uncharacteristically quiet. What a brave front she'd displayed for Jessie. She'd kept it together, but her creased forehead revealed her pain.

The EMT said Mia should physically recover after some stitches to her abdomen and cheek, plus a short course of oxygen. Her injuries could've been much worse. She'd lived when others often died in similar situations. He'd dragged her from a near death. Maybe a certain death. From searing flames.

He let out a shaky breath and raised his head.

Thank You for sparing Jessie's and Mia's lives.

Jessie should be fine, but was Mia in danger?

Was the fire the first of a chain of events that would escalate until she left Evergreen—or was killed for staying? How could she refuse to seek Russ's help and forbid Ryan from calling his brother?

All first responders, volunteer or not, were required to report crimes, certain statements, or potential threats and certain recipients of abuse. Like bullying. Sending a threatening letter via the post office was a crime, but receiving one wasn't. While no law was being broken this could be perceived as a threat, but reporting it was a judgment call at this point.

He would honor Mia's request. For now. But he would also find a way to get her to talk to Russ. And if Ryan failed to persuade her, he would go behind her back and report it.

He had no choice. Russ had to hear about the lurking danger before it caught up with her.

Ryan's phone rang. Jessie startled, her gaze going to his, panic alive and living in her face like flames of the fire.

"It's okay, Tater Tot." Ryan made sure to use the funny nickname he'd given her as a baby and smiled. "Just my phone."

He dug it out. His assistant at Wilderness Ways name appeared on the screen. Worst time ever for a call from Ian. Didn't matter. As the director of the outdoor counseling program for wayward teens, whatever was going on in Ryan's life, responsibility dictated he answer. Even if they didn't have teens on-site at the moment.

"What's up?" he asked.

"We have a problem." Ian's serious tone set Ryan on edge. "Paul just called. His mother slipped into a coma this morning, and he won't make the first week of the program, if he comes at all."

Man. This was all Ryan needed. With the drop in funding, he'd already had to cut one staff member and up the ratio of students to counselors. One less counselor and the kids had a better chance of ending up back in juvie than working through their issues, ultimately dooming this pilot program for juvenile offenders.

Not wanting to increase the anxiety level cutting through the ambulance, Ryan fought to keep the turmoil out of his voice. "How's Paul holding up?"

"Says he's okay, but you know, man. He's hurting."

"Make sure to tell him we're praying for him and his family."

"Already done." A breathy intake of air and long exhale followed the clipped words. "We have to figure out what to do. There's no way we can function short another counselor."

"You have any ideas?" Ryan asked.

"One, but I'm not sure you'll like it."

Ryan tucked the phone under his chin and used his free hand to massage a tight muscle in his neck. "Doesn't matter if I don't like it. Tell me anyway."

"Okay, but hear me out before you shoot me down." Ian paused as if he believed Ryan might object.

Ryan would consider anything if it helped the kids. "Go on."

"The other day when we were talking about that Mia chick taking over Evergreen for Wally, you said she was a counselor. I know there's some sort of history between the two of you, but you could ask her to fill in until Paul gets here."

Ryan let his free hand fall to the bench with a thud. His stomach sank along with it. He looked at Mia. He was all for trying to work things out between them to ease the tension, but how could he handle her daily presence at work? Living with the constant reminder of what could've been if she hadn't bailed?

Easy answer—he couldn't. "I don't think—"

"I knew you wouldn't like it," Ian said. "But you have to admit it's a good idea. Sure, she doesn't have the wilderness counseling experience, but she does work with teens. You can at least think about it, right?"

Could he? "What about training? Our program is unique, and she hasn't participated in anything like it."

"We've got enough time before the students get here to bring her up to speed. Even without experience, she'd be better for the students than no one."

Ian was right. Ryan had to consider what was best for the kids. "I'll think about it."

"Don't take too long. Our campers get here in two days."

Ryan said goodbye and ended the call. He didn't need a

reminder of the looming deadline and the need to decide quickly.

He stowed his cell. He had to make things right with Mia —and the best way to get her to listen to him was to spend time with her. As a bonus, it gave him an excuse to keep her in his sight and keep her from stepping recklessly into whatever danger loomed ahead.

4

In the minuscule hospital bathroom, Mia moved her portable IV pole to the side and stepped up to the sink. She needed a shower. She absolutely did. Nothing would work as well to fix her appearance. Too bad the shower was out of the question. Doctor's orders to protect her wounds for twenty-four hours.

Not what she had hoped for. She'd wanted a quick trip to the ER. But her continued low oxygen levels made him opt to keep her overnight as a precaution. Still, she couldn't spend the night without doing something to clean up.

She rubbed a rough washcloth over her face, scrubbing at the pore-clogging soot, making sure to avoid the big gash high on her cheekbone. No matter the amount of cleaning, the steaming hot cloth wouldn't wipe away emotional trauma.

Even if it could, what would she wipe away first? She had too many layers to deal with.

She leaned closer to the mirror and gently dabbed around the sutured laceration.

Had her father really done this to her? He blamed her

for her mother's death and avoided her at all costs growing up, but this? Could he have done this?

He hadn't started the fire. Jessie's description of the man she'd seen proved that. But was he so cruel that he could hire a man to commit arson in an attempt to scare Mia away? And if he did, how was she going to prove it? No one in town would think the good doctor Thomas Blackburn moonlighted as a criminal.

"Mia, you in there?" a male voice, deep and vaguely familiar, called from her room. "I need to talk to you."

She hated anyone to see her in this condition, but his urgent tone moved her to respond. "Be right out."

She draped the cloth on the sink and finger-combed her hair. Yuck. Caked-in ashes clung to her fingers. It would take several shampoos to eliminate them along with the stench. She replaced the oxygen cannula back in her nose and freed the plastic tube stuck under the IV pump to exit the room.

Standing by the door, a tall, muscular guy with short blond hair kneaded his shoulder as he looked down at his feet. He wore black tactical pants and a polo shirt. He had a gun at his hip and badge on his belt. Not a patrol officer or he would be wearing a uniform. He looked up.

Mia checked his eyes. Oh, yeah. He was a Maddox. He'd changed a lot in the past ten years since she'd seen him, but now that she looked carefully, she knew this man was Ryan's brother Russ.

He studied her, taking in every detail as she eased into the room. His intimidating presence seemed to draw the air from the space. He offered a stiff smile. "Don't know how we'll ever repay you for saving our little Jessie."

The tallest of the Maddox brothers, with a wide jaw and a sharp intensity, he was grimacing, maybe in reaction to nearly losing his niece.

Trauma Mia knew all too well, flashes coming back. Fire

35

sizzling all around and no rescue in sight. She suppressed a shiver. "I don't need any thanks. I'm just glad I came along when I did."

"Let's sit." He gestured at the pair of gray vinyl chairs by the window and issued a full smile. The lines edging his eyes—likely from the stress of a career in law enforcement —fell away, and the fun but often serious teenager she'd once known bloomed in front of her.

Lifting her oxygen lifeline over the bed, she navigated the IV pole toward the chair and sat.

"I'm real sorry for your loss," he said. "Wally was a cool guy and everyone around here will miss him."

"Thanks," she said and left it at that before she let her emotions get to her and started crying like a baby.

"It's been a long time since we've seen you in these parts." He perched a booted foot on the wooden edge of the other chair, choosing not to sit when he'd fairly demanded she do so. "With the way you shot out of here after high school, I'm surprised you came back. Guess the money you'll get when you sell Evergreen is a powerful motivation to return."

Oh right. She should've known. He still wasn't one of her biggest fans. He'd thought she was corrupting Ryan in high school and had tried to convince Ryan many times to cut his losses and dump her. She'd heard his sharp tone before. Plenty of times.

Did he think she'd react to it when she hadn't back then? And what was with his assumption that she would sell Evergreen at the end of the year? Snap judgments were common around here. One more reason she'd stayed away. Still, she wouldn't correct him. Her motives were pure. Respect for her uncle's last wishes had brought her back. That was all that mattered.

She resisted showing any emotion. "If you're trying to bait me like in high school, I'm not biting."

His expression cleared but a touch of angst lingered in the depths of his blue, piercing eyes. "I'm here to take your statement about the fire. Nothing more."

"Sounded more like you were interested in passing judgment on me. Something you were once good at doing."

"I didn't mean anything by my comment." His sharp glare drilled into her. "As far as I'm concerned, that's in the past."

"Easy for you to say. You weren't the one wronged."

He ran a hand around the back of his neck. "Look—I'll admit I was hard on you back in the day. I should have been more understanding, what with the loss of your mom and all. But when you and Ryan started dating and his grades took a nosedive, I had to make you see what you were doing to him. Keeping him out half the night or even all night. Skipping school. Getting into drugs."

"And you thought going behind my back and trying to break us up instead of talking to me was the right way to do that?"

He shrugged. "Might've used the wrong method, but I had the right motive."

"You were David's best friend back then. You knew how much losing our mother changed our lives. I thought you'd be more understanding."

"All I can say in my defense is at the time I thought you were totally out of control. Figured you'd soon be seriously breaking the law." He gripped his raised knee. "I couldn't let you take Ryan down with you."

Mia could appreciate Russ's concern for his brother, but he'd worried in vain. "As it turns out, that wasn't a problem."

Russ cleared his throat. "I'm sorry if I was rough on you

back then and didn't handle things right. What say we put all of that behind us and get on with your statement?"

His offer to make amends was out of character for how he'd treated her that last year of high school, but he could've changed. He'd been a friend until she really started partying, and other than not wanting her to date Ryan, he was a good guy. So making amends with him? Yeah, that was a solid plan.

"I'd like that. Fresh start and all."

"Okay then. Good. I appreciate it." He pulled out a notepad and pen. "Tell me exactly what happened today."

The searing flames. Suffocating smoke. Terrifying emotions. All came flooding back. She didn't want to recount them, but she had to comply. She launched into the story, skipping the warning at the post office and replaying the rescue of Jessie with concise comments devoid of the emotions still tumbling through her.

"I'm sure by now you've heard Jessie saw a man start the fire." She fell back into the chair, mentally exhausted over telling the story.

He leaned closer, his eyebrows furrowed then released. "Now that you've had time to think about the fire, do you have any idea who would want to do this?"

Idea? Sure she did. Like her father. A fact she wasn't ready to share. "Not really."

"Not really, or no?"

She shrugged and looked down to keep him from noticing her evasiveness. She'd had years of practice in subterfuge with her father, but that had been so long ago she might've lost her touch.

Russ drew in air through his nose and held his breath while looking at the ceiling. Letting out the air, his expression tightened. "You're keeping something from me. It'd be easier on both of us if you'd cooperate."

She would cooperate as far as she could and still keep the threats in the family. When she was released from the hospital, she would confront her father again and put an end to the mess. Then Russ wouldn't have anything to investigate.

She nodded. "I'll spend some time thinking about who might have started the fire and get back to you."

A knock sounded on the door, and he turned to face it.

Mia's dad? She planted her trembling hands on the arms of the chair. Sat motionless. Bit her lip. Held it.

Ryan pushed through the doorway, the suspenders of his firefighting gear hanging limp, a gray T-shirt snugged tight across his chest. He strolled into the space and beamed a confident smile in her direction.

He came to an abrupt stop and scrutinized them. "Looks like I'm interrupting something important."

Russ's foot hit the floor with a thud that echoed through the room, and Mia expected him to tell Ryan to take a hike.

"Actually, as a firefighter you can help," Russ said. "I was just about to share arson statistics with Mia. Specifically, that it's often committed by a property owner wanting to collect insurance money. You can confirm that."

"Well, yeah." Ryan crossed the room, regarding his brother with a skeptical look. "But if you're intimating Mia torched the barn for insurance money, you're way off base."

Russ's eyebrow shot up. "Are you sure about that?"

"Positive," Ryan said without hesitating.

Russ's eyes darkened and fixed on Mia's face like a mighty lion eyeing up lunch. "On the surface, it doesn't look like you'd benefit from the fire. Not when the property would be worth more with the barn standing. But maybe you can't wait a year for the cash from selling the place. By destroying the barn, you'll get a nice settlement from the insurance company right away."

Her mouth fell open. "You're seriously considering me?"

His frozen features said it all. He believed she was involved in setting the fire. "Got to check out all possibilities."

"You're wrong, bro," Ryan said.

Mia crossed her arms, careful not to tangle her IV tube. "This is unbelievable. I was almost killed in the fire and you suspect me of starting it. Guess you don't really believe your niece saw that man."

"Sure I do. You could've hired him."

"Right. I hired a man to burn the barn down then went inside and got stuck."

"Accidents happen. You arranged to have the place torched but didn't know Jessie would be in there." He paused dramatically. "You couldn't let her die, so you saved her. Got trapped. Wouldn't be the first time someone got caught in their own fire."

She wanted to sigh, but held it in. "Seriously, Russ, focusing on me is a waste of your valuable time."

"Maybe."

She lurched forward. "But you—"

He held up his hand. "Don't worry. You're not my only suspect."

"Good, then you'll find the guy Jessie saw and your case will be solved."

"Or maybe I *will* discover that you had a part in it." He let his hand drift to his weapon as if he was expecting a problem.

Ryan seared his brother with a heated look. "You should be thinking about how to protect Mia from the arsonist, not blame her for the fire."

Russ stared at Ryan so long Mia thought the brothers might come to blows. Their behavior reminded her of the year in high school with Ryan. Russ insisting Ryan break up with her. Ryan passionately defending her. The pair nearly duking it out before parting angry and hurt.

Without breaking eye contact, Russ slipped his notepad into his pocket, his movements deliberate and slow. "I appreciate your wanting to protect Mia, but you're overreacting. The fire wasn't about physically hurting her. If it had been, the arsonist would have made sure she was in the barn before setting the fire."

Ryan faced Mia. His pointed stare made it clear that he wanted her to tell Russ about the threatening letter. She gave a quick shake of her head and hoped Russ didn't notice the interchange.

If he did, the controlled expression on his face didn't let on. "I apologize if I'm pushing too hard, Mia. I'm simply trying to locate the person behind the fire no matter who it is. The best thing you can do to clear your name is provide me with a copy of the will and think about anyone who might be behind the fire." Directing a sharp look at Ryan, Russ tromped out of the room.

"Excuse me." Ryan spun and raced after Russ.

Watching him exit in hot pursuit of his brother, a burst of vulnerability brought tears to the surface.

Was someone other than her father behind the fire? *Was* her life really in jeopardy? *Was* it the right thing to do to keep the letter from Russ?

Or had she left herself unprotected and in the path of a lunatic?

~

Ryan charged down the hallway, gaining on Russ, who rushed away as if he hadn't fired such unbelievable allegations at Mia. She wasn't guilty of arson, and Ryan wouldn't let Russ accuse her of it. His brother was likely letting their past color his behavior toward Mia.

Or maybe he was letting his general grumpiness get in the way. He'd served in the Marines, and after he got out, he started in law enforcement, loved every minute of it, and threw himself into the job for Portland Police Bureau. He became a detective, then a child was murdered on his watch, and he blamed himself. Drowned his problems in a bottle for a couple of years. Ignored his son and wife until she filed for divorce and got custody of their son.

He'd climbed out of the bottle and had come a long way since the divorce was final, but was angry about not being able to see their five-year-old son, Zach, very often. So if anything threatened people he cared about in any way, like Jessie being trapped in a fire, he dug his heels in and behaved like a pit bull.

Ryan caught up to him near the nurse's station and spun him around by the shoulder. "You're crazy, bro, if you think Mia is involved in this. She gains nothing until her year is over."

"Are you sure? Have you seen the actual will or did she just tell you that?" He paused and let his words linger in the air. "Who knows. If it's true, maybe there's a loophole. Maybe she does get the cash now if insurance pays out."

Money never motivated Mia. She could have changed, but the warning letter pointed to someone else setting the fire. If only he could tell Russ about the threat, Mia would be cleared. But Ryan had promised to keep his big mouth shut. He would give her until the end of the day tomorrow to tell Russ, and if she didn't, he would.

He clenched his fists and let his fingernails bite into his palms to keep from revealing the secret. "Mia had nothing to do with the fire. Nothing."

"You can't know that." Russ raised a skeptical eyebrow. "You planning on making a habit of defending her again?"

"She doesn't need me to defend her. She's done nothing wrong."

Russ cocked his head. "Then it's not a problem if I investigate her."

Ryan's hands itched to throttle his brother, but how would that help? Russ was just doing his job, and Ryan needed to accept that. "Okay. I get it. You have to do this. Your job requires it. But you can go easy on her. She risked her life to save Jessie. She might've died if Mia hadn't been so brave."

Russ studied Ryan's face and didn't look away. Just held his focus until Ryan grew uncomfortable under the intense scrutiny and had to speak. "What's that look for?"

"I try to take that into consideration, but it seems odd you're defending her like this when she bailed on you."

Ryan had always given her the benefit of the doubt and believed she had to leave or suffocate under her father's mental abuse, but he didn't know that for sure, and he wouldn't say anything.

"And while you're at it," Russ continued. "Maybe you should ask if your guilt for not leaving with her is keeping you from seeing her involvement in the arson."

It wasn't that Ryan hadn't wanted to go with her to Atlanta. He had. Big time. But his mother had just been diagnosed with breast cancer, and he wouldn't leave her or his family at such a difficult time.

Russ clapped Ryan on the shoulder. "Don't worry. I'm not trying to railroad her. I'm keeping an open mind. She may well be innocent. If so, you can say I told you so all you want. All I ask is that you think about it before you rush to her defense without any evidence to support your position." He lifted his hand and saluted. "I'll catch you later."

He strode away as questions pummeled Ryan. Had he jumped to defend Mia without any thought as Russ had said? Was Ryan simply protecting her on instinct from their past relationship? Or was she really innocent and in danger from an unknown source?

She'd changed so much physically over the years that maybe her personality had drastically changed too. The woman he'd once known may not exist anymore.

There was only one way to find out. Spend time with her. Get to know the new Mia. See for himself.

He spun and headed back toward her door. Before going home and cleaning up, he would convince her to work with Wilderness Ways. That way, if Russ was wrong and someone had her in his sights, Ryan would be right by her side to defend her from all danger.

5

Weariness from a sleepless night oozed from Mia's bones, but she smiled at Nurse Karen as she straightened Mia's blankets before stepping up to a cart holding a computer. Nurses belonged on the top of Mia's chart of selfless giving people, and she was thankful for Karen's kind care.

"Once I finish this paperwork, you can get dressed, and we'll get going in no time." Humming quietly as if she loved her job, she input data into Mia's file.

Mia smiled over a melody as familiar as breathing to her. Her mom used to sing this same song when she was happy. Mia closed her eyes to listen and urged her body to relax. The notes rushed up the scale and plunged down, bringing with them the last good memory Mia had of her mother.

Mia could almost feel the warm breeze skipping off the lake and into their cabin at Evergreen. Their family had just arrived for a much-needed vacation, and her mom's face lit with happiness for the first time in months. Her parents didn't think she and David knew they fought over their father letting his job take priority over the family. Sure, he was a doctor and had to go in to work at odd times and he put in long days, but he'd chosen to be absent more than needed.

Their vacation was supposed to fix all of that.

They'd no sooner unpacked when her father dug out his laptop and sat at the worn kitchen table to work on a medical book he was writing. Mia's joy evaporated along with her mother's. She issued an ultimatum. If Mia's father spent his vacation days working on the book, the marriage was over.

Mia couldn't stand by and do nothing. She begged her father to take them for a ride around the lake. He agreed, and she was thrilled. She would keep their parents together. All was going well—they were laughing and joking—until she pointed out a deer bolting from the woods. Her father looked away long enough for the car to slip onto the steep shoulder. He tried to wrestle their vehicle back onto the pavement but lost control, and they slammed into a monster evergreen, killing her mother.

Mia sighed. Life would have been much easier if God had let her mother live. If her father never blamed her for the accident.

She was so tired. Tired of carrying around the lack of her father's love. Of her brother always siding with their father. Of her breakup with Ryan. Of having to flee the home and place she once loved to get away from it.

Now having to come back here and face it all again when she thought she'd come to grips with it. She didn't think she was this skittish woman. Living in the past instead of the present, and she'd do just about anything to make the heartache go away. All she wanted was love. The same kind of love she'd had for the first thirteen years of her life. Unconditional. Everlasting.

Except it didn't last. She'd learned her lesson the hard way. Most men disappointed her. No love or love so shallow it was followed with betrayal. And they always had a need to control.

Her father. David. Ryan, just beginning to show the tendencies before they broke up and proving it yesterday.

No way she'd remove the armor she'd developed. Not with any of them. They would only hurt her again.

Best remember that.

A knock sounded on the door, and Karen's humming ended.

Mia clung to the memories of her mom, but they drifted away with the music. Expecting Ryan, who'd offered to give her a ride home today, she opened her eyes.

Not Ryan. Her father.

He searched the space and took in her appearance. His eyes creased in a critical assessment before zoning in on the computer.

What was he going to say? Criticize now? She drew in a quick breath and held it.

"Doctor," Karen said, a hint of awe settling into her tone.

"I'll just have a quick peek at Mia's records." Head bent low over the cart, the sound of his fingers clicking on the keyboard pinged through the room.

Mia stared at a large void on the back of his head replacing thick black hair that had once thrived like shag carpeting. His profile didn't seem quite as intimidating anymore. More fragile and old. She released her breath. She could do this, right?

"Everything looks good, Mia." He waved a hand over the computer. "You should make a full recovery."

It was so like him to put up the facade of being a concerned father in front of others. She hadn't been able to stomach the two-faced behavior in high school and had rebelled against it, but after yesterday's stress, she didn't have the strength to fight him. Besides, if she hoped he would confess his part in the fire, she'd better not embarrass him in front of Karen.

Mia smiled tightly. "I appreciate your taking the time to stop in. Do you have a few more minutes to talk?"

His mouth dropped open. She hadn't responded positively to him in years. He probably didn't know what to make of her sudden about-face, and he didn't know what to say. An awkward silence descended on the room.

Karen cleared her throat. "If you don't need me for anything, Doctor, I'll get out of your way."

"Yes, of course." He flashed the nurse a kind smile reserved for those who met his exacting standards.

As Karen departed, Mia grappled with what to do. She wanted to say something to keep him looking open and receptive, but when the nurse exited the room his door of kindness snapped shut, and his hard shell returned.

"The barn burning down is most unfortunate," he said. "You're no doubt upset that it will reduce the value of the property."

Right. He would choose to comment on the structure instead of saying that he was glad she wasn't injured.

"I'm guessing Uncle Wally had insurance, and I can rebuild."

"You have the year to get it done before you sell, so why not?"

"I never said I was selling."

His eyes widened. "You're not? I just assumed you wouldn't want to stay here, that you would leave as soon as possible."

"Once my year is up, I don't have to live on the property to own it."

"Oh, right. Of course. I'm sure Ryan will want to continue his lease for Wilderness Ways and that will pay for your taxes and expenses of maintaining the place."

She hadn't really thought that far in advance, but she nodded. "I appreciate your concern. Especially as I'm certain you think David should've inherited the place, not me. Which is why you sent the threat."

His face creased in that look of utter disappointment in her that she'd seen so many times, and he stood wooden and silent for a long moment.

"The nurse will be in to discharge you shortly." He spun and exited as quickly as he'd entered.

What? He left. Just like that. He couldn't even respond to her comment. But why was she surprised? This was exactly what she'd expected from him but not what she'd hoped for.

Was she all wrong about him? Did he leave because he was innocent and she seemed too stubborn to listen? But if he didn't send the threat, why not outright deny it? Defend himself? Maybe he just couldn't be bothered. Didn't care enough to be bothered. Or maybe her defensive attitude had put him off. She didn't want to act this way around him. She wanted to reconcile, but the old wounds just had her saying the first thing that came to mind instead of thinking.

Had she just messed things up even more between them? How would she act if he were accusing her of the same thing? Not well.

Her lips quivered. Tears surfaced and trickled down her cheeks.

Even after years of his rejection, she'd hoped he'd deny the charges and declare he'd never hurt the daughter he loved and welcome her back. After all, that's what Wally had wanted when he structured his will to force her to live here for a year. She'd bought into his hope. Figured he had a reason for his plan and it had foolishly given her hope of reconciliation too. Her father didn't seem to have the same goal in mind.

No. It was time to face facts. Wally had died. His hopes died with him. She was alone.

All alone.

The finality of her loss swept through her like never before, and she curled into a tight ball of mourning.

～

Shaking his head, Ryan walked down the hospital hallway. Why in the world had Mia agreed to let him drive her home today? He shouldn't read anything into it. The lack of public transportation in their small town was likely her reason, and he was her only way out of the place. On the bright side, he'd asked her last night to fill in as a Wilderness Ways counselor, and she'd agreed to consider his request.

With the students arriving tomorrow, he hoped for a firm commitment from her today. The last thing she needed with everything going on in her life was pressure from him, but he wasn't opposed to encouraging her to accept. Turning her attention to the students could be the very thing she needed to take her mind off her own problems. Helping others had a way of doing that.

He rounded the corner and spotted Dr. Blackburn exiting Mia's room. Lips puckered, he slammed his hands into the pockets of his white coat and rushed down the hall. He didn't appear so much angry as dejected.

Was this a good sign? Conversations between Mia and her father had always escalated into fights so boisterous it was a wonder they didn't end in violence. If the same thing had happened today, he'd have been fuming and storming away.

At the open door, sniffling surprised Ryan and drew him into the room. Mia lay curled up, her moist eyes as vulnerable as little Jessie's had been when he'd left her with the

EMT yesterday. The large sutured gash on Mia's cheek kicked him in the gut again. He'd thought she'd look better this morning but her appearance was as delicate as the spider webs he often trekked through.

What could have happened to upset her to such a degree, yet not affect her father the same way?

Ryan hated to bring up the visit, but if she needed to talk about it, he was more than willing to listen. He sat next to her. Careful not to tangle the IV and oxygen tubes, he drew her into his arms. She didn't resist but snuggled close and her sniffling turned to sobs.

"Shh." He rocked her and inhaled her scent, a combination of tart hospital soap and caustic barn smoke with a slight hint of her sweet perfume. Her body shook, and she clutched the back of his shirt.

If Ryan could get a hold of her father right now, the man would pay. Something Ryan had wanted to do in high school, but had been too young. Her father had broken her heart more times than Ryan could count. Ryan had done his best to pick up the pieces, restore her confidence and prove she was lovable. All while her father seemed to go untouched by his behavior.

If Ryan lived the faith he professed, he would forgive the man for the way he treated his daughter, and should also be thinking about how to help repair the rift between them. So why did he just want to pummel the guy instead?

Mia snuffled, winding down her crying.

He gently released her and offered a box of tissues from the bedside table. "What did he say this time?"

"My father? You saw him?" Watery eyes fixed on his as she ripped out a tissue.

Ryan nodded.

"He only wanted to talk about the barn being destroyed. Not if I was okay. I mentioned the threat again and that I believe he sent it." She hiccuped and dabbed at her red-rimmed eyes. "He didn't deny it. Just bolted. That was the second time."

Not as bad as Ryan had imagined. "He didn't admit to doing anything. That's a good thing, isn't it?"

She sniffed. "Even if he didn't do it, he clearly wants nothing to do with me."

Ah, that's it. What set her off. Not her father's guilt but his continued rejection. This topic couldn't be resolved in a short conversation, and Ryan didn't think he could offer anything new after all these years. He could sidestep the rejection and keep discussing the fire. Then maybe she'd be open to telling Russ about the letter and consider other suspects.

Ryan shifted on the edge of the bed. "Sounds to me like you really don't believe your father's behind all of this."

She blew her nose and set the tissue on her lap. "I don't know what to think anymore. I can't imagine he'd hire an arsonist, but he's the most logical candidate."

She was right. He seemed to be the likely culprit, but Ryan had to plant doubt in her mind to get her moving forward. "Would your father really risk going to prison just to get you to leave town?"

She pulled out another tissue. "I know it doesn't make sense, but who else would've done it? David is the only one who will benefit if I don't last a year."

"I think he's a less likely suspect than your father, but we can't rule him or anyone out at this early stage. What about someone who works at Evergreen?"

She tapped her chin. "You mean like Verna?"

He nodded. "She's managed the resort forever and maybe she expected to inherit something from Wally. Or even Nico. He's been the caretaker for as long as I can remember."

"Yeah, maybe. But like you said, she's like family. Nico too. Still, my dad and David are family, and I'm considering them. Why not Verna or Nico? And they were hanging out by the fire at the end. Maybe watching their handiwork."

Now he had her thinking. "Can I make a suggestion to help figure this out?"

"Sure."

"We have a former FBI agent working in our family business. Colin Graham. He's a computer whiz. If Reid can free him up, Colin could dig into our suspects' backgrounds to try to find motives."

She cocked her head, her tears gone now. "You're thinking I should ask him to look into my dad and David."

"Yeah. And Verna and Nico. Maybe Wally too."

"Uncle Wally. But why?"

"Just to see if he has a reason for choosing you over David that you don't know about." She might not want to look into her uncle, but Ryan's law enforcement days told him people had things to hide, and they would do just about anything to keep them hidden. "Fair warning, though. If you ask for Colin's help, you'll have to be prepared for what he digs up."

She twisted the tissue in her fingers. "Doesn't look like the person behind the threat plans to give up, so I need to figure it out, and I'm not an investigator by any means."

"I'll get the ball rolling with him if you'd like."

"Please."

"And if he can't do it, I recently worked two investigations with a company called The Veritas Center in Portland. They're mostly a forensic lab, but they also have an excellent IT department. Maybe they'd take the job. Problem is, they're pretty expensive."

"I can't put a price on finding this person, can I?" She clutched her arms around her raised knees and rocked.

Ryan could hardly sit by and not comfort her, but he did. "No matter who did this, I'm here to help you through it."

She stopped moving. "You've been nothing but kind to me since I ran into you. I'm thankful for everything you've done—saving me at the barn and all. Really, I am. Not that you could tell. All I've done is snap at you."

He smiled. "I've probably come across as pushy. Telling you what to do. But all I want is for you to stay safe, and if I can help with that, I want to."

"I know. But you also know how being told what to do really sets me off. Always has since my dad took over after Mom died, and he pushed me around." She worked her lower lip and went silent for so long he thought she might have changed her mind and clammed up. "Do you want to talk about our breakup?"

He resisted gaping at her quick change in topic. "Now?"

She nodded. "I can't leave until the nurse discharges me. We might as well make good use of the time and get it all out in the open."

This was what he wanted, but he wasn't sure that he was ready to hear how she could have bailed on him. "If we hadn't broken up that night, what do you think would've happened between us?"

Her eyes widened.

He'd caught her by surprise. "This isn't a test or anything to see how you felt. Just a question."

"Well, you were starting college. My grades weren't good enough to get into a four-year school, so I would've gone to a community college or gotten a job so we could live close to each other."

He'd thought along the same lines. "And when I graduated, we'd get married and live happily ever after here in Shadow Lake, right?"

"Something like that. But I ruined that dream for both of

us. I couldn't stomach my father's control. It was getting worse by the day, and I wanted out of here more than anything except being with you." She looked up as if gauging his reaction.

He gave her a soft smile to encourage her to continue.

"I had to discover who I was without my father harping at me all the time. If you knew I wanted to spend the rest of my life with you, you would've tried to come to Atlanta with me."

She paused to take a long breath. "But your mother—your whole family—needed you. If I made you think I didn't want to be with you anymore, you would stay home with them without feeling guilty, which is exactly what you did."

Just as he'd thought. He regretted it happening, but from what he could see, the time away had been good for her. "And look at you. My gosh, just look at you. You're not working in some dead-end job with three kids and harboring resentment for your husband because he kept you here. You came back strong and independent. Able to stand up to your father. A professional counselor respected by your peers."

She sat unmoving, her attention fixed on his face. Tears began to slide down her cheeks. He didn't know how to respond. Were these tears of joy over her changes or tears of loss? Careful not to touch the angry gash on her cheek, he gently swiped his thumb over the tears, something he'd done time after time in high school.

She didn't pull away, and a nervous laugh escaped her throat. "And now this is the part where you forgive me for hurting you because you realize I did what I did because I loved you."

"You had a good reason, and I can forgive you." Second nature with her had him reaching out to take her in his arms, but he let his hands fall.

He wanted to hold her until her tears stopped again, but he wouldn't risk reconnecting as they had in high school. Couldn't risk caring for her again. She'd nearly died yesterday, and this nightmare wasn't over.

She was still in danger.

If the man who set fire to the barn wanted to hurt her, Ryan wasn't sure he could stop him. Losing Cara had proven his limitations, and despite his best efforts, any woman he loved could die.

6

Mia wished she'd known about the condition of Ryan's vintage truck before she accepted a ride home with him. Under the noontime sun, the vintage vehicle rumbled down the winding country road to the rattling of soda cans on the floor. Flies had succumbed to the quicksand of dust and grime on the dashboard, and cracks populated the seat with tufts of stuffing eager to escape.

Redressed in her fire-ravaged clothes, Mia matched the interior, but not Ryan. Today he wore an emerald green shirt highlighting his dark coloring and coordinating perfectly with khaki tactical pants and hiking boots. He had a day's or more worth of stubble on his jaw, and as he climbed into the truck, a hesitant, little-boy-lost look had crossed his face and made it hard to keep her eyes off him.

He'd been so helpful, and she was now even more grateful for running into him. But was he what he seemed or did he really have his own agenda?

Last night when she'd tried to fall asleep in the noisy hospital, her thoughts kept drifting back to the ambulance ride. Back to his loving expression as he answered Jessie's questions and calmed her fears, much as he'd comforted Mia after her father's many rampages.

Then she had to go and dream about Ryan too.

Not just him, but them as a couple again, married and with a family. The whole American dream wrapped up in a neat little package. Two children, a boy and a girl, living in the big lodge at Evergreen, and of course a dog romping around the place. Foolish, but she liked it. Even wide awake with all of the turmoil of her life, she liked it.

She glanced at his strong profile. How could she spend day after day working alongside him at Wilderness Ways and not wonder what their life would've been like if they'd never broken up?

He slowed the truck at a stop sign and glanced her way. "You thinking about the fire again?"

She wasn't about to admit the truth, so she lifted her shoulders in a shrug.

He seemed to buy her vague response and clicked on the blinker. "I don't have to tell you that people who survive an experience like a fire often start to ponder the meaning of life and why they were spared. I'm not sure how you stand on God these days, but He can help you through this if you turn to Him."

She swiveled toward Ryan. "You've embraced religion?"

His lips tipped in the briefest of smiles. "I started living by my faith again, if that's what you mean."

She peered past him and out the window. Here she was fantasizing over getting back together with him, and he clearly wasn't the same person she'd known in high school. Back then, he believed in God. So did she, and they'd each attended church with their families, but live it day-to-day? No.

"Would you mind if I tell you how it helped me get

through some tough times?" he asked, seeming undaunted by her skepticism.

She'd embraced her faith to get through things until her mom died and her father ignored her. Then she couldn't help but believe God had left her. Nothing over the years indicated that had changed no matter how much she would like it too.

If anyone could change her mind it would've been Wally. He lived his beliefs. That included service to the community and compassion for those who were down on their luck. She could and did embrace those same traits, only she wasn't motivated by faith, just by doing the right thing.

She looked through the front window to avoid seeing Ryan's disappointment in her that surely would follow her response. "Now's not a good time. God keeps taking away the people I love most. We're further apart than ever."

Out of the corner of her eye, she saw his knuckles tighten on the wheel, turning white. He didn't speak, and the miles rolled past.

Something inside urged her to take back that comment. To lift a hand to touch his arm and end the uncomfortable silence. To return the carefree guy from before this conversation, but she held herself in check.

No good would come from revisiting her stance on God. After all, she'd tried it a few times, and the end result was the same. She believed in Him but didn't think He had her best interests at heart, and she feared He never would.

～

Ryan set aside Mia's reaction to his suggestion and replaced it with the resolve to try again later. She believed in God. At least enough to blame Him for the loss of her mother. Ryan got that. Many people felt the same way when things went wrong in their lives. But it meant Ryan had a chance of helping her let go of her blame and perhaps move her toward God again.

Not now, though. Clearly it wasn't the right time. Now he would let her see that as a Christian, he wouldn't take her rejection personally.

"So," he said, putting a cheerful tone into his voice. "Did you have a chance to think about helping us at Wilderness Ways?"

She arched a perfectly plucked brow. "I'm not sure it would be a good match. I'm not much of an outdoor girl anymore. The thought of camping for days without a shower makes my skin crawl."

Her reaction didn't surprise him. After all, he'd have to be blind not to notice the change in her appearance to a real girly girl. But he was way ahead of her. Last night he'd thought of all the reasons she might say no and prepared a defense for each one of them. She didn't stand a chance.

"Actually." He turned what he hoped was a high-wattage smile on her. "Last night, I decided it wouldn't be wise to send you into the field with students. With the injuries you suffered, I'm not sure you're up to the physical demands that kind of trip could place on you."

Her eyes narrowed. "So why ask if I still wanted to help?"

"I have another plan for you." With his free hand, he pretended to twist a handlebar mustache like a villain.

She laughed as she always had, rewarding him when he'd worked hard to brighten her mood. "And what plan might that be?"

"I'll shift staff so you can work with the students at the base camp. We start each session with initial evaluations when the students arrive at camp. This provides the field staff with a risk assessment for each student. They work with the kids on the treks, but every few days we return to base camp to clean up and hold a round of one-on-one counseling."

"You didn't have to resort to your dastardly villain routine to get me to agree. I would love to do that." She kept her gaze on him. "But if I do this, you have to agree to keep things professional between us."

Great. She was on board and he would do his best to meet her terms. "Whatever you need, I can do that."

"Good. Then I'm ready and willing to help."

He glanced at her, and their eyes met. Her passion for helping others radiated in waves and warmed him far more than was good for him. They'd always shared a drive to help the underdog, and now they made their living that way.

He looked back at the road. "It's amazing we both ended up in the same line of work."

"I wasn't at all surprised when I heard that you were the director of Wilderness Ways. You're a natural counselor. So how long have you been working with the program?"

"About a year and a half."

"After you quit being a deputy." She swiveled to face him.

He could feel her questioning gaze burning into his face. He had to concentrate on the road, so he didn't find himself telling her more than he could handle revealing.

"I went to grad school in Eugene and then came back here to work at a small clinic before I became a deputy." The same clinic Cara had worked for. The clinic she died in.

His chest tightened the way it always did at the memory of responding to the call coming over his radio. A rookie deputy then. Finding Cara on the floor of her office. The blood pooling around her. Her face pale, her pulse barely there.

He sucked in a sharp breath and gestured at Evergreen's

main entrance to direct Mia to check out the scenery. "We're here."

But he failed. She saw right through his plan and didn't look away. She would probably question him about this subject later. But at least he'd bought some time before he had to recount the day Cara's life ended at the hands of a crazed patient.

～

Mia let Ryan's evasive behavior pass. He didn't want to talk about something. Maybe he had a secret. Or maybe he had no desire to dredge up their old wounds. At least not more than she already had. She could appreciate that, and she would respect his privacy.

She'd come through the private gate yesterday, so she sat back to enjoy the scenery that greeted visitors when they arrived. They reached the small green check-in hut used during the peak summer season that ended after Labor Day, and Ryan slowed to let the attendant get a look at them. Next came a grouping of cabins that had been on the property for as long as she could remember. Further in, the office/convenience store and a large recreation center were all located near a wide beach on Shadow Lake.

"Everything looks the same." The longing in her tone caught her off-guard. Until the shell of the barn came into view and a wash of fear erased the warm feeling.

Ryan tipped his head at the carnage. "When I got home last night, I closed up your car and brought it up to the lodge and your things inside. And I had Poppy stock the fridge and pantry too."

"Thank you." She let her voice ring with sincerity at his continued kindness. She was learning a lot about her old boyfriend. Except for the religion thing, she liked what she saw, and honestly, she was happy that he could live his faith because it seemed important to him.

She was all for his happiness. "So I take it Poppy still cooks for your parents."

Ryan shook his head. "She lives with Reid and Jessie and also cooks for the guests at the beginning of our training camp."

"I remember her meals. Especially her bread. The best ever."

"Still is." He grinned and made the last curve to approach the lodge.

A patrol car, black sedan, pickup truck, and two SUVs lined up like dominoes in front of the large log building.

She flashed him a look. "What's going on? Do you think something else's happened?"

"Don't jump to conclusions and start worrying. There's likely an innocent explanation." He smiled at her, but the truck picked up speed, mimicking her new sense of urgency.

Her stomach tightened. Maybe something had happened to Jessie. Could the man in the barn have learned she could identify him and come after her?

If only God heard Mia's prayers she would offer one for Jessie. But He didn't, so what was the point? She'd prayed the second the family's car hit the tree and her mother didn't respond. He didn't spare her mother then. Or even Wally when he hadn't recovered from the stroke. God wouldn't spare a child simply because Mia requested His help. And He didn't seem inclined to keep Mia safe either. True, she survived the fire, but it seemed like there was a threat against her life.

The vintage truck rocked to a stop in front of the rustic two-story lodge. She slid out and took a moment to look at the massive swing and the cane-backed rocking chairs filling the huge wraparound porch. She'd spent hours sitting there in the cool summer shade with Wally. Fun, joy-filled hours. The only real joy she'd found with family after her mother died. But he was only in town for summers, and the winters seemed so very long without him.

The enormity of losing him hit harder than ever. Those pesky tears wanting to flow again. She gritted her teeth to stop them.

"C'mon." Ryan came up behind her. "I can hear people laughing inside. If something was wrong, they wouldn't be having a good time."

But could she face a good time when her heart was aching over her uncle? When she was about to enter his summer home? Their place of refuge together when she was younger?

The door flashed open. Jessie, holding the leash of a small white dog with eyes circled in a mask of black and wearing a plastic cone over his head, raced down the stairs.

"Get control of him, Jessie." A man whose intense blue eye color identified him as a Maddox and whose parental tone identified him as Reid, lingered at the door.

He was tall like his brothers, but he was leaner like Ryan. He dressed similar to his brothers in tactical pants, but he had on a green polo with a Shadow Lake Survival logo on his broad chest.

Jessie barreled into Mia, surrounding her waist in a tight hug.

Mia lurched back in pain, but regained her composure and managed to smile at Jessie to keep her from knowing the hug cut into her sore side. The innocent fragrance of baby shampoo enveloped the sweet child's head like a halo.

Oh, how thankful Mia was to have saved this precious girl's life. "I'm so glad to see you're doing okay."

Jessie gazed up with hero worship Mia knew she didn't deserve. She'd just been in the right place at the right time.

The dog yipped in excitement giving Mia the chance to turn the focus in another direction. She squatted and reached into the cone to cup the dog's head. "Hey, little fella."

He ran his pink tongue over her palm, and she scooped him up. "Is he your dog, Jessie?"

"Kinda, but not really. Daddy won't let me have a dog. He says he doesn't have the time to take care of anyone but me." Her lower lip shot out, and she plopped onto a step.

Jessie's pain hung in the air like the smoke from yesterday's fire.

Were Jessie and Reid living the same life Mia'd had with her father? Mia continued to stroke the dog, but looked up at Reid.

Ryan leaned forward and whispered, "I know what you're thinking, but it's nothing like what you went through with your dad. Jessie is oversimplifying things. Reid's a great father, but he's really struggling to cope as a single parent, and a dog is just too much right now."

Mia nodded to let Ryan know she understood that this situation was nothing like her past. For that Mia was grateful as she had come to care for Jessie and wanted the child to thrive.

Reid came down the stairs and held his hand out. "It's good to see you again, Mia. I'll never be able to repay you for saving Jessie." His voice caught, and he cleared his throat. "I hope you don't mind that we took over the lodge, but we wanted to bring a few friends over to say thanks."

Mia hid her surprise by looking at the dog and stroking her fingers down his back. "And does that include this cutie?"

Reid cast a concerned look at Jessie. "We didn't know Bandit would be here."

Jessie popped up and pointed at the bandage wrapping

his rear leg. "He got a bad 'fection and had to stay at Doc's for a really long time. Now he's better enough to come home, and Doc brought him."

Ryan stepped forward. "Bandit was Wally's dog. When Wally was up here in the summer to run the camp, Bandit lived in the lodge. When Wally went back to Atlanta, Bandit stayed in the barn, and Jessie and our staff took care of him."

Jessie crossed her arms. "I took *good* care of him."

"You did at that, Tater Tot." Ryan grinned at Jessie.

"I'm not a Tater Tot." She wrinkled her nose.

"But you *are* little and one of my favorite things."

"I know, but when I grow up I won't let you call me that."

"Of course not." Ryan gave her a very serious nod, but his eyes crinkled with humor as he turned to Mia. "Since Bandit no longer has a home in the barn, we were hoping you'd keep him at the lodge for now."

Jessie looked up at Mia, her expression hopeful. "If you keep him, I can help you take care of him."

Her lower lip came out, and she tilted her head, her ponytails dangling, her freckled nose wrinkled.

Ah, how could anyone say no with that pleading face? After this poor child had been through so much in her young life? As a counselor, Mia knew that she shouldn't give into a big thing like this for a child without contemplating her decision first, but Ryan had considered the idea and thought it sound. She'd never owned a dog and had no idea what it entailed, but Jessie did, and she could benefit emotionally from the pup.

"What do you say, Bandit?" Mia cuddled him against her chest, his black-tipped tail thumping like a pendulum on her arm. "You want to live with me?"

His tongue lapped at her but couldn't connect due to the cone.

Still smiling, she looked at Ryan. "How about we try it for a few days to see how things go?"

"Yes." Jessie pumped up her fist and jumped up to dance around.

"Thank you," Reid mouthed.

Jessie grabbed Mia's hand and tugged. "C'mon. Let's go to the party."

"Slow down, Jessie," Reid warned. "Mia needs to take things easy for a few days."

"Okay, I'll take Bandit." Jessie extended her hand for the leash.

Mia set the dog down, and Jessie jogged up the steps with the cute dog.

Mia smiled at Reid. "She's going to love coming over to see Bandit."

He connected gazes. "I want you to know how thankful I am for your intervention in the barn. If there's ever a way I can repay you, let me know."

Ah, the opening Mia had hoped for. "Just take good care of Jessie. She seems pretty traumatized by the fire and should talk to someone about it."

Reid gave a firm nod. "She's been seeing a counselor since her mom died, and I'll make sure the counselor knows about the fire."

"Perfect. Sounds like you have things under control."

"Under control? Hah!" His voice skated higher. "I'm winging it. One day at a time. Sometimes one hour at a time."

"Having Bandit to take care of and bond with will help her."

"Thank you for that too." He frowned. "You probably think I'm lame for not taking the dog home with us, but we just can't care for him right now. Her counselor said a dog might help too, but that we shouldn't make any changes that could set us up for failure. I would hate to bring Bandit home only to have to relinquish him. That would make things worse for Jessie."

"Sounds like you're doing the right thing, and she can still spend time with him over here. You're welcome to bring her over anytime."

Jessie came to the door. "C'mon, Mia. Hurry."

"Patience, Bug." Reid smiled fondly at his daughter then looked at Mia. "Thanks again. I'll be in touch."

Mia climbed the steps, her heart overflowing with warmth from being able to help Reid and Jessie. At the door, Jessie took Mia's hand and pulled her into the lodge. Mia paused in the entryway to look around.

Ten years away and the family room was exactly as she remembered. Heavy, rustic furniture filled the space. The same sturdy leather sofa angled in front of a massive stone fireplace was home to many long discussions with Wally. Same chunky coffee table made from old barn wood that had held game boards and cards still sat in front of it. Wally's same worn leather recliner hugged the corner.

Ah, yes. This was good. Finally. Memories of happy times.

She faced the intimate groups of people mingling in the large space connected to an open kitchen, a big island filled with potluck dishes. The guests turned one by one to look at her, and she recognized many of the locals. An undercurrent of unease surged through the air. People in Shadow Lake had never seen her in a positive light due to her rebellious ways, and they had definitely never thrown her a party.

She didn't deserve one. Or even their kindness or respect. She'd pushed them all to the breaking point and for that she was sorry. If she could have a do over for those rough years, she would hope she would've found a way to work things out with her dad instead.

From the far side of the room, Russ stood with an older couple and kept his eye on her.

Ryan placed his hands on her shoulders and gave a comforting squeeze as if he was telling the others he supported and approved of her. Man, he was really stepping up for her and even more, she didn't deserve that.

She offered him a thankful smile and let herself linger for a moment in the depth of his caring. How she had loved him. Beyond measure, but she couldn't get caught up in that now only to leave and hurt him again.

She looked back at her visitors.

"Move over, Uncle Ryan." Jessie's lips morphed into a cute little pout. "You're hogging Mia."

He ruffled Jessie's hair. "Don't worry. I'll share her with you."

"C'mon, Mia." Jessie tugged harder on Mia's hand. "There's a present on the table for you. Daddy says we haveta show it to you before we can eat, and I want pie. So I can help you open it if you need me to." Jessie pointed toward a box covered in multicolored balloon paper sitting on a small table near the fire where she'd played chess with Wally. "See?"

Mia stifled her laugh over the pie comment and moved toward the table. The guests watched her with expectancy, and her steps faltered. She'd often fantasized about over-coming the negative reputation her teenage rebellion had brought. But in those dreams, she'd never been dressed in burnt and torn clothes with scraggly hair.

She ran her free hand over the tangled locks. "You really didn't have to do this."

They glanced at one another in confusion. Embarrassed looks followed.

Reid laughed nervously. "Wish we *had* thought to get

you something for all you did. We found the package sitting on the table when we got here."

Oh, no. They didn't bring the gift. What did etiquette dictate in a situation like this? Should she open the package or ignore it? Who would've had a key to drop this off? Wait... had the door been unlocked? It had to be because none of these people would have a key. Including Ryan and Poppy, who'd both stopped in last night.

So what did she do with the package?

If she opened it, the attention would shift to the gift and she could relax. Maybe.

"C'mon, Mia." Jessie tugged harder, making Mia's final decision for her.

She made eye contact with her visitors. "I'll just see what this is." She dropped Jessie's hand and rushed to the package. "No card. Maybe the sender put a note inside."

"Can I help open it?" Jessie pleaded as she skidded to a stop at the table. Unable to stop as fast, Bandit slammed into Jessie's leg and looked dazed.

Mia smiled fondly at Jessie. "Why don't you pull off the paper?"

Jessie handed Bandit's leash to Reid and ripped the wrapping into shreds, tossing the fragments on the wide wooden floor planks. She put her hand on the box and telegraphed her desire to pull up the flap.

"Jessie," Reid warned. "This is Mia's present."

"That's okay," Mia said. "I'd love Jessie's help. Go ahead."

The child started to lift one flap when a sheet of white paper slipped free and drifted to the floor.

"Hold on, honey." Mia retrieved the paper. "Let's see who it's from before you open it."

A giggly Jessie danced in place as Mia unfolded the paper.

No. No.

Letters cut from a magazine, very similar to the warning she'd received in the post office, filled the paper.

Mia's stomach twisted, but she forced her eyes to stay on the page and scanned the message.

Sever your claim to Evergreen Resort or I'll sever it for you.

Jessie reached for the flap.

"Don't!" Mia shouted. "Don't touch it."

Jessie's mouth opened wide, and she looked ready to wail. Bandit raised his head and issued frantic barks.

Mia had scared them both, but if the box contained something awful, Mia didn't want Jessie to see it. Mia eased between the child and the box and clamped a hand on the lid.

Russ came forward, lowered himself to one knee, and settled Jessie on the other one. "It's okay, squirt. Mia was just surprised, and she didn't mean to scare you."

"I didn't. I'm sorry...I..." She blinked at the box wondering how to get it out of Jessie's view and see what might have accompanied the latest warning note.

Russ smiled at Jessie. "What say we sneak a cookie from the kitchen?"

"Yes, please." Jessie's face brightened.

"Wait," Mia said, making that smile disappear again. "Stay here. I have to take this..." She grabbed the package and carried it to the end of the kitchen island away from all the food brought by her visitors, and most importantly, out of Jessie's eyesight.

"Mia, what is it?" Ryan started her way.

She couldn't wait for him to arrive. She opened the flaps and peered inside.

Oh, no!

She dropped the note into the box, covering the horrible sight, and slapped the lid closed.

Her stomach roiled. Acid burned.

"Don't let anyone see," she managed to get the words out for Ryan as nausea sent her bolting for the nearest bathroom.

Near the claw-foot bathtub, she dropped to her knees and lay her head against the cool cast-iron tub to wait for her stomach to cease cramping.

Who was behind this latest threat? The fire? The first letter?

She couldn't answer that. Not at all. But she did know one thing.

This perpetrator wanted her gone, and his note and present claimed he was willing to go to extreme lengths to make it happen.

7

Mia's colorless face when she rushed past Ryan tightened his chest. He started to follow her. Russ clamped a hand on his arm and drew him toward the box. Russ picked the note out of the box and held it open for Ryan to read along.

Sever your claim to Evergreen Resort or I'll sever it for you.

Ryan turned from the warning of cutout letters similar to the note at the post office and looked into the box. A bloody severed hand lay on a bed of tissue paper.

No. No. He slammed the lid.

Wait. Had he seen right?

He opened the box. The hand was made of rubber. Fake blood dripping down it. A very good fake. Mia likely thought it was an actual hand.

"She didn't hang around long enough to discover this isn't real," Ryan whispered to Russ.

"Real or not, we need to end this party," Russ said in a low voice. "I'll clear this place. You stay here to make sure no one touches this box."

Russ stepped into the room and clapped his hands together. "Okay, folks. This party wasn't a good idea so soon after Mia got out of the hospital. She needs to rest. I suggest we all go on home."

His official sheriff's voice stirred the guests to speculate on what had happened but didn't get their feet moving.

Ryan faced the hallway Mia had run down, and it was all he could do to stand guard over the box and not go after her.

"C'mon, folks. Let's give Mia some privacy." Russ strolled through the family room and herded the guests toward the exit.

The minute the door closed behind the last guest, Ryan bolted down the hall. He knocked on the bathroom door. "The hand isn't real. It's one of those fake rubber ones."

Silence. He could almost hear her thoughts. The same thoughts weighed heavy on his mind. Fake hand or not, the person sending the letters made sure Mia knew he wouldn't hesitate to harm her if she didn't comply with his demands.

Ryan's words sank into Mia's brain. The hand wasn't real, but the sender had made his point. Vividly. Terror had engulfed Mia for the time she'd believed it to be real. That fear lingered.

The letter conveyed the sender's intent to keep after her until she left, raising the ante each time she ignored him.

She stared at her reflection in the mirror for the second time in as many days. Who was this woman peering back at her? Was it her? Oh, the physical appearance with a few added scrapes and a long suture was the same but gone was the confident woman she'd become. The wall she erected to keep pain and hurt out was crumbling. Fast. She hadn't felt so vulnerable since high school and then she had Ryan to turn to. Sure, he would let her turn to him now, but she wouldn't put him in that position.

74

She had to admit the person threatening her had won. For now. The insecurity looming large on her face, and her tight gut proved that.

Well, no more.

She pushed back from the mirror. She wouldn't let years of hard work disappear in less than a day. She would take charge of her life again. Find the person behind these threats. Nothing would deter her from completing her uncle's wishes that she spent a year at Evergreen, and then she would return to Atlanta to resume her real life.

That was exactly what she would do.

She pulled her shoulders back and marched into the family room.

She spotted the empty table where Jessie had been so excited about opening the brightly wrapped box, and her heart skipped a beat. Poor baby. Mia had scared her when that was the last thing she would want to do.

She forced her gaze from the fearful sight to Bandit, who lay on a plush bed in the corner. Across the room, Ryan leaned against rustic pine cabinets in the kitchen, a phone to his ear. Russ and her visitors were nowhere in sight, and the offensive box was gone.

Russ had likely taken it with him when she expected him to wait and grill her again.

Ryan waved her over.

She padded to the open kitchen where a wrought-iron pot rack swarming with worn copper and cast-iron cookware hung above a long island and separated the two rooms.

Ryan held his hand over his phone. "David."

Her new plan started by finding the person behind these incidents, and getting David's take on things was near the top of her list. His accounting firm managed Evergreen's finances, and she needed to speak to him about that anyway. She could get his opinion on the threats at the same time.

"I need to talk to him," she answered.

Ryan eyed her. "Are you okay?"

She let her lips form what she thought was a brave smile. "I'm fine."

His eyebrow rose. "Are you sure?"

"Positive."

He tilted his head in question then shook it and held up a finger before resuming his conversation.

She slipped onto a counter-height stool, glad to see he'd put the refrigerated food away or that the guests had taken it with them. Her stomach curled at the mere thought of food. She turned to Ryan and watched bright rays filtering in from a picture window flicker on his wavy hair.

He looked up and flashed a hint of a smile, probably from catching her watching him. He crossed to the island and held out the phone. "Your turn."

She reached for his cell. He pulled the phone back against his chest and issued a playful dare.

She raised an eyebrow at his response and took it from him.

Had their reconciliation made him think she wanted to start something with him? If so, she would end that notion when she got off the phone with David. If she planned to resume control over her life, she certainly couldn't fall for him again.

She turned her attention to the call. "David."

"I was out of town and just heard about the fire." His concerned tone was exactly what she'd hoped to get from her father. "Ryan tells me you're doing okay."

"Ryan's right—I'm fine." She felt Ryan's gaze on her as he took the stool next to her, but she wouldn't look at him. Not when she had to concentrate on talking to a brother she wanted to reconcile with. Even if he did take their dad's side all the time, she hoped that had changed.

Not something she would discuss over the phone. Instead, she would focus on the threats to her life. "Who all has a key to the lodge?"

"I'm not sure. I know Verna does, and I assume Nico does too."

"It makes sense that Verna and Nico would have keys, but do you or Dad?"

"No."

"That's odd. I figure Uncle Wally would've given you both keys for emergencies."

"We weren't close to Wally like you were."

Was David telling the truth? Wouldn't it make sense for Wally to give them an emergency key? She would keep this in the back of her mind for now. "Do you have time to get together this afternoon so we can talk about the accounts?"

She heard papers rustling in the background of the call. "Sorry, I've got appointments until late tonight. The soonest I can see you is eleven tomorrow morning. Could you stop by the office then?"

"Sure. I'll see you then." She clicked off and handed the phone to Ryan. "What did David want with you?"

"When he heard about the fire, he tried calling you to check up on you, but you didn't answer your phone. So he called me." He pocketed his cell. "You're seeming pretty calm after what just happened here."

Great. She was doing a good job of faking it. If he only knew the truth. He just couldn't see the fear lodged deep in her chest. Correction, she wouldn't let him see it or he would go all Mr. Protector on her, and she might lose it. "I can't live afraid all the time like I've been doing since I got here. I have to take charge of my life again."

He rested his elbows on the counter. "After what's happened, I'd think you'd get that you can't control things."

He was right, but she didn't like it. She crossed her arms

to protect herself from the emotions simmering under the surface. "It's been a difficult day for sure, but my life has been out of my control since Uncle Wally died. Having to do what he wants—not what I want. But I won't disrespect him by not following through. What I can do is refuse to let these threats control my life."

Ryan searched her face for what seemed like an eternity. "That's what scares you the most, isn't it? Not the danger you're in, not your father's attitude, but that you've lost complete control of your life."

She didn't expect him to question her determination. True, he might see this strength as her way of standing up to him, but he should be proud of her resilience.

She squared her shoulders. "You sound like there's something wrong with trying to plan. To be in charge of your life."

"Planning is one thing, trying to control things is another," he fired back and added a challenging stare. "You can have every minute of every day planned and things you don't want to happen will still come to pass."

"Hah! Don't I know it, but if I have a plan to follow when these things occur, I can get back on track." She paused to catch a breath. "I can't afford to live any other way. I'm all alone in this world." She couldn't stand to see him curling his fists and the uncertainty on his face, so she bolted from her stool and went to the massive window overlooking the lake.

Children and parents floated on rafts, laughing and splashing water. She remembered similar days here. Summer vacation. Her mom planning and keeping everyone active and engaged. And then she died and the whole concept of family died with her.

"Mia." Ryan's voice came from behind her.

She wanted to face him, but if she did, he could sway her

decision to take charge. "I really have a lot to do, so I think you should go now."

"I can't leave you feeling this way." He gently turned her by the shoulders.

At his tenderness, her throat went dry, and she couldn't tell him to back off.

She started to move away, but he tightened his hold and rested his forehead on hers. "You don't have to be so tough all the time. You're not alone. I'm here to help you through this."

She inhaled the sweet musky scent of his cologne and slowly exhaled. What could she say with him so close? Too close. Even if she could find the words, her mind couldn't form a coherent thought other than...what would happen if he kissed her?

What a fool she was. Someone was going to great lengths to chase her away, her father still hated her, and all she could think about was kissing the man she'd left in the lurch. Where had that resolve gone from just a moment ago? Did this wonderful man still have such a strong hold on her? It was looking like it.

She dug deep for strength and pulled back.

"Mia, don't. Let me help." He reached up to cup the side of her face.

She peered into his eyes and saw the hope and healing waiting for her if she could only let go of the past, but it was so ingrained in her by now that she lived with distrust for any man. "I wish I could trust you not to hurt me like others have."

"I've never hurt you before," he said.

"I know, but I figure it's just a matter of time before you do something like every other man in my life."

He drew in a breath and seemed to withdraw mentally as he physically stepped back. He glanced around as if looking for a way to change her mind. He was wasting his time. She'd gained control again, and she wouldn't let him back in.

He went to the island and picked up a manila folder.

"This is Eddie Kramer's file. He's the student I told you about yesterday." Ryan forced the heavy folder into her hands. "If you can fit him into this new life you're planning, take a look at the file. I'll be at the rec center all afternoon, and I'd appreciate it if you'd stop by for a short orientation on our procedures."

Ryan plodded out the door and down the stairs. Her heart tightened and the urge to run after him nearly had her feet moving, but she hadn't worked so hard to build a life for herself to toss it away on a whim.

No. She was back in control and ready to put her plan into action. Find the person threatening her. Fulfill her dear uncle's wishes and then move on.

Ryan stormed down the stairs and hopped into his truck. Mia had rebuilt the wall she was so famous for putting up when trouble threatened. A tall wall. An unscalable wall. One he'd never been on the wrong side of before, and he didn't know *how* or even *if* he wanted to bring it down.

He shoved the key into the ignition and backed the pickup around. On the driveway, he spotted Russ's car and a tow truck at the barn. *Curious.* Russ hadn't said anything about the truck or who owned it. Did he know something new on the investigation?

After Mia's latest rejection, Ryan had half a mind to go straight to the rec center and let her find the person behind the threats by herself. After all, she'd made it perfectly clear that she didn't need or want his help.

So what? He wasn't the kind of guy who could leave a damsel in distress alone to fend for herself. Never had been. Never would be.

He groaned and swung the wheel left toward the barn. It didn't mean he was helping Mia. He was just curious. That was all.

At the barn, he exited his vehicle near Russ, who leaned over the hood of his car and filled out a form on a clipboard. The barn's charred rubble sat like a hulking reminder of the danger to Mia, the stench of burnt wood lingering in the air.

Ryan stepped up to Russ. "You ID the truck's owner yet?"

Russ looked up in surprise. "If you're down here that must mean Mia came out from the bathroom. She doing okay?"

Ryan's turn to be surprised. His brother's sincere concern when he'd been tough on her so far was a twist Ryan hadn't seen coming. Russ was a great guy. Usually very compassionate, but for some reason he had a thing about Mia. Ryan got it. She'd once been a bad influence, but he could've resisted the things she wanted to do. If he'd wanted to, but he hadn't. What he'd done was spend every waking hour with her. If that meant going to parties and skipping school, then he'd done that.

"She's hanging in there," Ryan answered. "You never said if you found out who owns the truck."

"Not yet. Looks like it was stolen and whoever boosted it was smart enough to remove plates and VIN numbers. Likely a pro."

"And that makes him a pro? The average Joe knows enough to take plates and that little tag off the dashboard."

"Yeah, but the average Joe doesn't know the number is etched on various parts of the vehicle." He tipped his head at the tow truck driver securing chains on the truck. "Bobby just told me they are all filed off."

Ryan looked at Bobby and the destroyed truck. He swung his head back toward Russ and caught sight of the package Mia received sitting on the front seat of Russ's patrol car. If the man was a professional at stealing trucks, had no qualms about torching the barn, and sent a message like the one in that box, what was he capable of doing to Mia if she didn't comply with his demands?

Perhaps kill someone. Someone like Mia.

"Learn anything else?" Ryan asked.

Russ shook his head and ripped the top page from his clipboard to hand it to Bobby.

"Thanks, man," Bobby said, heading back to his vehicle. "Truck'll be at my shop if you need to look at it."

Russ opened his car door and glanced at Ryan. "Later, bro."

"Wait," Ryan said. "I've been thinking about the package. Whoever put it inside the lodge had to have a key, right?"

Russ leaned on the open door. "Wally might not have locked it. We found the place open when we got here."

"Odd. I found it unlocked last night when I brought Mia's car and her belongings up to the lodge. But I locked it after I left. So whoever left the box must have a key."

Russ gave a sharp nod. "Or knows how to pick a lock. But I'll dig deeper to see who all might have a key and check the lock for signs of damage."

"Mia just asked David about keys. He mentioned Nico and Verna for starters, but sounded like he and their dad didn't have a key."

"Like I said. I'll look into it." Russ dropped into his car and drove off.

Ryan wanted to stop his brother and shake free any details he might be withholding, but Ryan knew his brother couldn't share every investigation detail and there was no point in getting frustrated over it.

He went to his own truck and took the private road leading to their family resort. Still called Valley View, the property abutted Evergreen's eastern border and also had lakefront access where two large three-bedroom cabins sat. Ryan lived in one. Russ in the other. To the west, the property was wooded and rustic, and the perfect place to take clients to learn to survive in the wilderness.

He stopped at the gated entrance to enter his security code. The gate swung open, and he started down the narrow drive. This part of the property had once been an open area, but since they'd invested in tons of valuable equipment, including guns, they'd secured the perimeter with a stockade fence and the two entrances with electronic locks. Not only did it protect their equipment, it gave the clients who were by nature untrusting more of a sense of security.

He passed the big log lodge with a wide wraparound porch sitting in the middle of the space where Reid and Jessie lived and took the fork toward ten smaller log cabins located deep in the trees. The three other Shadow Lake Survival staff members, including Colin, lived in these older cabins, and the others housed clients. Further down the road sat their meeting facility and equipment garage, along with a barn and corrals for their horses. And in the other direction by the lake were his and Russ's larger three-bedroom cabins.

What he wouldn't give to be coming here to ride his favorite horse. Or even take a group on a trek in the wilderness. Maybe paddle around the lake in his favorite canoe.

But despite Mia saying she didn't need him, he wouldn't let her fend for herself, and her safety came first.

Vehicles had been parked outside each of the small buildings. Meant they had a full class right now, and Colin might not be available. Wouldn't deter Ryan. Not one bit.

He swung into the drive by the third cabin where Colin

had parked his big black truck. Ryan got out and inhaled the fresh air, filling his lungs and trying to release some of the day's tension as only the outdoors could do for him.

The building sat in the shade, and the temperature felt refreshingly cooler. He took a few more breaths then knocked on the door and stood back, hoping Colin wasn't teaching a class.

He was in luck. Colin pulled open the door. He wore their team uniform of khaki tactical pants and a deep green polo shirt with the company logo on the chest.

He eyed Ryan and ran a hand over short dark hair. "You never visit. What gives?"

"I have a favor to ask," Ryan said.

"I'm late for a session so you'll have to walk with me." Colin pulled the door closed behind his back and started down the Hosta-lined trail. He set a quick pace toward the meeting facility, and Ryan had to hoof it to keep up with the guy who matched Ryan's height of six feet.

Colin glanced at him. "So what's this favor?"

Ryan shared about the fire, the boxed hand, and the need for his help. "If you could do a deep dive on Verna, Nico, Dr. Blackburn, and David Blackburn, that would be great. Wally too."

Colin came to a dead stop and fixed an intense look on Ryan. "You know I don't do that anymore, right?"

This wasn't going at all like Ryan had hoped. "I'm sorry, man. I know you left the FBI because you were burning out."

"Burning?" Colin's right eyebrow rose to join the other one. "Come on. Admit it. I was crispy fried when I got here."

"You were, and I hate to ask because I get it. I don't like rehashing my old law enforcement days either." Ryan had been living that life again since Mia came back and could totally relate. But he had a vested interest. Mia. And he wouldn't give up easily. "I wouldn't ask if it wasn't important. Mia's life is on the line."

Colin widened his stance, his hands drifting to his waist and planting firm. One on his sidearm, which they all carried when working with clients since they'd had one go off on them and threaten lives. He scratched his wide jaw covered in whiskers.

Okay, the guy was going to say no. If he did, Ryan wouldn't beg. No way he would force Colin to do something that he really hated to do. Ryan would move on to Nick at Veritas even if Ryan had to pay the guy himself.

Colin huffed out a breath and started walking again. "I have sessions until six today, but I can start on it tonight."

Ryan clamped down on his lips to keep his mouth from falling open.

"Thanks, man." He clapped Colin on the back. "I'll make sure Reid and Russ know that you're working on this in case it gets in the way of one of your classes."

"No way I'd let that happen. I can do both."

But could he do it on a timely basis?

Ryan hated to push, but... "This guy coming after Mia seems pretty determined, and I'm concerned for her safety. The sooner we have the information the better."

"Understood. Now I really gotta go." Colin saluted and took off in a jog.

Ryan watched his teammate rush toward the large pole barn structure and remained standing in place. He had to hope he'd convinced Colin of the importance of doing this research on a timely basis.

If not, the arsonist could strike again, this time taking a life.

8

Mia closed Eddie's folder and laid it on the table next to the sofa in the lodge's family room. Man, that kid had a history more troubled than her past. It should probably scare her off, but it steeled her resolve to help him. Even if it meant spending every day with Ryan. No cost was too great to keep Eddie from ruining his life more than he already had.

Poor kid had been dealt a tough blow. He'd been a model student until his mother had been mowed down by a drunk driver. She'd been a single mom, and his dad was completely out of the picture. Eddie had bounced from foster home to foster home for the last three years and had a rap sheet filled with misdemeanor offenses.

Mia had never been arrested and wasn't an orphan, but the way her dad treated her, she'd often felt back in the day as if she was all alone in the world. And she'd come close to being arrested. Should've been more than once. Maybe God had been watching out for her. But if so, maybe He should've let her be arrested to teach her a lesson. Who knew His plans? Surely not her.

Resolved to help, she got up. She would meet with Ryan on Wilderness Ways procedures. On the way back, she could check in with resort manager Verna Swann about filing an insurance claim for the barn and get her take on the fire. Kill two birds with one stone and all of that.

"Here, boy," she called Bandit.

He hopped up from the fuzzy bed in the corner by the fireplace and charged across the room.

"I'm so glad to have you." She snuggled him tight and laid her cheek against his soft body. "I need a friend who doesn't try to persuade me to do something I don't want to do, but just listens."

She walked past the counter where the box holding the hand had last sat and shivered. She'd replaced it with her purse and a folder holding Wally's will and the warning letter from the post office. She would make a copy for herself in the office so she could give the original to Russ. If she really wanted to get to the bottom of things, it was time he knew about the first letter. She didn't have to tell him that she suspected her father.

She gave Bandit one last hug and eased his coned body through the door of his crate. He whimpered, but didn't put up a terrible fuss when she stepped outside.

She went through the attached breezeway to the garage, the late afternoon sun breaking through puffy clouds and shining through the windows. The green John Deere utility vehicle sat in the only clean area of the oversized space, keys dangling from the ignition. Leave it to Wally to leave keys in vehicles. He'd been one of the most trusting people she'd ever met.

"Oh my gosh!" She slapped a palm against her forehead. "That's it."

Wally didn't lock anything. So no surprise that the lodge had been unlocked for the package delivery. But why had the barn been locked yesterday? Not with a simple little padlock but a massive chain. She didn't think anything of the locks at the time other than they were barring her way out of the fire, and she hadn't mentioned it to anyone. And she never thought to ask Ryan if the south end was chained too or even ask how Jessie got in. Or the arsonist. Sure, Jessie said he drove a truck in, but did he have a key or cut the chain? Maybe Verna could shed light on the locks too.

Mia might be getting somewhere, and she eagerly reached for the key.

Her phone chimed. A text from Ryan.

No longer available. Need to meet with staff. Will text you when we finish.

She typed a quick acknowledgment and would go straight to the office to talk to Verna. After a few false starts, the engine caught and the cart sputtered from the garage. She raced down the twisting drive, enjoying the cool breeze whipping into her face in the hot afternoon. She crested the hill leading to the lake and let the vehicle coast to the bottom.

How many times as a child had she run down this hill to the water and jumped in, splashing, playing with David and the Maddox boys? Happy, fun times with her whole family. But that was before her mother died. Before and after, which was basically how her life was broken down. That one horrible moment defining the rest of her life.

She shook off her thoughts and looked at the rustic office. One car sat in the parking spaces, an electric-blue Chevy Bolt. Not the color of car she could picture the more reserved Verna driving.

Mia swung into the space next to it in front of the long log building that held the resort office on one side and a small store on the other. Verna and the office assistant manned the store during the off-season. In the summer months, they hired high school kids to staff the shop.

Unlike Wally, she pulled the key from the ignition,

grabbed her folder, and went to the solid wood office door. She pushed it open, and a bell tinkled above. Verna's neat desk sat empty.

"Mia? Mia, is that really you?" A high voice, not at all like Verna's gruff tone, called from behind the door.

Mia stepped beyond the door to see a young woman with straight blond hair rushing around the assistant's small desk. Khaki pants emphasized her long legs, and she'd paired them with a white button-down shirt. She'd finished off the conservative outfit with a pair of leather boots Mia would kill to own. She obviously knew Mia, but her identity was a mystery.

"Oh, my goodness, it *is* you." She flipped her hair over her shoulder. "I heard you were back, but I refused to believe it until I laid eyes on you."

Mia returned the woman's infectious smile. "Do I know you?"

"Sydney...Sydney Tucker."

Tucker? Mia knew the name, but the Tuckers in Shadow Lake multiplied faster than bunnies. She could belong to one of any number of families.

"Clueless, huh?" She laughed. "I'm Adam's cousin and was a few years behind you in high school."

Cousin to her friend? Really? *That* girl? "But you're so...so..."

"Normal-looking?" She tossed back her head and laughed. "Gave up the piercings after high school. The shock value no longer got what I wanted."

"I would never in a million years have guessed your identity."

Sydney mocked a runway pose. "I'll take that as a compliment." She suddenly sobered. "I'm so sorry for your loss. I didn't know Wally well, but from what I knew, he was the best."

"And now you work here," Mia said absently to avoid the sadness of Sydney's condolences.

She nodded. "Part-time. I'm finishing my associate's degree in criminal justice then off to the police academy before I start work as an officer for Shadow Lake PD."

"Police department? That *is* a change from high school."

"Don't you know it." She laughed. "I suppose you're here to see Verna."

"I am. Is she around?"

"Nah." Sydney frowned. "Lucky for you the warden is taking a long lunch again today."

A warden and long lunch? Not the Verna Mia recalled. Maybe things had changed around here. "I remember her as being pretty nice if a bit reserved."

"Maybe at one time." Sydney perched on the corner of her cluttered desk. "Things were cool until Wally died. Now every little thing sends her ballistic."

Mia's radar beeped at full alert. Why would Verna's attitude change when Wally died? Mia had always thought Verna was close to Wally, but the behavior Sydney described didn't sound like a typical way to express grief.

So what then?

The door flew open and crashed against the wall. Heart racing, Mia spun.

Verna, carrying a large box, trudged into the office. She eyed Sydney with a stern reprimand. "Come get this shredder. If you have time to stand around and gossip, you have time to help me clean this place up."

Sydney passed Mia, giving her an I-told-you-so look on the way.

Mia followed Sydney. "It's good to see you, Verna."

Verna let her purse slide down her arm and plop onto her desk. "About time you decided to stop in."

Ooh, she *was* testy. That wouldn't deter Mia from asking about the barn, but she would ease into it.

Mia held up her folder. "I was wondering if I could make some copies."

Verna jabbed a finger at the far wall and sat in the squeaky chair behind her desk. "Copier's over there in the corner where it's always been."

"Thanks." Mia crossed the room and started her copies, the older machine humming efficiently.

"We were all sad to hear about Wally's passing," Verna said, sounding like the kind woman Mia remembered. "I know you were like a daughter to him and will miss him."

"I will," Mia said, keeping her tone casual but wondering why Verna didn't say she would miss him too. "Say, I was wondering when you started locking the barn."

Verna's penciled-in eyebrows arched. "We never lock the barn."

"The doors were chained on the day of the fire."

"That's news to me." She slowly laced her fingers together and stared at them in fascination.

Mia changed pages on the glass. "Any idea who might have locked it?"

Verna's gaze darted around the room then lighted on a pack of Lucky Strikes that had fallen from her purse. She tapped out a cigarette and dangled it from the corner of her mouth, but didn't light it.

"Nothing in there worth locking up." She leaned back in the sagging chair. "Now if you don't mind, I have work to do."

Good one, Verna. The best non-answer Mia had ever heard. Was the manager hiding something?

Mia searched her face, but her expression hardened. So fine. Pushing more for answers would only spook the woman. Make her close down more. Mia didn't want that.

She would have to come back later and find a way to better ease into the topic.

Mia put the documents into her folder. "One more thing before I go. Did Uncle Wally handle the insurance on the property or did you?"

Verna dug in her purse and extracted a blue lighter to set it on the desk "Wally didn't handle much of anything."

Did Mia detect a note of frustration with Wally? She would have to watch for that. "Have you filed a claim for the barn, then?"

"The fire just happened yesterday. I ain't no miracle worker." The cigarette bobbed with each word.

"Do you think you can get to it today?" Mia replaced the will with the letter, making sure to hide the cutout letters from Verna's and Sydney's view.

"Like I said, I ain't a miracle worker."

"If it helps, I can file the claim," Sydney offered.

"No." Verna gave her a stern look. "You've got enough to do as it is. I'll make time for it."

Mia took out her last copy and slipped it into the file. "I'll check back tomorrow to see if there's anything you need from me."

Mia waited for Verna to reply but she didn't speak, so Mia smiled at the older woman and turned to the door. She mouthed thank you to Sydney and waved.

Mia climbed into the utility vehicle and stared at the office. She hadn't learned anything to help with the investigation. Not really. But Verna's attitude? She was hiding something.

What an interesting development. Verna wouldn't inherit Evergreen under any circumstance, but she just earned a place on Mia's suspect list, and Mia was eagerly looking forward to what Colin's deep dive into the resort manager might unearth.

In the rec center, Ryan checked the cage-covered clock from his seat at the head of a long table surrounded by his staff. Through two hours of status updates, he'd had to force himself to keep his mind off Mia and on his hard-working staff members. Mia had always done that to him. Consumed his thoughts and left zero room for anything else.

"Did you hear me, Ryan?" Ian asked, a hint of irritation in his tone.

"Sorry, what did you say?"

"I asked if you think the fire and that weird hand incident at the lodge will have any impact on our program."

Ryan wasn't surprised at the question. Gossip spread fast in a small town, and his staff members weren't immune. "These incidents are targeted attacks not directed toward us, and we always keep the students in sight. Though I'm not concerned, I would say to stay vigilant and report anything out of the ordinary to me."

His phone chimed. He looked at the screen—Russ.

"Sorry," he said to his staff. "I've got to get this. Let's call this meeting for now. If something else comes up we can get together again."

Ryan stepped outside and out of everyone's earshot.

"Hey, bro." He kept his tone purposefully light to try to keep the conversation less argumentative than they'd been since Mia arrived.

"Do you remember Mia ever owning a charm bracelet?" Russ asked.

A charm bracelet?

Ryan ran through the hours they'd spent together. She'd dressed like a tomboy and didn't wear much jewelry. Just unique earrings. The only time he remembered her not wearing torn jeans or cut-offs and T-shirts was when they

93

went to prom. And the only thing on her wrist that night had been the orchid corsage he'd given her. "I remember crazy earrings but no bracelets."

"I'm talking about the kind of bracelet she might not wear but keep in her jewelry box. Girls collect charms from special events and put them on a chain." He sounded baffled as to why girls might do this.

"Sorry, bro, don't remember anything like that."

"When's her birthday?"

"October fifteenth. Why?"

"My evidence tech found a bracelet stuck in the tissue paper in the severed hand box. Looks like whoever sent the package tried to strap the bracelet on the wrist, but it dropped into the tissue. It has a birthday cake charm with October 15 engraved on it. It also has several charms from the Atlanta area that Mia might've collected. All were dated before her mom died."

An uneasy feeling settled into Ryan's gut. If she owned such a special memory of her mom, she would've shared it with him. "This can't be hers. I would've known if she had one."

"Maybe you don't know as much about her as you think."

Ryan might be on her short list of people to avoid right now, but he knew her as well as anyone could. Maybe better than anyone else. At least he used to, but now he couldn't be sure. "I don't think it's hers."

"Well, we'll soon find out. I'm heading to the lodge to ask her about it."

If it did belong to her and somehow the creep threatening her got ahold of it, she would need Ryan by her side whether she thought she did or not. "I'll meet you there."

"This is official business." Russ's stern older brother tone had been used to try and keep Ryan in line more times than Ryan would care to admit. "You need to keep out of it."

Just like their days living at home together, Ryan ignored his brother and disconnected before Russ made him promise to stay away.

Russ was right. This was official business but no way Ryan would miss seeing the bracelet and learning why the creep threatening Mia thought it would cause her pain.

9

The steep incline on the drive from the rec center had forced Ryan to keep his speed down. He was making the last curve when he spotted Russ's squad car parked near Mia's garage. Ryan had hoped to arrive at the lodge before Russ, but at least the trip had given him time to pray for a positive outcome.

Prayer or not, he still wanted to beat Russ into the lodge. He pressed the accelerator, sending throat-clogging dust into the air. In an effort to cut Russ off, who'd climbed from his car and was heading toward the lodge, Ryan slid into a parking spot closer to the lodge. Truck still rocking from the sudden stop, Ryan hopped out and hurried toward the walkway.

"Thought I told you to stay away from here," Russ said as he reached Ryan.

Ryan shrugged. "This is a free country. I just stopped in to see Mia."

"Short of arresting you, I can't stop you from going in. But not a word. Even if you think I'm picking on Mia. Got it?"

Ryan nodded, though if Russ got too difficult Ryan fully intended to step in.

Russ climbed the lodge stairs and pounded on the door. Ryan followed.

Fierce barking sounded from inside, but Mia didn't answer.

"You think something's wrong?" Ryan asked.

"Don't overreact." Russ pounded again.

Nothing but Bandit's high yips.

Russ twisted the knob.

Unlocked. What in the world was she thinking?

Russ pushed the door open. "Mia!"

No response. Bandit's barking turned frantic.

Russ withdrew his gun from his holster. "Stay here."

Stay here?

No way. Ryan hadn't reacted fast enough for Cara, and she'd ended up dead. He wouldn't make the same mistake with Mia.

Please let her be okay.

They cleared the family room and kitchen. No sign of an intruder or violence. Russ pointed at the hallway leading to the bedrooms, and Ryan followed him. Bandit had stopped barking and was whimpering and scratching at the door of his crate.

Russ stepped into the first bedroom. Ryan moved toward the next one.

"What's going on?" Mia appeared at the end of the hallway, folder in hand, purse slung over her shoulder.

Ryan let out a long breath, but worked hard not to let her see how worried he'd been. "We came to see you. Bandit started barking, and you didn't answer the door. We figured something was wrong."

"We?"

"Russ is in the first bedroom."

Despite Ryan's residual concern, he had enough presence of mind to enjoy the sight of Mia dressed in a green jogging suit in that soft fuzzy kind of fabric he didn't know the name of.

Russ stepped out. "You're here. Why didn't you answer the door?"

"I was down at the office and just got home." She turned to go back to the family room.

They followed her. She set her purse and folder on the counter then bent down to Bandit's crate. He danced and whimpered until she opened the door and picked him up. She gave the dog an innocent child's smile. A wide dazzling smile that stole Ryan's breath. She looked downright sensational, and he had to plant his feet to keep from crossing over to her and giving her a fierce hug.

"Hey, little fella." She reached into the cone and scratched under his chin. He ran his pink tongue over her hand. "What's this I hear about you barking?"

Her gentle and loving tone sent a pang of jealousy coursing through Ryan. It'd been years since a woman had talked to him with such affection. He missed the companionship. Maybe he'd been too hasty when he'd sworn off dating. But could he even do it? He would have to let go of Cara's tragic death first and that didn't seem likely.

Mia finally set the dog down then moved to the island and rested her hands on the folder she'd placed there. "So what did you two want?"

Russ moved closer to her. "First off, I wanted to tell you we ID'd the owner of the truck that burned in the barn."

"But all the VIN numbers were removed." Ryan joined the pair by the counter. "Can't see how you could do it that fast."

"Belongs to Orrin Jackson." Russ squatted to pick up Bandit and pet him.

"He owns a rural property not far down the road. He came back from vacation today and discovered it was stolen."

"Orrin, huh." Ryan processed the news. "He have any idea who might've taken it?"

"Not at this point. But his house was ransacked and his gun cabinet emptied. He's an avid hunter, which means we're talking about three rifles and two handguns."

Mia's face blanched. "So this man, the one who wants me to leave, is now armed?"

"Maybe." Russ's calm expression seemed more like he was reporting a traffic violation not arson and burglary that involved stolen weapons. "More likely the intruder plans to sell the weapons."

"But you can't be sure," Mia said.

"No, I can't be sure." Bandit squirmed, and Russ set him down.

"I could be in real danger here, then." Mia turned away but not before Ryan caught a glimpse of the raw fear in her eyes.

She was right. Guns could now be involved. Rifles. Handguns. Her life perhaps even more on the line.

Visions of Cara's lifeless body had Ryan swallowing hard. He could never survive losing someone like that again. Never. Best to forget those thoughts on dating he'd just had and stick to the single life.

He curled his fingers into fists and faced Russ. "What do you plan to do about it?"

Russ didn't seem troubled by Ryan's pushiness. Just stood there and took it. "Got my team on the burglary, and I'll do my best to resolve this investigation as quickly as I can."

Not good enough. "What about calling in Sierra Rice at Veritas to do the forensics at Orrin's place? The barn too?"

"Budget, man."

"I'll pay for them," Mia said.

Russ shuffled back a step. "Not sure how that would work or how much it would cost."

"Cost doesn't matter. I want this resolved, and I'll pay for as much as I can afford. Uncle Wally had quite the savings that he split between David and me. I'll use that money."

Russ gave a nod of approval and shoved his hand into his pocket. "Then I'll give Sierra a call as soon as we finish up here."

Such easy cooperation from Russ was unexpected. Maybe he wasn't going to ask about that bracelet after all.

He dug a plastic evidence bag from his pocket and laid it open on his hand. A shiny bracelet settled into his palm. *Right.* He hadn't forgotten or changed his mind.

He stepped closer to Mia and held his hand out to her. "We found this in the box with the hand. I'm certain it's yours."

Mia stared at the bracelet, and Ryan checked it out. He'd never seen this piece of jewelry before, of that he was sure.

She blinked frantically and backed up until she bumped into a stool. She sank onto the seat and clutched her hands together.

"Is this bracelet yours?" Russ shoved his hand closer.

She didn't speak, and Russ moved into her personal space. Her head snapped up. At her pained stare, Ryan's instincts urged him to step in between them, but he wanted to hear the answer as much as Russ did.

"It's not m—"

"Before you deny it, the charms have dates engraved on them," Russ said. "Dates like your birthday." He maneuvered the charms around and jabbed his index finger at a birthday cake.

She turned away and covered her mouth. Ryan couldn't

see her expression, but her body trembled, giving them a nonverbal answer.

This was Mia's bracelet.

~

Mia wrapped her arms around her waist. How could anyone have gotten a hold of her bracelet and put it on that hand? And how did it relate to the threat or the fire?

Could this be a setup of some sort? Or was Russ trying to trick her into confessing to being behind these incidents? But she had nothing to confess. Nothing other than the fact that she'd once owned this bracelet. She had to tell him that, but the words were stuck in her throat.

Didn't help that Ryan was looking at her like she had two heads. Did he think she'd been hiding this bracelet from him? She had to set that right.

"I had a charm bracelet when I was a kid." She spread the bag with the thick chain across her open palm. The cool metal slashed a line across her hand. The bracelet seemed alive, like a snake reaching out to bite her.

She couldn't hold it any longer. She thrust the bag back at Russ. "It's my bracelet, but I don't know how it ended up in that box. It was disposed of the summer I moved here."

"Disposed of?" Russ asked. "How? Where?"

Mia had never talked to anyone outside of a therapist about the summer she'd lost her mother. Not even Ryan. She probably should have, but she only told him about the accident. Not her father's unbelievable behavior immediately following it.

She would certainly never share the gut-wrenching details with Russ now. But she could give him enough information to understand that barring a miracle—barring the fact that the evidence was in his hands—this could not be her bracelet.

She would make the telling brief. She rattled through the details of the car accident then stopped to fight back the tears that always threatened when she remembered her mother. She looked at Ryan. Found compassion. Guilt for the way she'd treated him when she'd left ate at her, so she turned to Russ. His sympathetic expression was nearly her undoing.

She looked at her feet to get through the telling. "My father was distraught over Mom's death. He didn't want to see anything that reminded him of her, and he certainly didn't want to go back to our home in Atlanta. After deciding we would live here, he convinced Uncle Wally to get rid of everything we owned in Atlanta. Sell our house and dispose of all of our stuff. All Dad let us keep were the things we'd brought up here. Minus Mom's stuff, of course."

"Sounds harsh," Russ said.

"It was. But we got over it." *Liar. You're still carrying the pain of his ruthless treatment around.*

"What if Wally didn't get rid of everything?" Ryan asked. "Maybe he kept the bracelet."

"Not likely. Uncle Wally had a picture of my mom. He gave it to me at her funeral. When my dad found out, he threw it in the fireplace and threatened to kill Uncle Wally if he gave me anything else. There's no way anyone would want to stand up to that rage again."

"So if Wally didn't keep it, who does that leave?" Russ asked.

"No one. My dad would never have asked for the bracelet. All of the charms were from special times with Mom. It would bring him too much pain. And David was fifteen. No teenage boy would want his little sister's bracelet."

"Then maybe someone had a replica made," Ryan said more to Russ than to Mia, as if he felt the need to defend her. "To hurt Mia. To get her to leave."

She thought about the charms. Could they be duplicated? She ticked them off one at a time, mentally stroking them as she traveled along the length of the silver chain.

When she reached the end, the answer struck her. "Check the penny from Stone Mountain. When you smash a coin in one of those machines, it stamps the year into the copper. They could easily smash the penny, but how would they replicate that date?"

Russ laid the bag on his palm and flipped the penny over. Mia stared at the bracelet. As it moved, piercing rays shooting through the window glinted from the charms as if the bracelet were sending out a warning.

"It says 1999. This is the real deal." Head bent, Russ jiggled the charms again. "Assuming, and this is a big assumption, this warning and the fire are related, then the bracelet points toward someone from your family. Access to your old bracelet would most likely be restricted to your family and, of course," he looked at Mia, "I need to keep you on my list."

She stared at him. What was with his need to consider her a suspect, and what could she do about it?

He shoved the bag back into his pocket. "We might be able to get prints or DNA from the bracelet. Especially if we get Sierra Rice on board."

"Count on me to pay whatever it costs." She let relief color her words. "I haven't touched that in so long my prints won't likely be on it and this will clear my name."

"Not necessarily," Russ said. "I don't want to have to say this, but you could have hired someone to put the bracelet in the box just like you did to start the fire."

What? She did not expect him to go in that direction.

Ryan's jaw tightened. "You saw her legit reaction to the hand, bro. Move on. Mia's not involved in this."

She came to her feet. "He's right, and I can prove it."

"I'm listening," Russ said, cocking a brow.

She reached across the counter and thrust the will and threat into Russ's hand. "Here's the will. Once you read it, you'll know I don't gain anything until the year is up. And in the envelope is a letter that was waiting for me at the post office yesterday."

Russ tucked the will under his arm then opened the envelope and scanned the letter. "Okay, so how does this prove you aren't involved? You could've sent it to yourself."

"Look at the postmark. I was in Atlanta when it was sent."

Russ rolled his eyes. "So the guy you hired to start the fire mailed the letter."

"You're unbelievable," Ryan snapped. "Can't you at least acknowledge you could be wrong and someone is threatening Mia?"

"Despite what you both think about me," Russ paused and looked at them in turn, "I have an open mind. I'm more than willing to entertain another suspect, but so far there's no evidence to point to anyone else."

"You can get prints and DNA from the letter I just gave you, right?" Mia asked. "That could give you that other suspect."

"Yes, but since you've been handling it without gloves, yours will be on it as well."

"I touched it too," Ryan said. "Does that make me a suspect?"

"Not a strong one, but yes. Anyone who touched this letter except me is a suspect."

Ryan advanced on his brother. "How about Mia's father or David for that matter? You could at least look into them."

"And why would I do that?"

Mia held her hand in front of Ryan. "Ryan, don't."

"I'm sorry, Mia, but he needs to hear this." Ryan explained her father and David's motive.

Russ fixed a hard stare on her. "Why is this the first time I'm hearing about this?"

"She hopes to one day reconcile with her father, and she doesn't want people in town to gossip about her like they did back in high school," Ryan answered for her. "Accusing Dr. Blackburn of these crimes would only make him more angry."

"Can't be helped. They both sound like viable suspects."

"But I..."

"You can't have it both ways, Mia," Russ straightened to full height. "Either I consider them suspects or that leaves only you for now."

"I don't want to believe they could do this," she said.

"And that's admirable," Russ said. "Especially given the things your dad has done."

A compliment from Russ? She appreciated it, and yet her stomach was knotted over ratting out her own family to law enforcement.

Russ tucked the letter into the envelope. "I'll talk with your dad and brother about this. If I have additional questions, I'll get back to you."

She watched him leave and dug deep to find the confident woman who bolted for cover as she always did when her father was involved.

"You don't look so good," Ryan said.

Her head shot up. "It hurts to think my father might hate me this much. Plus you've probably started the ball rolling for the news to be spread all over town."

"I'm sorry, but the stolen guns are most worrisome. Even if I don't think your family is behind this, I had to tell Russ about your dad and David. He has to realize they could be threatening you and stop wasting time trying to prove your guilt."

Ryan spoke the truth. She got that. But right then, it was a better choice for Russ to blame her than to interrogate her father and David. After Russ questioned them, all hope of reconciling would end.

She would be without a family forever.

10

Mia had agonized over the bracelet for hours as she paced around the lodge, unpacking and taking stock of the supplies. She couldn't keep up the pace or she would burn out. She dropped into a chair near the large stone fireplace. Bandit crossed over and curled at her feet as best he could with his cone. Her mind went to Ryan. She'd hoped he would be the one guy who wouldn't let her down. But her history said, it was just a matter of time—going against her wishes and telling Russ about her father's potential involvement in the threat.

Men did that, didn't they? They were by nature fixers. Took charge even if she wanted to handle things on her own. Or at least the men in her life. All except Wally, who let her figure things out for herself. Let her fail and make mistakes even if he could've stepped in. Taught her that she wasn't always right and having things her way all the time wasn't necessarily a good thing.

Problem was, she only applied that to Wally. Gave him the benefit of the doubt because he'd never pushed too hard. But really, putting that year of residence at Evergreen in his will was big-time pushing now, wasn't it?

She sighed and looked at Bandit. "No point dwelling on any of it. Not when Ryan could be right and my life could be in danger."

Her phone rang. She grabbed it to see an unidentified caller, but she answered anyway in case it was related to the investigation. "Mia Blackburn."

"Hi, Ms. Blackburn," a pleasant female voice said. "This is Sierra Rice at the Veritas Center calling to talk to you about payment details on the Emerson County investigation."

Wonderful! Now they would get somewhere. "Please call me Mia, and thank you for agreeing to handle the forensics for us."

"Glad to help. I understand you will be paying for the investigation in full."

"That's right."

"Before we proceed, I wanted to clarify that our contract will be with Sheriff Russ Maddox of Emerson County and all findings will be given to him and not shared with anyone else including you."

"I'd be lying if I didn't say I would've loved to get your reports, but I expected this to be the case, and I'm fine with it."

"Oh, good. I find it's always best to set expectations right up front."

"Agreed," Mia said, liking this woman already for her thoroughness and strict standards.

"As a new customer, we'll require a deposit to get started on the project. I'll have our bookkeeping team give you a call to set that up. You should hear from them in the next hour or so. If all is good, then I can arrive sometime tomorrow afternoon."

"Sounds great," Mia said, though she wished Sierra could get there in the morning instead.

Still, she would arrive tomorrow, and then Russ might have the information he needed to stop considering Mia as a suspect and arrest the real person behind the threats and fire.

~

Ryan moaned and pushed back his chair. Enough was enough. He'd spent hours in the rec center preparing for the students' arrival tomorrow, and he couldn't concentrate. Not with thoughts of the stolen guns and Mia's bracelet weighing heavy on his mind.

He'd reached one conclusion. They had to seriously consider that her father and David could be behind the threats. Ryan didn't believe if they were sending the threats that they would follow through and kill her. But if someone else stole the guns, someone they employed to start the fire, then Mia's life was truly in jeopardy, and he couldn't go on with his normal life.

He'd done that with Cara. Look how that had turned out.

He had to talk to Mia. Figure out how to bring this to a close—before guns were used.

He hurried outside and waved at his staff who were gathering at the firepit for their daily social time before having dinner together. Smoke swirled into the air with the smell of grilling burgers. The staff's laughter reached him. He would normally join in, but no way his mood allowed him to be social.

He climbed into his truck and raced to the lodge. The sun still hung high in the sky and cast shadows through the trees onto the rustic building matching Ryan's cloudy mood. He parked, took the porch steps two at a time, and then knocked on the lodge door. Bandit's nails clipped across the wood floor inside, and Ryan stepped back for Mia to answer.

A loud thump was followed by laughter and Mia saying, "You silly dog. You need to be more careful, or you'll get brain damage."

She pulled open the door, and Bandit charged out. He circled Ryan and danced on his hind legs. Ryan bent to scratch his back. His happy yips made Ryan smile despite his mission.

"I'm surprised to see you." Mia tilted her head and watched him carefully.

Right. Not nearly as open to his visit as Bandit was. "Can we talk for a minute? I just can't quit thinking about the bracelet and feel like we're missing something. We can talk out here if you want." He moved out of her way and gestured toward the first cane-backed rocking chair.

She settled into the chair.

He took the chair next to her but turned it to face her. "My mind keeps coming back to the fact that Wally must've kept the bracelet. There doesn't seem to be any other possible explanation for how it could have shown up here."

She didn't answer for a long while. Just tapped her chin. "I'm leaning the same way, but then why didn't Uncle Wally give it to me when I moved to Atlanta to live with him? My dad had no hold over either of us then."

Ryan shrugged. "Who knows what he might have been waiting for. But we need to assume he brought it to Evergreen and someone around here got a hold of it. Who could've found it and realized what it was and how important it was to you?"

"Only one person had unrestricted access to Uncle Wally's stuff up here and that's Verna." Mia's face lit up. "She knows all about our family, and she was acting weird when I talked to her this afternoon."

Interesting twist. "Weird, how?"

"Gruff. Bad-tempered. And you know Uncle Wally never locked anything around here, right? Well, the barn was locked the day of the fire, and I asked her about that. She gave me a vague answer then acted all secretive."

He was hard-pressed to think of Verna as a criminal but he caught Mia's enthusiasm and went with it. "You think Verna locked the barn to hide something in there? Or to keep someone from seeing something she stored in there?"

Mia twisted her hands together. "I'm not even sure both doors were locked. I can only vouch for the one I saw."

Had they been locked? He thought back to when he'd gone in to check for a survivor in the truck. The doors were toast by then, but he'd taken a good look around, catching sight of the rear door. "There was a chain hanging on the other handle, but I don't remember seeing a lock."

Mia jumped to her feet. "We can check right now."

Ryan held up his hand. "Not so fast. I know you want to do something, but how does finding out it was locked help us to move forward?"

"If the padlock is still there and the chain is intact, we know the arsonist had to have the key to get in. If he had a key, then maybe that connects him to Verna. And maybe Sierra Rice can get DNA or fingerprints from them."

"If Veritas even agrees to help," he said.

"They did. Sierra called me to arrange payment, and she'll be here tomorrow afternoon."

"Finally, some good news."

"C'mon." She danced in place.

He didn't like walking around in the shell of the barn. Could be hazardous for them both. But he did want to determine if the doors had been locked. "Okay, but we do it my way. Rutting through a burned building is dangerous. We'll go together, but I'll do the looking."

Her excitement deflated, and she settled down. "Fine."

He stood. "Let me get a pair of boots from my truck. And you might want to put Bandit inside or leash him. Don't want him getting into trouble."

"It'll do him good to go for a walk. I'll get his leash."

She went inside, and Ryan crossed to his truck. He slipped into protective boots and retrieved thick leather gloves. He doubted looking at the chain would pan out, but when he saw the excitement on Mia's face, he'd have offered to pick up every charred hunk of wood in the barn to find a clue.

Mia clomped toward him wearing an old pair of green rubber boots that looked three sizes too big. Likely Wally's boots. "Ready?"

Before he could answer, Bandit shot off, jerking the leash and pulling Mia along at a fast clip through recently mowed grass that emitted a fresh and earthy odor.

"I probably shouldn't have said I'd keep Bandit." She laughed as she tried to rein in the frisky animal. "I don't have the first clue how to take care of or train a dog."

"I can give you some pointers when we get done here."

"That would be great." She looked at him with the same admiration she'd had for him in high school, and a warm feeling spread through his chest. He was honestly looking forward to working with her and getting to know her again. "Have you had a chance to look at Eddie's file?"

She shifted the leash to her other hand and faced him. "I did."

"We can review the notes before your first session if you'd like."

She cocked her head. "Do you do that with your other staff?"

"Only if they ask," he answered honestly.

She studied him carefully. "You said we would keep this professional, right?"

He'd said that, but could he really follow through after seeing her need for a friend? For him? He raised his face to the tall pines, listening to the chirping birds. Searching for answers.

"Ryan? Can we work together?" Her voice had gone soft like she was afraid to hear his response.

He watched a hawk soar through the trees, and he ran a hand through his hair. "You want the easy answer or the truth?" He let his gaze fall on her face again.

"The truth." The words slipped from her lips like the wind rustling the trees.

"I'll do my best to keep my promise. I honestly will. But I'd be lying if I didn't say I want to be sure you realize I'm not like the other guys in your life who've let you down. You can trust me." He waited for her to bolt, run for cover at his honesty, but she kept her focus pinned to him.

Softness claimed her vibrant green eyes before they drifted closed and long lashes lay on her cheeks. "I'm not there yet, but I hope at some point I'll be ready to do that."

He wanted more than her hope for a change, but he would settle for anything at this point. "That's all I can ask for."

She gave him a tight smile, and he sucked in a breath to shake off the heaviness that had settled over them. As a counselor, he knew they'd already made amazing progress, but she needed more time. Still, she gave him hope and a sense of urgency to move forward and restore her faith in him surged through his body.

Why was this suddenly so important to him? So pressing?

Was it Cara? The loss. A vision of her lying in her own

blood on the floor with a knife lodged in her stomach, chilled him.

Life could end in a flash and the warnings were growing more threatening. He couldn't let Mia meet the same fate. Wouldn't let her die.

~

Mia couldn't stand still any longer. Not with the way Ryan was tensing up. She started for the barn and engaged him in conversation about Wilderness Ways to lighten the mood. It didn't take him long to relax and settle into a comfortable conversation with her. A warm current floated around them and reminded her of when they were so well-connected in high school.

Bandit tugged on his leash, and she shifted toward the barn. Her mood soured. The north wall where she'd been trapped remained standing, but the rest of the barn huddled on the ground in mounds of ashes and charred wood. The closer they came, the stronger the noxious scent grew. The water-laden ground sucked at her boots. She picked up Bandit to keep his injured leg clean and moved on. Each step took concentration to keep from slipping into the slimy muck.

Sadly, this reminded her of the way she'd felt since Wally died. Like all her positive energy had been sucked from her, and she had to fight with each step to keep from going under.

Ryan suddenly faced her. "This is as far as you go."

Mia wanted to argue, but he was giving of his time to help her. "Be careful."

He slipped on gloves and picked his way through the debris. He took slow, measured steps until he reached the spot where the main entrance would have been located.

"The door is still partially intact." He bent to dig through the charred wood.

She tried to be patient but as he squatted without a word she had to see if he'd found anything.

Careful not to fall, she tiptoed closer. "What's going on?"

He stood. "No chain."

"There has to be one." She studied the area. "You said you saw it the day of the fire."

He stepped through the debris to join her. "I did, but there's nothing there now. Maybe Russ took it for evidence."

"Not likely Russ even knew the lock had any significance."

"Only one way to be sure." Ryan pulled off his gloves and stuffed them in his back pocket then reached for his cell.

He was going to call his brother. Was that a good idea? "Are you sure you want to ask him? It might make him come back here again."

"I can ask in a way that he won't suspect a thing." Ryan dialed, but Mia's mind went to the puzzle and tuned him out.

Assuming Russ didn't take the chain, why would it be gone? Did someone come get it to hide the fact that the barn was locked?

Mia halfway listened as Ryan smooth-talked his brother, but she kept pondering the missing chain and potential lock. They needed to look for the other lock and padlock too so Sierra could process it for prints and DNA.

Ryan ended his call. "He didn't take it."

"This is really odd." Mia stared at the charred lumber. "We should go check the other door to see if that chain is gone too."

Ryan tucked the phone in his pocket. "That's too danger-ous. Even for me. The remaining wall could fall with a slight breeze in either direction, and I won't risk either of us getting trapped under the debris."

"But we have to know."

His gaze met hers and held. "Not today, we don't."

"There has to be a way." Disappointed, Mia looked away.

"I'll call the chief and see if he can get the crew together to safely bring the wall down in the morning. Then, and only then, will we check on the lock."

She didn't like his answer, but she respected his professional opinion.

"Mia." He gently clasped her shoulders and angled her to face him. "I mean it. Keep away from the barn."

She would listen to him. For now. But if he didn't arrange to have the wall brought down tomorrow, she would have to find a way to check it out. Regardless of his concern, she had to see if the lock was still there.

11

An hour later, Ryan approached the front door of his parents' house, and Mia led Bandit alongside them. Or was Bandit leading Mia? Hard to tell who was winning right now. The night air had cooled some, especially with the sun behind thick clouds and hinting at potential rain.

Ryan glanced at her. "Bandit needs to learn you're the alpha dog and respect your leadership."

She narrowed her eyes. "I don't know if I can do that. I just look at his sweet little face and want to spoil him."

"I get that, but dogs are pack animals, and he really will feel more secure if he believes you're in charge. It's something you're good at, so just ignore that cute face until after you've taken control."

"I'll try."

Ryan opened the door and stood back for them to enter. With Russ suspecting Mia of being behind the threats, Ryan had been tempted to skip the usual weekly family dinner at his parents' house. But he liked the idea of having Mia in eyesight instead of her being alone at the lodge, so he'd convinced her to join them. She agreed under two conditions. No talk of the threats and that she be allowed to bring Bandit to cheer Jessie up.

Ryan readily agreed to both.

His mother rushed into the entryway. Her long blond hair was in a braid down her back, and she wore one of her usual big dresses that hung to the floor. He always thought they looked like brightly patterned sacks with a head hole and did nothing to flatter her fit shape. But she loved them.

Mia cast a smile at his mother. "Thank you for inviting me and Bandit, Mrs. Maddox."

His mom waved her hand and gave Mia a big hug. "Please. It's Barbie."

Everyone was welcome at this home. Including the woman who almost led him too far astray in high school for him to get into a good college. His mom didn't judge. Didn't criticize, but lovingly corrected. She was the best mom a guy could ask for. Even if when he was younger her hippie tendencies and a name like Barbie led to some bullying at school.

"Jessie's dying to see Bandit." Ryan's mom circled her arm around Mia. "Let's take him to the family room. Just a warning. Everyone's already here, and the boys are getting up to their usual antics when they come together."

Mia chuckled, and the pair headed down the hallway. Ryan appreciated his mom's usual lighthearted mood more than ever, though he'd be just fine if she stopped calling them boys.

The house smelled like onions and some sort of browned meat, along with the tantalizing scent of fresh bread. His mom wasn't the greatest cook, but she could make a mean pot roast and baked all kinds of delicious breads and desserts.

The whole family, as predicted, was sprawled around the large family room filled with an overstuffed sectional and comfy chairs. Jessie and Russ were on the floor by the coffee table playing checkers.

His dad sat in his recliner, feet up, smiling over his family. He flipped down the leg rest and got up to shake Mia's hand.

"Now, Hank." Ryan's mom swatted at his dad's hand. "No need to be so formal."

He looked confused. Ryan got it. His dad was a formal handshake kind of guy. An accountant, he was pretty straightlaced. Until you took him out in the wilderness. Then he let go and relaxed. Found his joy and real passion there.

"Handshake or not, welcome." He dropped back into his chair.

"Bandit!" Jessie rushed forward.

"Oh no you don't." Russ caught her. "You can't escape the game because you're losing. I'll have to exact my punishment."

He started to tickle her. She giggled and turned to throw herself into Russ's arms. "I love you, Uncle Russ. You're so much fun."

"Backatcha, squirt." He released her, and she ran to Bandit, dropping to the floor and letting the dog climb all over her as she giggled.

"Thanks for bringing Bandit over," Reid said.

"Of course."

"Go ahead and sit," their mother said. "We have about ten minutes until dinner, which should give Jessie time to wear little Bandit out."

Mia took a seat next to Reid on the big sectional couch, and Ryan sat on her other side, thankful to have her here with his family. Despite the past, she seemed relaxed and like she fit in. Much the way Reid's wife, Diane had. It'd been a sad day in the Maddox family when cancer had taken her life. Still was sad, especially on holidays and family dinner nights.

Reid smiled at Mia. "Seeing Jessie's happiness is such a good thing. It's hard to come by some days. Thank you for helping with it."

"I can relate to that," Mia said.

Reid narrowed his eyes. "I know your experience with your mom could help her. Maybe once your current issue is resolved, you could share some of how you coped when you lost your mom."

Mia smiled at Reid. "I'd be glad to. We can bond over Bandit."

She so readily accepted Reid and was willing to help him, and yet, there was still a tension with Ryan. Would that ever go away? He wasn't sure, but he knew he wanted it to.

"I wish I could commit to keeping Bandit at our place," Reid said. "But as I mentioned, it's just too much right now. The business has taken off far stronger than we thought, and even with the extra guys we hired, we're still slammed."

"A good thing, though, right?" she asked.

"Absolutely, and we're very blessed by it." He looked at Jessie. "But she needs a lot of my time too, and I don't ever want to shortchange her."

Mia frowned. Ryan knew her thoughts. Her dad not only didn't mind shortchanging her, he chose not to spend time with her and had even avoided her whenever possible.

Jessie charged over to Mia, Bandit nipping at her feet. "Grammy says I need to take Bandit out to do his business before dinner. Want to come with me and see the special play structure Grammy and Grandpa got for me?"

"Sure," Mia said readily.

Reid gave Mia a you-don't-have-to-go look, but she waved him off and took Jessie's hand.

Ryan knew how much she loved kids. Always had. They

accepted her for who she was and didn't try to change her as everyone else in her life had done. Everyone except Ryan and Wally.

But since they'd reconnected, he'd been pushing hard to change her decisions and actions. Maybe as unpalatable to her as trying to change her. He should probably back off, but how could he with her life at stake?

"I suppose Mia told you that she fronted the money for the Veritas team," Russ said. "Was a big chunk of change."

Ryan nodded, not that she'd shared the amount. "That should tell you she's not hurting for money then and burned the barn for insurance money."

"It does."

"So you no longer think she might be behind the fire and threats?"

"Didn't say that." Russ placed the red checkers into the storage box. "I read the will this afternoon, and there's a loophole."

Ryan did his best not to look shocked. "She didn't mention one. Maybe she doesn't know about it."

"Don't be naive, bro." Russ closed the box. "She must've read the document many times by now. Or at the very least, Wally's attorney would've explained the clause. She just chose not to tell us about it."

Ryan didn't like his brother's tone but resisted dropping to the floor and punching him in the shoulder as they'd often done growing up. Because, more likely what Ryan didn't like is that Russ spoke the truth.

"What's this loophole anyway?" he asked.

"She can leave at any time if she's in danger or if the property becomes uninhabitable."

"The threats make it seem like she's in danger," Reid joined in. "But the uninhabitable part makes it sound like

Wally was thinking more of natural disasters, not someone threatening her."

"You could be right," Ryan said, letting the information settle in. "Wally couldn't have predicted something like this. No way."

"What happens to the property if she takes advantage of the loophole?" Reid asked.

"Immediately, reverts to her. And the term danger is so vague that she could probably make it hold up in court if it came to that." Russ sat back. "Now it makes even more sense that she's behind things. Stay for a day or for a year. If you hated being here, which would you choose?"

Mia looked at Ryan across the dinner table. He'd been tense all through the tasty meal of pot roast, veggies, and fresh hard rolls. She tried to enjoy the food that tasted as savory as the aroma filling the air, but an undercurrent had run through the room that hadn't been there before she'd gone outside. Seemed like something—and not a good something —had happened when she'd helped Jessie with Bandit.

She set down her fork and took a long sip of the cool iced tea made to perfection then looked around the table. Unease in the room or not, the Maddox family was still the ideal family in Mia's eyes. She'd been jealous of Ryan's family, but he'd not only taken it for granted, he'd rebelled against his parents in search of adventure. She'd been more than glad to help him find it back in the day and make a little family unit of her own with him.

But what did she want with him now, if anything?

He was still an amazing guy. That had become clear. Kind. Funny. Dependable. Good-looking. A real catch.

So why hadn't he settled down?

A question for the ride home for sure.

"I hate to eat and run," Reid said. "But Jessie looks like she's going to fall asleep at the table."

"Aw, do we have to go?" The little girl rubbed her eyes. "I want to spend more time with Bandit and Mia."

Mia didn't want to be the cause of this little munchkin missing much-needed sleep. "I need to be getting home too. It's been a long day, and I have to work tomorrow."

Russ arched his eyebrow. "Work?"

Mia didn't like his suspicious look, but she would answer anyway. "I'm doing some counseling for Wilderness Ways."

Russ glanced at Ryan.

"Paul's MIA," Ryan said as if he thought Russ needed an explanation. "His mom's sick."

"I'm filling in for him," she added, as she didn't want Russ to think she'd committed to something full-time and planned to stay here after her year had ended. On day three-hundred-sixty-six, she was headed back to her life in Atlanta.

She pushed her chair back and smiled at Barbie and Hank. "Thank you for dinner. The food was excellent and so was the company."

Barbie came around the table and drew Mia into her arms, holding her tightly. She smelled of garlic and cinnamon. An unusual scent, but it was comforting at the same time. "You are always welcome here, sweetheart. With or without Ryan. Remember that."

Tears pricked Mia's eyes, but she batted them away and stepped back. "Thank you again."

Ryan said goodbye to his family, and she nearly ran to Bandit where he lay curled on a rug. He hopped up and pawed her leg. She remembered Ryan's instructions and despite her desire to spoil him, she didn't reward the dog for his behavior.

"Sit," she said and squatted to press his rear end down to the floor, telling him what she expected. He tried to play, but she remained firm until he was sitting. Only then did she strap on his leash and praise him.

"Good job," Ryan said.

His simple compliment meant more to her than she could say.

She'd been ridiculously fragile since returning home, her emotions on the proverbial roller coaster ride. Up. Down. Over. Under. But mostly, her old insecurities that she'd thought she'd dealt with were resurfacing and winning over logical thought. When she got home, she was going to have a long talk with herself and work on not letting them win. When she let them take charge, she made bad, horrible decisions, and she didn't need to be making bad choices when someone was threatening her life.

"I really like you," Jessie said to Mia. "Bandit too. Can we come over tomorrow?"

"You're welcome anytime I'm not working."

Jessie flung her arms around Mia, and Mia's heart felt complete in a way she hadn't experienced since her mother died. The child somehow cemented a sense of family in Mia's heart.

"We'll let you know if we can fit it in our day." Reid smiled and opened the door.

"We haveta do it, Dad." Jessie marched through the door. "I mean we just haveta."

"We'll see."

Her continued pleading trailed behind her as she and Reid went to Reid's pickup.

"She's a tenacious one," Ryan said and closed the door behind them. "Reminds me of you."

Mia wasn't sure how to reply, so she just set off through the dark night and sharp wind coming from the west and climbed into his truck. She waited for Ryan to get the vehicle moving then faced him.

Before she could speak, he met her gaze. "Why didn't you mention the loophole in Wally's will?"

Shocked at his topic, she watched him for a moment before answering. "No point in saying anything about it, I guess. I doubt it will ever come into play."

"Then you're not sending threats or starting a fire in the barn to make it seem like you're in danger so you can leave?"

She blinked at him. "Now you think I'm behind it all too?"

He glanced at her and held her gaze for a moment. "Look at it from my side. These threats and incidents could get you off the hook."

"Not really. I asked Uncle Wally's attorney about the clause, and he said my uncle put it in just in case there was a fire or flood. Even a tornado. If I wanted an uninhabitable place to live per the requirements, I would burn the lodge— not the barn."

"But you could probably use the danger aspect to leave now."

She hadn't even thought about it. "Maybe, I guess. But I won't. It's not really what Uncle Wally wanted, and this is all about honoring his wishes. Barring a natural disaster, I'll be staying."

She took a long breath. "I assume Russ told you about this while I was outside with Jessie, and he's eager to grill me again."

"He did, and he could be. He didn't say."

They fell silent and not the comfortable silence of old friends. Thankfully they didn't have far to go, and he soon pulled up to the lodge. She didn't want to come home to a dark building and had left the outside light on and one turned on in the family room too.

He shifted into park and killed the ignition. "I'm coming in with you to check things out."

She thought to argue, but she didn't mind having a former law enforcement officer look for any danger. Then when he left, she would lock up tight and take her little watchdog into her room for the night.

She handed the key to Ryan. "Go ahead and check things out. I'll take Bandit to do his business."

"*We'll* take him first. Together." His firm tone told her there would be no point in trying to argue with him.

"Then let's go." She looked into the sky, marveling at the millions of stars that were never visible in the city. "I forgot how beautiful it is here."

"I take it for granted at times, but then a new batch of teens arrive for the program, and they're in awe. Lets me see it through their eyes again."

"It's a good thing you're doing with Wilderness Ways." A gust of wind kicked up and carried her words into the wind.

"I like to think so."

"In fact," she said heading into territory she probably shouldn't go. "You're quite the catch. Why hasn't any woman snapped you up?"

He didn't speak, and she looked at him to find him frowning.

"Not a good subject?" she asked.

"Not particularly."

"Want to share?"

"Want to, no. Will I?" He shrugged. "I guess so."

"You don't have to," she said quickly as the pain in his tone left her concerned. She had to admit to being more intrigued now though and hoped he would fill her in.

"I'm not embarrassed to admit it took me a long time to

get over you. If I ever did." He peered into the distance. "But that's not what's holding me back. I was engaged a couple of years ago to a wonderful woman named Cara."

Oh, wow. She didn't know that. "What happened?"

"She died," he said matter-of-factly. "Was stabbed at the clinic where she worked by a guy looking to score drugs."

"Oh, Ryan." Mia tugged Bandit to a stop to rest a hand on Ryan's forearm and look him in the eye. "I'm so sorry for your loss. That must've been terrible for you."

"You know, lots of people have said that to me over the last few years, but I've wondered if they understood." He started walking again. "With the loss of your mother, you know how the sudden loss feels." He shook his head. "Sort of, anyway. I was a deputy then and was on duty. Responded to the call but got there too late. I should have been there for her."

Mia squeezed his arm and released it. "Blaming yourself for what happened is a heavy burden to carry. Take it from me. No matter what happened, you weren't at fault. You didn't kill her. You need to let it go or you'll never be able to move on. Never fall in love again."

"No worries there. I don't plan to. Won't be hurt like that again." The bitterness in his tone ended the conversation and left Mia with a lump in her throat.

Was she feeling bad for him or for herself? For them? For the possibilities they might've had? Possibilities that ended all because the pair of them had closed down any hope of the happily ever after most people dream of finding.

And what did that leave them with?

12

Mia's palms sweated as she opened the door to David's CPA practice the next morning. She hadn't seen him in so long. What would he be like? Would he still unwaveringly support their father and ignore her needs? Probably.

Her heart started pounding. She'd given herself a long pep talk this morning about her insecurities brought on from being back in town. Hadn't she gained a foothold over them? Each step closer to seeing her brother told her no. Not at all.

Focus on the place not the person.

The office held upscale modern furniture, hinting at the successful practice she'd heard about. Her dad likely beamed with pride over David's accomplishments. If he took the time to get to know Mia, he could beam over her too, just not for earning big bucks. For changing lives.

She approached the receptionist whose nameplate read Olivia, and inhaled the rich scent of freshly brewed coffee swirling up from Olivia's mug.

"I'm here to see my brother, David." Mia tried to sound strong—in control—but her voice came out fragile and weak.

"Mia. Good." The sweet young woman smiled. "David's been looking forward to seeing you from the moment he heard you were coming home." She settled back into her chair, her size dwarfed by the tall leather back. "Go on in. He's in Kurt's office. The last one on the right."

In his partner's office? But why? If he was looking forward to seeing her, why wouldn't he meet with her alone? Maybe he was uneasy about seeing her too. They'd not parted on the best of terms, and even if they had, a ten-year absence would be awkward for most anyone. Wouldn't be unusual for another person to want someone to help break the ice.

"I'm not interrupting anything, am I?" Mia asked.

"Not at all." Olivia waved a hand. Her fingernails, painted in a plum color, glistened in the light and matched her blouse. "Kurt handles Evergreen's accounts, and David figured you'd want to meet him while you were here."

"I do. Thank you." Mia set off down the hallway and hoped Olivia was right. That David really *was* happy she'd come to visit. She reached the office with Kurt Loomis, CPA, on an engraved bronze plaque mounted outside the open door. She quickly scanned the room through the open door.

A man Mia assumed was Kurt sat behind the desk covered in paperwork that looked as if a tornado had blown through the space. A large ornate frame holding a picture-perfect family of two young girls and a boy accompanied by a smiling couple hung on the wall behind him.

David, his back to her, sat beside the massive antique desk. The men were engaged in an animated discussion about return on investment, their tones speaking to the love of a job Mia couldn't imagine choosing.

She knocked on the door and waited to be invited in.

"Come in. Come in." Kurt stood, a wide smile pulling up full lips. He smoothed his fingers over a white dress shirt snugged tight at his neck with a navy tie that accented his fair coloring. He had a kind face, welcoming her into the room.

David rose and pivoted. He wore a power business suit with a white shirt and striped green tie. He held his shoulders back in a rigid stance as his appraising gaze gave her a thorough once-over.

Mia's hand flew to her mouth. Thankfully it did or she might've said something she'd regret. Her brother had turned into a photocopy of a younger version of their father. His expression, his eyes, his lips. The entire package screamed Dad. She wanted to run. Fast and far. But she planted her feet.

He adjusted his tie, and his expression mirrored her discomfort. Was he picking up on her reaction? Likely. She forced a blank look to her face. He approached and lifted his arms as if he might try to hug her.

No. Not that. Not yet. She thrust her hand out and looked him in the eyes. "Good to see you, David."

His charcoal eyes darkened, but he didn't lose a beat and firmly clasped her hand. She shook but quickly withdrew and pushed the strap of her handbag higher on her shoulder to mask her sudden action.

David opened his mouth but nothing came out.

"I...um...uh." He gestured at Kurt. "This is my partner, Kurt Loomis. Since he handles Evergreen's accounts, I asked him to join us. Hope you don't mind."

"Not at all, and I'm happy to meet you, Kurt," Mia said with honest enthusiasm and held out her hand to him. "I don't know the first thing about running a business. I have to count on Verna to do the bookkeeping and you to do whatever it is you do."

"Actually, Verna doesn't really do the bookkeeping anymore." Kurt's hand was warm and dry, his face earnest and welcoming. "When we took over the accounts a few years back, we set up a system to be more GAAP friendly."

Mia's mind went blank, and she looked at David for help.

He chuckled. "GAAP is an acronym for generally accepted accounting principles. In this case, we separated the duties of taking in the money from spending the money. So Verna takes it in, and Kurt pays the bills. I reconcile the accounts. Keeps everyone on the up and up." David clasped his hands behind his back. "So what is it you wanted to see us about?"

"Ah...no...I didn't actually come to talk about the business. This is more of a personal call."

"Oh." David's eyes widened.

Mia instantly regretted her visit. Why did she think her brother wanted to have anything to do with her? Not when he'd always sided with their father. Seemed like that hadn't changed.

She would give him an out. "If you don't have time, I can go."

"No. No. That's fine. Let's head to my office."

"Nice to meet you, Mia," Kurt said. "David and I are preparing financial reports for you. Once we've gathered a comprehensive look at the business, we can get together to review it."

Mia crinkled her forehead and faked a shudder.

Kurt laughed. "I promise to help you understand them."

"Thanks." She smiled, and it wasn't hard to do. She liked David's partner. He seemed down-to-earth and friendly. Maybe once she and David broke the ice, he'd warm up the same way.

"And I'm sorry about Wally's passing," Kurt added. "I enjoyed working with him."

Mia smiled. "I love hearing how much people liked him."

"He was one of the good ones for sure," Kurt said.

"This way," her brother said and led her down the hall to an office similar to Kurt's in size, but causal in design. He'd decorated in muted beiges with blue accents. With a slight nod, he urged Mia to sit.

She sat in a leather and chrome chair while looking at the multitude of family pictures perched around the room. He'd placed on the table next to her a candid shot of their father with two adorable girls. They were grinning at him as he returned the smile with the love Mia had always wanted to see reflected at her. She swallowed a gasp and almost ceased breathing.

"That's Dad and my girls after Easter services," David said. "Now that you're back, it would be great if you came over to meet Penny and the girls."

Mia swallowed a few times to recover from the shock of seeing the picture before she was able to speak. "You have daughters?"

"Figured Wally would've told you about them."

"We didn't talk much about what was going on here. But it would be nice to meet them. Your wife too." Maybe Mia wasn't all alone and could have a family after all.

David sat back, crossing his legs and acting as if she'd simply taken a little time away rather than ten years. Like a long vacation.

Had he forgotten about their tumultuous past? Why she'd left? If so, he wouldn't think their father had any part in these events.

"I know you must miss Wally," David said. "I will too, but you were always so close to him."

She nodded but couldn't trust her voice so didn't speak.

David picked fuzz from his pant leg and flicked it away, a

habit way too much like their father's behavior for her comfort. "What did you want to talk about?"

She reached into her purse and pulled out her copy of the threatening letter. "You said you'd heard about the fire, but there's something else I need to tell you about. I was wondering if you could look at this. It's a copy of a letter I received in the mail. The envelope has a Shadow Lake postmark. Do you have any idea who might've sent it to me?"

David unfolded the paper and his head quickly popped up. "Do you think this person set fire to the barn?"

She nodded. "Any idea who'd want me to leave town this badly?"

He ran a hand through thick hair gleaming with some sort of product and leaving behind little tufts standing at attention. "I guess if you're looking for someone who would profit from your leaving, it would be me. But I don't want Evergreen. You deserve it." A sincere smile curled his lips. "You and Wally were close. We weren't. As far as I'm concerned, he should've left everything to you, even the cash, and I hope you don't think I'd do something like this."

Mia wanted to return the smile, but he looked so much like their father she couldn't bring herself to follow through. But it did help her gather the courage to continue. "I was kind of wondering if Dad might've sent it."

"Dad? No way!" David's back straightened. "How could you even think that?"

"He's never made it a secret of the fact that I embarrass him. Seems like he'd be happy if I didn't stay around here and sully his reputation more than I did in high school."

"That's crazy." David firmed his shoulders into a hard line.

Okay, fine. He didn't believe her at all. She had to tell him everything. "There's more. I also received a package with a second warning. The box contained a fake severed hand and my old charm bracelet. Remember that bracelet with all the charms I collected?"

David nodded but his face drained of color. "Wouldn't Wally have gotten rid of it with all of our other stuff?"

"Exactly. I haven't seen it since before Mom died and suddenly it appears on the wrist of a severed hand."

"So where did it come from?"

"I don't know. I'm guessing Uncle Wally must have kept it. Then someone got a hold of it. Someone who knew how much it meant to me and used it to scare me."

"And you think Dad did this?" David frowned.

"I don't want to, but who else knew how much the memories would hurt me?"

David sat in silence, his eyes distant.

"Think about it, David." She leaned forward to encourage him to look at her. "Dad's the logical choice."

"Not to me he's not." David set his jaw. "Look. I know the two of you didn't get along, but after my girls were born, he talked to me about the mistakes he made with you and told me how sorry he is that he treated you so badly."

News to her. "Then why didn't he try to contact *me*? Tell *me*?"

"He didn't think you'd take his call."

"That's a lame excuse." Anger coursed through her. So many wasted years, when he could've picked up the phone, and they could've at least talked. Maybe not fixed things. But talked. Made it better. But now? Now what?

She shot to her feet. "I refuse to believe he wanted to make up with me and then didn't even try. I have to proceed by thinking he's behind these threats and go from there."

David looked up at her and handed her the letter. "You do what you have to do, but please don't accuse Dad of this. He's already hesitant when it comes to reconciling with you, and he may never try if you accuse him of something this horrible."

Mia slipped the letter back into her purse and said good-bye. She'd be more than happy to entertain David's advice, but she couldn't. The damage had already been done.

~

Ryan leaned over Mia's shoulder in the rec center. Her perfume drifted upward as if inviting him to move closer as it had for the last few hours of the orientation session. Or was it the memory of her stricken expression after returning from her meeting with David that tempted Ryan to give her a hug?

She wouldn't tell him what had happened. Not that he really needed details. Her expression said it all. She was vulnerable right now. Hurting. In need of a friend, not an ex-boyfriend hitting on her. Worse yet, if he did ever hit on her, he had no plans to follow through. What kind of guy would that make him? Not a very ethical one for sure.

He needed to remove the temptation. He moved to the end of the table to perch on the corner. Made it look casual, not like he was running. But he knew he was and so did God.

Is that what You want me to do? Stop running? One of the reasons You brought Mia back here?

He shook his head. He had to pay attention to the job. "That last form is a release for the documentary."

"What documentary?" She glanced up at him and then back at the paper.

"I thought I'd told you about that."

"No." She angled her body away from him.

Right. She didn't trust him with anything. He had to explain. "With increased cuts in funding, I have to find new

135

revenue sources to keep the program running. I hired a documentary crew to film this session, and I plan to use it in fundraising. Not the private counseling times, but group and wilderness activities. You probably won't end up on video, but we need your permission just in case."

"Fine by me." She turned back to the form and trailed a finger down the page as she read.

He studied the top of her head. He'd loved her crazy red hair and wished she hadn't changed it, but seemed as if she wanted to leave every bit of her past behind—including him. The natural color reminded him that a temper matching it lurked inside of her, and she was known to let it fly at times. Much the same way she had with him since she'd arrived. More than that, though, the memory of how easy it was to slide his fingers into the tangles and draw her close for a kiss pounded his brain.

He lurched to his feet and went to the other side of the table, feeling better having an obstacle between them.

Her cell lying on the table vibrated. She cast a wary glance at her phone. "It's David. Mind if I take this?"

"Go ahead." Ryan went to the window to find something to look at other than her. He listened to her side of the conversation. Apparently, David was inviting her to dinner that night, and she was trying to wriggle out of it.

Ryan opened the blinds and peered out over the lake. Sharp explosive cracks blasted through the air. Probably teens playing with firecrackers at one of the beaches. Such fireworks were illegal in Oregon, but that didn't stop people from firing them off any more than his determination not to get involved with Mia had tamped down the fireworks between them.

Her resigned tone grabbed his interest, and he turned to look at her.

She massaged her forehead and sighed. "Let me check with Ryan."

"David wants me to meet him for dinner at six. Will we be done in time?"

Ryan nodded.

"I can come," she said into the phone, followed by another sigh. She listened for a few moments, her eyes closing like clenched fists and then reopening before she handed the cell to Ryan. "He wants to talk to you."

Ryan took the phone. "David."

"With all the crazy things happening around there," David said. "I'm concerned about Mia being out at night by herself. Would you be willing to come to dinner with her?"

Ryan suppressed a groan. He didn't need to be in her company for more time than absolutely necessary.

"I'd come pick her up myself, but I have a late appointment," David continued. "Who knows what could happen if she was out at night alone."

David was right. Of course he was. Ryan couldn't let Mia go off on her own. He'd left Cara to stay at work alone at night to catch up on paperwork while he'd gone in for a double shift, and she'd died.

He wouldn't risk Mia's life too.

13

—————

Mia took the phone from Ryan. His eyes were narrowed, and his breathing had deepened. She wanted to question David about his brief conversation with Ryan, but wouldn't. Not with Ryan standing nearby.

She finalized her plans to go to dinner at her brother's place and ended the conversation before facing Ryan. "So you're coming to dinner tonight too?"

His head bobbed in one sharp nod, then he glanced at the clock. "Time for your session. I'll get Eddie for you." Ryan held her gaze, lingering like he didn't want to leave before he took off for the door.

What was with that last look? Was he upset because he didn't want to go to David's tonight? Or was this somehow a reminder of his loss of Cara?

She could easily imagine how he was suffering from that. She'd had plenty of practice with how dark emotions could impact life. Even if her dad hadn't heaped tons of guilt on her after the accident, she'd already blamed herself. But Wally persuaded her to go to counseling when she moved in with him, and she'd worked through it.

But Ryan? He was a protector. Had always been and

would carry an extra measure of guilt for not being there for his fiancée. It could even be the reason for his fluctuating behavior since they'd reconnected. Was surely behind his need to keep Mia safe. She would like to help him. She couldn't though. Not even if she understood his motives. She couldn't alleviate his guilt. Only he could do that.

She clenched and relaxed her hands to ease her tension. Things between her and Ryan were far too complicated and too personal. They promised to work together as professionals, but only a few hours on the job, and the possibility was waning fast.

No matter. She couldn't disappoint Eddie and the other students Ryan had assigned to her. She would simply have to make sure she and Ryan kept things strictly businesslike in the future so neither one of them got hurt again. And now she would do her best for Eddie. Devote herself to him and him alone for the next hour.

She rose to get some fresh air so she wasn't closed down for the session.

She stepped from the office into the main rec center and searched the space for Ryan and Eddie. Didn't find them. Instead, she spotted her father and a nurse talking near medical screens set up in the corner. Her steps faltered as she studied him. Ryan had told her a doctor examined the students to confirm their ability to handle the extreme conditions before they could join in.

He hadn't said her father was that doctor.

Rattled, she resumed walking toward the door, picking up speed. Her athletic shoes squeaked on the wood flooring, and a group of students mimicked the sound, magnifying the noise. She glanced at her father. He'd spotted her. She assumed he would ignore her, but he handed a folder to the nurse and started in Mia's direction. They met near the exit blocked by students and counselors filing out of the room.

"Mia," her father said. "I heard you were working with the students." He spoke as if they were friends.

How odd. "I hadn't heard the same about you."

"Dr. Rucker had an emergency. I'm filling in for him." He twisted a rubber band between his fingers. "This is a good thing you're doing here. Helping these kids. I'm real proud of you."

Proud of her? She didn't know how to respond other than to gape at him.

He tipped his head at the corner with the medical screens. "Looks like I have a student waiting on me. Keep up the good work."

Completely unsettled, she gawked at him as he crossed the room. Was it possible he really did want to reconcile with her as David had said? Or was this just a way to make her doubt his involvement in the threats?

The room closed in on her, and she needed air even more. She squeezed through the remaining students at the door and crossed the lawn. Sydney, pacing and checking her watch rushed forward. She grabbed Mia's arm and dragged her behind a stand of junipers.

Sydney planted her bright pink athletic shoes in the dirt behind a thick tree trunk. She wore pink shorts and a striped lime green and pink knit top, looking more like someone who worked at a resort office than the other day.

She peeked out behind the tree and gulped air, nearly panting.

Something was wrong. But what? "What's up?"

Sydney pursed her lips and glanced around the area. Was she worried about someone overhearing them?

She faced Mia. "I just heard you'd be working with these kids. My little sister, Nikki, hopes to major in filmmaking after high school. She'll be shadowing the documentary staff for the next few days."

Why would that bother Sydney? "That'll be a good experience for her."

Sydney waved a hand. "Oh, I know that, but Nikki's kind of flighty, and I'm worried about her hanging around the kids in the program. Do you think you could keep an eye out for her and tell me if she's getting into any trouble?"

Sydney's little sister sounded far tamer than Mia and Sydney ever were in high school, but Mia could understand Sydney's concern. "I'm happy to help."

Sydney pointed toward the driveway. "That's Nikki. On the sidewalk by the big guy with the camera."

Mia studied the girl's pixie face with three pounds of eye makeup. She had auburn hair and was cute in a high school girl kind of way, but Sydney with her blond hair softly framing her face devoid of makeup was stunning.

Nikki looked up, and Sydney pulled Mia deeper into the trees. "I don't want her to see us talking."

Mia gave a solemn nod she believed Sydney's sisterly concern deserved.

Sydney peeked around the tree again. "Nikki's facing the other way now. Gotta go before she sees me. Catch you later. And thanks." She skittered away, staying under the cover of trees lining the driveway.

Thankfully, Sydney's drama took Mia's mind off her father's odd behavior long enough to regain enough composure to go back to the students. She eased out of the trees and rounded the corner while keeping an eye on the parade of students.

Pain radiated from some faces, anger and frustration from others. Ryan stood at the end of the sidewalk deep in a discussion with a counselor. He'd dressed much the same as yesterday—khaki tactical pants, hiking boots, and a green polo shirt, all giving him a rustic male charm that was far too attractive.

He listened to his counselor with a keen interest. His heart for these students and the counselors who worked for him sang through in his warm expression. Man, he was something. Had really turned into the fine man she'd always thought he would become.

Maybe her leaving town had been good for him. Who knows what she would've done if she'd stayed here instead of living with Wally? She might've continued to lead Ryan astray. Get him into trouble. Serious trouble.

And what about her? Wally was the one who nurtured her and encouraged her to follow her passion for helping the underdog and get a degree in counseling. Where would she be if she'd remained here?

Ryan glanced at her and offered a quick smile before turning back to his conversation. A conciliatory smile. All business as he'd promised. As she wanted.

So why didn't she like it?

He clapped his hand on the counselor's back, and seemingly unaware of her discomfort, he joined her and tipped his head at a scowling male student. "There's Eddie. I'll get him."

Ryan escorted the boy closer. He had blond hair pulled back in a short ponytail and wore drooping camo shorts and a black T-shirt. His untied shoes sloshed on his feet, and his shoulders sagged as he walked.

But it was his fierce glare that captured her attention, and a moment of unease settled in her gut. Not in the same way Ryan's earlier behavior had. He seemed to have put aside whatever had been on his mind and kept his professional hat on as he introduced Eddie.

So as she led Eddie into the building, why did Ryan's behavior bother her? Did she want this attraction to him to go somewhere after all?

Thirty minutes later and Ryan couldn't miss seeing Eddie storm out of the rec center and down the hill. His body was rigid, face tight, anger oozing from his pores. Could be a good sign or bad. Depending on the reason for his mood.

Ryan left the firepit and approached the boy. "Session go okay?"

He scowled. "Was lame. She wanted me to talk about my feelings."

"That's what you need to do. Get your feelings out so you can move forward."

"Ooh, feelings." Sarcasm dripped from each word like wax from a melted candle.

"Listen, Eddie." Ryan took a step closer. "You have to cooperate if you want to stay in this program and not go back to juvie. And that means taking the counseling sessions seriously. Go ahead and join the group, but take some time to think about this and decide if you really want to be here."

Eddie stomped off, his untied shoes sending up dirt puffs. No way the kid wanted to go back to juvie so hopefully this little talk would help.

Ryan turned to face the rec center where Mia stepped outside.

She crossed over to Ryan, her shoulders drooping. "That didn't go so well. He didn't open up at all."

"I talked to him. Told him he needed to get with the program if he wants to stay in it. He doesn't want to go back to juvie, so maybe he'll listen and tomorrow will be better.."

"Maybe." Mia rubbed her forehead and squinted into the sun. "I'm getting a headache. Would it be all right if I waited to write up my notes and head back to the lodge?"

"Sure, I'll drive you in the UTV."

She opened her mouth as if to say it wasn't necessary but gave a sharp nod instead.

"Give me a second to tell Ian where I'm headed." Ryan rushed over to his second in charge and made the telling short and to the point before Mia changed her mind. He joined her in the vehicle and drove her home.

"I'll put it in the garage for the night and jog back."

"I can get the door." She hopped out and rolled up the squeaky door.

He puttered inside and turned to her. "Can I come in and check the place out?"

"Sure," she said and led the way to the door of the breezeway leading to the lodge.

Her easy acquiescence should be a clue to her fatigue or disappointment in her day. She entered the breezeway, her feet dragging. She really was down about the session. That should be expected as it was the one positive thing she had happening in her life right now and it didn't go so well.

Ryan opened his mouth to remind her that tomorrow's session could have a better outcome, but she hurried inside before he could speak.

In the kitchen, she looked over her shoulder. "I'll just grab some Tylenol while you check the place out and get back to the kids."

He would do as she asked, but when he finished he would find a way to stay with her until her mood had improved. How, he didn't know and he only had the time it would take to clear the rooms to figure it out.

14

Mia released Bandit from his crate then poured a glass of water and found Tylenol in the cabinet where Uncle Wally had always kept it. She took two tablets and sat on the barstool.

She looked at her computer on the counter. She should open it and start to document Eddie's brief session while it was fresh in her mind, but she just couldn't officially record her failure with the boy yet. He'd slouched in the chair across from her, a sullen expression firmly lodged on his face, his tattooed arms tightly crossed. Occasionally, he'd offered a sarcastic response to her probing questions but said nothing to give her insight into his true feelings.

She could certainly identify with his actions. She'd behaved the same way after her mother died and her father retreated into his own world. Then why couldn't she find a way to help the teen? He definitely needed it or he was headed down a one-way street of self-destruction, and she wanted to help him.

She rolled her neck, stretching stiff muscles strained when rescuing Jessie from the fire. The fire. That was something she didn't want to think about either. Especially the terrifying minutes ticking by while trapped in the blazing barn, her thoughts consumed by her imminent death. Thoughts that continued to hover near the surface.

She'd been lucky. She had stiff muscles, a few gashes on her abdomen, and a cut on her cheek, but she was alive. Alive and embracing all of her old habits exactly like Ryan had said.

She wanted to control everyone and everything around her.

So what? It had served her well. It was the only way she'd endured the pain and turmoil life continued to throw at her. Sure, after surviving a tragedy many people experienced a rebirth or change in priorities, and she hadn't, but that didn't mean anything. Right?

Maybe she didn't feel like a survivor yet and wouldn't until the lunatic terrifying her was caught and put in jail. If he was caught.

No. Don't think that way. He would be located. Russ was a determined guy. Once he stopped concentrating on her as a suspect, he would keep digging until he arrested the creep before he tried something else.

Ryan returned and came to lean on the counter. "Can I make you a cup of tea?"

"I'd love some tea, but I'm not very good company right now."

"That doesn't matter to me." He went to the electric tea kettle on the counter and held it up to confirm it held water then plugged it in. He turned back to her. "Did you want to talk about Eddie?"

She'd first wished Ryan would go, but he was being so kind and caring and she had to admit it felt good she wanted him to stay for a while. "I just have to find a way to connect with him. Do you have any idea what he might be interested in?"

Ryan shook his head. "He's pretty much been devoting himself to getting into trouble and that's all I know."

Oh, man. She knew those days. In high school, she didn't have time for much else outside of classes except partying and hanging with Ryan. "Perhaps I can get him to tell me what he used to do before his mother died."

"I hope so. And I hope my warning about going back to juvie is the jumpstart he needs."

The kettle whistled.

"Earl Gray still your favorite?" he asked.

She smiled at him, and her heart warmed over him remembering her tea preference. "It is but I think I'll have chamomile. It's calming."

A boom sounded outside. Bandit wailed. The door splintered and something whizzed behind Ryan.

"Gunfire!" Ryan lurched across the counter, grabbed her in his arms, and took her to the floor.

He landed on his shoulder, holding her tight and taking the brunt of fall.

Her breath left her body. She dragged air in, her mind awash with fear and questions. "What's going on?"

Bandit lifted his head and howled.

Ryan held her tightly in his arms. "Someone's firing at the lodge."

"A gun? Someone's firing a gun. At us?"

"Yes."

"Then we have to go. Get out of here."

"We have to stay close to the floor. Crawl behind the island." He looked her in the eyes. "Can you do that?"

Fear paralyzed her muscles, but she had to do as he asked to stay safe. "Yes."

"On the count of three I'll roll off, and we go. Belly crawl if you can."

"Okay." She took a deep breath.

"One. Two. Three." He rolled away.

Feeling even more vulnerable, she flipped over and scratched her way across the wood floor.

Bandit whimpered.

"Come here, Bandit," she said, but didn't stop to look back at him.

Another report sounded. Another bullet whizzed through the door.

They reached the other side of the island, and Bandit trotted toward them but stopped short.

"Bandit come here, boy. Come on." She leaned toward him.

"No. Don't move." Ryan retrieved his phone from his pocket. "Stay as low as you can. I'll call 911."

He tapped his screen.

Bandit whined and slunk across the room in the opposite direction. She wanted to help him, but wouldn't call out while Ryan was on the phone. Her heart thumping erratically, she listened to his conversation. She could easily tell he'd been a deputy at one time. He sounded calm. In charge.

Not her. Her heart continued to race at top speed, and her hands trembled.

Another blast sounded. She jumped and cringed.

A bullet pierced the door and lodged in the island.

"We're still under fire," Ryan said. "Get someone here now."

He ended the call. "A uniform is two minutes out, and they'll let Russ know what's going on."

"Can I crawl over to Bandit?" she asked, feeling odd to be lying prone on the floor and having a conversation.

"No. Try to get him to come over here."

She turned her head. "Here, Bandit. Here boy."

She held out a hand. He moved a few inches then sat again.

"C'mon now," she cooed in her best baby talk tone. "I've got a treat."

She was lying, but that didn't matter if it got him to move to a safer location.

"Been a bit since the last shot." Ryan's tone held a good dose of worry now.

"You think they left?"

"Could be."

"Or?" she asked, hearing more in his words than he was sharing. "There's something you're not saying."

"Or they could be coming to see if the shots hit their target."

"Here? Coming in here?" She couldn't control the panic in her voice, and Bandit whimpered again.

"Maybe it's just warning shots not meant to hurt you. Just to scare you off."

"But if the shooter is coming in, then what?"

"I need to get to Wally's gun safe. Do you have the key?"

"On a ring in the corner drawer of the island."

"You stay put. I'll grab the key and make my way to the cabinet."

"No, please. They could hit you."

"They seem to be firing only at the door, and I can avoid that area." He pushed up and staying behind the island, reached for the key then dropped back down to belly crawl across the room.

Her heart kicked in even faster. Panic threatened. She couldn't watch. Instead, she tried to coax Bandit over to her. He finally gave in and trotted her way. She had to roll to her side to hold onto him with the cone in place, but she was still low to the floor, and she eased Bandit down low. She stroked his fur and offered calming words all the while straining to hear the gun safe open, and fearing the sound of footsteps on the porch.

Sirens blared from the distance then the driveway. She relaxed a fraction. Hopefully the arrival of deputies would send the shooter in retreat if they had not already departed.

She peeked around the island at Ryan. He grabbed a handgun and ammo and was dropping back to the floor. He loaded the gun then slid against the wall behind the gun safe and faced the door, weapon outstretched.

"You're staying over there?" she cried out.

"I want to be a position to take out the shooter before he gets anywhere near you."

And draw his fire, she thought but didn't say it because there was no point. Ryan the protector was on scene, and despite what she might ask of him, he would do what he had to do to keep her alive. Even give his life. That was a certainty.

Another siren joined the first one and raced closer. Could it be Russ? Would all depend on where he was when the call came in, she supposed. But for the first time since she'd returned to Shadow Lake, she would be glad to see him.

She soon heard footsteps on the porch and fists pounded on the door.

"It's Russ," his voice came out loud and strong.

"Come in," Ryan yelled back, but didn't relax the arm holding the gun.

Mia peeked around the island. The door opened.

Gun in hand, Russ strode in. "We all good in here?"

"Fine," Ryan said. "Go after the shooter."

"Roger that." He spun and took off down the steps.

Face pale, Ryan raced across the room, set the gun on the countertop, and grabbed her in a hug. He held her tight for a moment then pushed back to brush her hair from her face. "You're okay?"

"Yes."

"Thank goodness." He pulled her close again and held her with arms that felt like iron bands.

She should push back but she let him hold her for now. He drew her closer and tightened his arms as if he never intended to let her go. A shuddering breath shook his body.

Wow, he was really worried about her.

She pulled back to look at him, but something red on the door caught her attention. "Did you see the door?"

"No, why?" He turned.

She marched over there, her legs wobbly and threatening to collapse under her.

Pinned to the door was a large red target with a picture in the bullseye of her wearing the same clothing she'd worn on her first day in town. It was taken outside the lodge. Starting at the outer circle, bullets had pierced each ring leading in to her photo.

A message said, *Leave town or my next bullet is for you.*

She gasped and grabbed Ryan's shoulder for support.

Not a single shot had missed the target. It was now clear. Whoever was trying to scare her had the ability to end her life in a split second if he chose.

15

On the lodge's front porch, Ryan glanced across the yard at Russ. He was talking to his deputies who were clearing the area, ensuring Mia's safety from any gunfire. At least while they were on site.

She'd seemed to take the latest warning in stride and sat in a rocker cradling Bandit in her arms. She stroked his fur and cooed softly to calm him down, but Ryan could see her hands tremble.

He wanted to get in her face, tell her to forget about the dog, and talk about the danger surrounding her. He wanted to, but he didn't have the heart to hurt her more. He would just have to double his efforts to protect her, even if it meant not letting her out of his sight.

Russ finished giving instructions to his deputies and headed their way, his steps firm and purposeful. Ryan planted his feet in preparation for any news Russ might have. Ryan didn't much want Russ bugging Mia, but maybe he would break through her thick shell.

Russ climbed to the top step, planted a boot on the porch, and eyed Mia. "The little fella doing okay?"

Mia's shoulders drooped. "He's still shaking."

"Hope it's not something that sticks with him."

Ryan cared about Bandit as much as his brother seemed to, but at the moment, he wanted details of the investigation more. "Any leads?"

Russ frowned. "All we know at this point is that the slugs recovered from the door are .30-06."

"Could the shooter have used one of the stolen guns?" Mia asked.

"Could have." Russ locked his gaze onto her face. "One of the stolen weapons is chambered for that caliber, but we won't know for sure until we locate the rifle used. Odds aren't in our favor in that. Hunting rifles are chambered in any one of hundreds of different calibers, but the .30-06 is very common for a hunting rifle. Don't have to tell you how many hunters we have around here."

"So, what happens next?" Ryan asked.

"Sierra Rice is due here any minute. We'll have her set this scene as top priority. Maybe we'll finally catch a break." Russ peered at Mia. "Have you thought of anything else I need to know since we last spoke?"

Mia stroked Bandit's back and shook her head.

Ryan took a step closer to his brother. "Did you talk to her father and David?"

"I did." Russ crossed his arms. "But I have to say I don't like either of them for this."

Mia's hand stilled on Bandit as she watched Russ. "And what are you basing that on?"

"Gut instinct." Russ released his arms and lifted his chin. "Experience has made me an excellent judge of people, and they both seemed sincerely glad you've come home."

"But your gut says I'm guilty?" Mia asked.

"I don't have a choice but to consider you." Russ ran a hand around the neck of his shirt. "If it helps, I'm sorry about it. Not for thinking you might be behind this. Not when facts tell me to look in your direction. As the sheriff, I have to do that."

He made strong eye contact with her. "But I will admit I haven't been impartial. That I might be letting our past dictate the way I've been talking to you. Maybe believing the worst of you. And for that I am sorry."

Shocked, Ryan eyed his brother. "And now?"

"Now, I'll do my best to be impartial." He looked at Mia. "But I have to say, it's hard to do when you failed to tell me about the emergency clause Wally included in the will."

Her eyes widened. "But only because I really don't think it's relevant. I explained that."

Russ's hand drifted to rest on his sidearm as if he felt a need to remind her of his legal standing or he thought she might take off. "Consider it from where I'm standing. You don't want to be here. Wally gave you an out. A way to leave in a matter of days instead of years. You seem to hate it here. Why wouldn't you try to use the clause?"

She sat forward in her chair and put Bandit down, her firm expression preparing Ryan for an argument.

"My goal here is to honor Uncle Wally's wishes above everything else," she said. "According to his lawyer, he only added that clause in case of a natural disaster. So barring a tornado destroying the property or something like that, I won't be leaving. Besides, I was at the rec center when these shots were fired."

Russ tilted his head, the stubborn expression Ryan had seen for years tightening his brother's face. "Again, you could hire someone. Maybe the same guy who set fire to the barn."

"I would need to have cash to pay this guy off. You can check my bank accounts to see I haven't withdrawn money other than to pay the Veritas Center."

"We are. But until we can get a full picture of your

finances, I can't take your word for this. You could say that you don't plan to use the clause just to encourage me to stop investigating you. How can I be sure you're not setting this all up to give you a reason to leave?"

She gripped the rocker's wide arms. "I get that you have to consider me, but please don't focus on me and neglect other potential suspects."

Russ relaxed the hand on his holster. "You must mean your dad and David because we have zero other suspects."

"What about the man who set the fire?" She jutted out her chin, reminding Ryan of times they'd argued in the past.

"Sure, he's a suspect," Russ said. "But since we don't know who he is yet, we can't determine if he's acting on his own or at someone else's request." Russ dropped his foot from the porch to the top step. "We'll just have to keep going in the same direction and hope we get the lead we need from forensics."

Ryan appreciated Russ's apology for overstepping and his willingness to try to be more openminded. He was a man of honor, and when he was wrong, he said he was wrong. But what if he was right about her father or David, and neither were involved in the incidents? That left some crazy stranger as the prime suspect.

Someone who'd proved he was an expert shooter and was targeting Mia. Someone Ryan had no idea how to find, let alone stop before he took Mia out.

16

Mia breathed in deeply and let air whoosh out as she set Bandit on the grass and held firm to his leash. She hoped letting him run off his residual fear from the shooting would help relax him. She wished that would work with her too, but a simple walk wouldn't calm her down.

How could it after seeing the target pierced by bullet holes? Sharp, life-threatening shots. This threat wasn't a vague warning like the others. Not at all. The bullets in the target could kill and were a direct threat to her life.

How did she go on from here? Could she act like nothing had happened and resume her life? She'd put up a good front for Ryan and Russ so far, but she couldn't continue for much longer. At least not without any positive movement in finding the perpetrator. If she had any hope of moving forward, she needed to use this walk with Bandit to gain control of and reorder her thoughts. Find her center again like she taught the teens she counseled.

And she had to stay near the area that Russ and his deputies had cleared to remain under the watchful eye of Russ and Ryan. Not that the shooter was likely anywhere nearby at the moment. Not with the law enforcement presence. But what about later? When they'd gone? Then what?

She shivered even in the eighty-degree day filled with brilliant sunshine and traipsed behind Bandit, leaving Ryan and Russ to set up a perimeter around the lodge with crime scene tape.

An army green utility vehicle came up the drive, sending gravel spitting and dust flying. She probably should be concerned, but their suspect wasn't going to drive up to them in broad daylight with law enforcement present. The vehicle came closer and parked.

A large guy dressed in cargo pants and a green polo shirt with the Shadow Lake Survival logo on his broad chest stepped down, a thick file folder in his hand.

Must be Colin.

Bandit started yipping, and she picked him up to save the guy from an overly eager greeting.

He offered his hand. "Colin Graham. I'm the guy digging into your suspects."

"Thank you for that." She shook his hand and set Bandit back down.

"It's what neighbors are for, right?" He smiled, broadening his narrow face.

Footsteps came from behind, and Ryan and Russ joined them.

"You have something for us, Colin?" Ryan asked.

"A few things." He held up his folder. "Starting with the caretaker, Nico."

"What about him?" Mia asked, doubting they could find anything on sweet old Nico.

"Ryan mentioned the recovered bullets from the door are .30-06. Nico owns a rifle chambered for that caliber."

"As do half the men in this county." Russ stared at Colin, a look many men would back down from.

Not Colin. He returned Russ's gaze and widened his stance. "But do half the men in the county have a grudge against Wally?"

"Grudge?" Mia asked, her mind racing over what it might be.

Colin shifted to face her directly. "Goes back a few years. Nico wants to retire, but he didn't save enough money. Wally said he would build a cabin on the property for Nico to spend the rest of his days in rent free. Wally never delivered. Nico confronted Wally on his last visit. Wally said he just forgot about it and would get the construction process started. But Wally didn't and told no one about it. Not his attorney, Verna, or even his accountants. Verna did say if it was up to her, she and Nico both deserved a place to live after all they've given over the years to this business."

"Not sure what I think about that, but it's worth considering that it could be a motive for revenge," Mia said. "I didn't find any plans for a cabin or permits or anything to suggest Uncle Wally planned to start building."

"And he didn't leave any money in his will for it either," Colin said.

"But wouldn't Nico just come to me and ask about it instead of trying to get even?" Mia asked.

"Makes sense, yeah," Colin said. "But maybe he thought you wouldn't follow through either."

She shook her head. "I refuse to believe he would do this unless he talked to me first and I shot him down. Even then I find it hard to believe.."

"I need to talk to him," Russ said.

Mia nodded. "Me too."

Russ shot her a frustrated look. "Leave this up to me."

"You go ahead and do your thing, but it's my duty to ask about this for business reasons."

Russ frowned but didn't argue, so she moved on. "What about Verna? Find anything on her?"

Colin nodded. "She's in debt up to her eyeballs. Looks like it's all recent. From medical expenses for her daughter."

"She has a Down syndrome daughter," Russ said. "She's a few years older than us."

"Yeah, thirty-four and still lives with Verna," Colin said. "The daughter had a scare with cancer. She's in remission but the bills trashed Verna's finances."

Russ frowned. "Means Verna could be looking for a quick buck to save her hide."

"Exactly."

Mia looked at the men. "But scaring me away won't provide her with any cash."

"Insurance would pay for the barn, and if she was stealing from Evergreen, she could take advantage of the sudden cash windfall," Russ said.

Mia shook her head and explained the separation of accounting duties. "And she's dragging her heels on filing for insurance. That doesn't suggest she's eager to steal that money."

"Then I don't see how her finances could be behind this." Colin handed the folder to Mia. "These are the background reports on both of them plus David and your dad. I don't see a red flag in either of their finances and no associations with men who they might've hired to threaten you. I was unable to look into David's business. The records will be hard to access without permission."

"No way I can ask him to open his books to us other than Evergreen's accounts," Mia said.

"What about Wally?" Russ asked. "Anything of interest there?"

"A few things actually."

"Really?" Mia resisted gaping at Colin. "He was the most

uncomplicated guy I've ever known. How could he have something worth looking into?"

Ryan locked gazes with her. "You can't know everything about a person. You know that from counseling."

"Yeah, but this is Uncle Wally." *My father figure. The one man I trusted. Loved unconditionally.*

Colin arched an eyebrow. "Did you know he had a falling out with David, and they were estranged for a few years before they reconciled last year?"

"No," she admitted, knowing Wally didn't tell her because she'd specifically told him she didn't want to hear anything about her family.

"Not something that ever made the grapevine, which is odd," Russ said. "Means neither one of them talked about it."

Colin looked at Mia. "But David's receptionist overheard him talking to your father, and she told me about it."

Russ wrinkled his forehead. "She's loyal to David and Kurt. How did you get her to talk?"

"I had to meet her for coffee." Colin grimaced. "You owe me for taking one for the team."

Mia wanted to chuckle but Colin looked legitimately horrified. "Not sure how we can repay that."

"Stop her from calling me." He shoved his hands into his pockets. "I've sworn off relationships for a while. Told her that, but she isn't getting the message."

"I'll do my best but not sure what that might be," Mia said. "What did she tell you?"

"David wanted his girls to be able to enjoy this place whenever they wanted to like he did as a kid. That couldn't happen as long as Wally continued to lease to Wilderness Ways. David got that Wally needed the revenue generated during the summer months by private guests, but Wilderness Ways is paying far below the going rate for their lease, and David believed Wally was being taken advantage of."

"Wally always said this was his way of giving back," Mia said, defending her uncle.

"David wanted us gone?" Ryan honestly sounded hurt.

Colin nodded. "So much so that he threatened to make sure charges were brought against one of the teens who'd taken off and broke into a house near David's home."

Ryan grimaced. "We dealt with that situation. Carlos went back to juvie."

"David claimed that the locals were unsafe with these kids in the area, and he could rally the people around his cause." Colin shook his head. "Wally walked out on their conversation. David did nothing, but they didn't speak for a few years."

What else might she not know about? Could her perceptions of things be all wrong because of so many years of shielding herself from news of her family?

"What happened to change that?" Mia asked, still shocked at what happened.

"Wally agreed to reduce time with Wilderness Ways by three weeks to create exclusive family time at the resort."

Ryan rubbed his jaw then shook his head. "So that's why Wally changed our contract. He said it was for maintenance."

Russ zeroed in on Colin. "Maybe David really hasn't gotten over it and wants more time here. Maybe even wants to own the place."

"Maybe," Colin said, shifting his attention to Mia. "Your dad took David's side and also didn't speak to Wally after that. They never reconciled."

"I didn't know that either." Sadness over the finality of that estrangement set in, and she actually felt bad for her father.

"That's not all." Colin's expression changed, and his eyes gleamed. "Most interesting is that Wally was paying money to a private investigator. A Franklin Springer from Dunwoody, Georgia."

Mia blinked a few times as she processed the information. "That's Fuzzy. He was Uncle Wally's good friend. In fact, I sat with him at my uncle's funeral."

Ryan's shoulders stiffened. "Why would Wally need a private investigator?"

Colin shrugged. "I tried calling him, but got voicemail so left a message. Hopefully, he'll call back soon, and we'll have that answer."

Mia couldn't believe she hadn't known any of it, but it was time she learned everything. Her life could depend on it. "Anything else?"

"Yeah."

"Really? There's more?" She couldn't control her surprise now, and her voice had shot up.

Colin nodded. "Your dad and David bought the vacant lot next door during that time. They still own it."

"What?" Mia cried out. "Why in the world would they do that?"

"And how did they keep it secret?" Ryan asked. "We never even knew it was for sale, much less that someone bought it."

"The real estate transactions were recorded, but the owner is a company they formed together called DT Holdings. They own several properties in the area so I think it's just a real estate investment, but it could be more."

"Like what?" Mia asked.

Colin leaned forward. "Like a location where they could keep an eye on what was happening at Evergreen."

"You could be right." Russ's rapt attention was pinned to

Colin. "I don't have just cause to get a warrant, but we need to get eyes on the place. See what's going on."

Ryan planted his hands on his waist and looked at Colin. "Get the team together. We need to scout the lot. Look for cameras and any other activity that might point to Dr. Blackburn and David's involvement in these crimes."

Mia swallowed hard. Here she'd been looking for things that actually suggested her father or David's guilt, and now she finally had something that could be actionable. And did it make her feel good? Not at all. The pain in her stomach cut her like a sharp knife, feeling almost as agonizing as the day her mother had died.

Mia stepped onto the lodge's porch where the six-man Shadow Lake Survival team were goofing off and talking. Included were the three Maddox brothers, Colin, and two other men she hadn't met before. Jessie sat on the floor and played with an overly excited Bandit. Mia could be upset with Ryan stepping in and taking over the conversation with Colin, but she wasn't a former law enforcement officer. He was, and he knew how to move forward. Or maybe she was feeling better about relinquishing some control.

Maybe.

Reid cleared his throat, and the men instantly stopped joking around. "Mia, you haven't met our other team members. I'll start with Devon standing next his brother Colin."

The intense-looking young male had dark hair like Colin, but he had a close-cut beard where Colin was clean shaven. Both were around six feet tall with broad shoulders and both obviously worked out.

Colin swung an arm around Devon. "Dev's my baby brother."

Devon fired an irritated look at his brother. "You know I hate it when you say baby."

"Yeah." Colin grinned. "Why do you think I say it?"

"You always skip the fact that I'm your only brother." Devon rolled his eyes and held his hand out to Mia.

She took Devon's punishing grip in stride and tried not to wince. "Nice to meet you, Devon."

"Call me Dev like everyone else does." He released her hand.

"Dev's a former Clackamas County deputy and expert in water rescue," Reid said. "He teaches all of our water skills."

"You want to learn how to survive in a water accident or how to safely maneuver most any watercraft, I'm your guy." He smiled a most pleasant smile that had to make women's hearts flutter.

"That could come in handy living on a lake and with a river on the property too," she said.

"So far I haven't had to save any of these bozos, but I know the day is coming." He chuckled.

Colin groaned. "Full of yourself much?"

"I could say never hire siblings," Ryan said. "But then look at the three of us."

"Yeah, a barrel of monkeys," Russ said.

Reid rolled his eyes. "Then we have Micha Nichols. He's an expert in weapons."

Russ cast a look at Micha that conveyed secret knowledge. "We served together in the Marines. Weapons maintenance techs."

"Basically, meant we got to play with guns all day." Micha laughed.

"Yeah, except it was way more than that, and Micha excelled at it." Russ frowned, and Mia sensed some unease about that job that Russ wasn't sharing. "I don't eat, breathe, and sleep weapons like Micha does."

"I really don't sleep with them. They're close by, but..." Micha grinned, his serious expression flooding away and revealing a very good-looking man with his dark hair and square jaw.

She shook hands with him. "I can respect the job you do. I know how to shoot. My Uncle Wally taught me."

"We're all real sorry to lose him," Micha said. "He was a special guy."

"Everyone loved him," Russ added, surprising Mia. "Maybe we could have a night at the campfire and share our favorite memories of Wally."

Wow, Russ wanting to share in public. This was the guy she'd once known, and he'd lightened up some, but she knew he took his job very seriously. As David's best friend, Russ had often hung at their house, and she hoped to see more of that fun-loving side of him once this was all over.

"We'll be doing a grid search of the property," Ryan said. "See what we can find."

Mia nodded her understanding. "And I'll be anxiously awaiting any news and probably stuffing my face with the cookies someone left the other day."

"I wish I could stay here," Jessie said.

Reid looked at his daughter "Sorry, Bug. Not today."

Jessie eyed her father. "You ruin all the fun, Dad."

Reid held up his hands. "Don't want to ruin your fun. You can have a good time with Poppy."

Jessie looked up at Mia. "Poppy usually takes care of me when Daddy works, and she cooks for us too. She's really old like Grammy, but I like her."

"Best cook I know," Russ said. "And if anyone tells Mom I said that, my handcuffs will come out." Russ ran a serious gaze around the group then chuckled.

The guys laughed.

"She cooks for the business too," Reid said. "We'll have you over for dinner so you can see she hasn't lost her touch."

Jessie looked at Russ. "Grammy would be sad if she knew you didn't like her cooking."

Russ knelt by Jessie. "Grammy is a good cook. Poppy's just better."

Jessie wrinkled her nose. "I don't like some of the things either of them makes. The stuff they call healthy and say is good for me."

They all laughed, and Jessie cast a bewildered look around the group.

A UTV pulled down the driveway. Mia came to attention.

"Relax," Ryan said. "It's just Poppy here to get Jessie."

"Aw, I don't want to go home." Jessie's lower lip came out. "I want to stay with Mia and Bandit."

Mia smiled at the child. No way she would tell her it just wouldn't be safe to stay here alone with her when she had a target on her back.

Reid took his daughter's hand and helped her get up. "You can come back another time."

She gazed up at her father. "Promise?"

He gave her a fond smile. "Promise."

Mia hated to end the conversation as she enjoyed the lighthearted turn at the end. Enjoyed being part of a group of people in Shadow Lake who accepted her for who she was. But they had a job to do.

Reid escorted Jessie down the steps to the older woman with braids driving the UTV.

Ryan looked at Mia. "Would you please go inside now and make sure you lock up?"

"Of course," she said, knowing she was doing her part so Ryan didn't have to worry about her.

She opened the door and called Bandit to enter the house with her. She glanced back as the men strode down the steps. Six men. Each a force to be reckoned with. Now that she had these strong professionals on her side, she would soon know who was trying to hurt her. Wouldn't she?

17

Ryan led the guys across the tall grass and through a shortcut in the woods that separated the two properties. On the far side of the thick stand of evergreens, he paused until everyone cleared the trees.

He looked at the guys. "We'll do a grid search. I'll be moving slow. Don't want to miss a thing. Form a line to my right. Don't get in a hurry and overlook something."

Russ stepped into place next to Ryan, Reid on the other side of Russ.

Russ looked at Ryan. "Guess you're taking charge."

"I'm just protecting you, bro." Ryan resisted grinning. "Without that warrant you mentioned, you shouldn't be doing this."

"None of us should," Reid said. "We'll be trespassing."

"Hey, we're just a group of guys out for some fun, and we accidentally crossed the property line." Ryan grinned at his brothers.

They both shook their heads.

Ryan looked down the line of men. "Let's move."

They started forward, each using a stick picked up on the walk through the wooded area to sweep it through the long grass. They picked their way across the empty lot and turned back four times. A few scrub trees had to be skirted, but mostly they had direct paths from one side of the lot to the other through knee-high grass and weeds.

"Stop." Ryan held up a hand and squatted. "The grass has been fractured here. Trail starts at the driveway and looks like it goes all the way to the woods."

Russ got down next to Ryan and spread the grass apart to reveal muddy soil. "Boot print. Fresh."

"Large," Reid said from above. "Probably male."

Ryan nodded as his excitement built. "And the grass hasn't recovered, so it has to be from today."

Russ stood. "Could be our shooter. Let's keep moving. See what we find ahead."

Ryan got up and looked at the team. "Be even more diligent in your search."

They proceeded, the pace even slower. They neared the tree line and a reflective object glinted in the sun.

Ryan pointed at it. "There. Looks like a bullet casing. Distance to the lodge door from here is right for our shooter."

Russ held up his hand. "No one go any closer."

"I'll take a better look." Ryan retrieved his phone and aimed it ahead, using his fingers to zoom in with his camera. "It *is* a casing."

"The shooter didn't police his brass?" Russ's incredulous stare mimicked Ryan's surprise.

"That tells us something for sure," Reid said. "Either someone disturbed the shooter and he didn't have time to retrieve his brass, or we're not looking at a professional hitman."

"If he'd been disturbed and had to bail, we would likely see a different exit path," Ryan said. "More frantic from running, but he exited on the same path he came in on, and it's a pretty straight line."

"Still," Russ said. "Seems odd that he's careful to take one path but leaves his brass."

"Maybe he wasn't being careful, but lazy," Colin said. "Takes more work to plow down tall grass than to follow a path he'd already flattened."

"Could be." Russ stared at the brass. "That casing will be visible from Mia's property. Gives me cause for a warrant. Our spur-of-the-moment search ends right now, and the official one begins."

～

Ryan had insisted on accompanying Mia to Nico's workshop, but she wanted to talk to Nico alone. So she left Bandit with Ryan outside the building and entered the tiny space that smelled like gas, oil, and pine, the same scent she'd always associated with Nico. She didn't know how long he'd worked at Evergreen, but she couldn't remember a time he hadn't been fixing something or other that had broken on the property.

He spun from facing his workbench, a wrench in his hand. His silver glasses slid down a large nose, and a sprinkling of gray whiskers covered his narrow chin.

"Mia. Hi." He smiled, his full lips turning up. "Wondered if you might stop by."

"Good to see you, Nico." She looked at the cluttered bench in front of him. He'd mounted an outboard motor for one of their rental boats on the side of the bench.

He dropped the wrench and grabbed a rag to wipe his grease-covered hands. "Stupid motor keeps quitting on me, and we don't want to buy a new one. Every penny counts, right?"

"Right," she said.

He pointed at a teakettle in the corner. "Can I make you a cup of tea?"

A rush of guilt swamped her. Here she was planning to interrogate him, and he was offering her tea. "Thanks, but I won't be long."

"Uh-oh, sounds like you got something serious on your mind." He leaned back against the counter, but his expression remained sharp.

She would come right to the point. "I heard you and Uncle Wally had a disagreement."

"You could call it that." He dropped the rag and shoved his hands in a thick apron he wore over a denim shirt and worn jeans. "He promised to build me a little cabin on the property so I could retire. Never did it. When I asked, he said he just forgot. But then he still didn't do it."

He shook his head. "These old bones can't keep up with the full-time work anymore. Told Wally I would help whoever he hired to replace me and wouldn't expect to get paid. I want to keep busy, just not this busy." He waved his hand over the bench.

"Do you have any witnesses to this promise?" she asked, hating to do so.

He frowned. "Nah. Just between us, but you know me, Mia. Most of your life. I live my faith, and I'm a man of my word."

"I do know that, but it's not like Uncle Wally to promise something then not follow through. Makes me wonder what he was thinking."

"Agreed, and I can't explain it. But if you could see your way clear to building a little place, I'd help with the work. Put in as much sweat equity as you would want from me."

She might be mad in his situation, but he was his usual calm, laidback self. "You don't sound angry about it."

"Angry, nah. Hurt that Wally didn't follow through, yeah."

"So not angry enough to shoot up the lodge or send me threatening messages?"

"No way." He pushed off the bench. "You gotta believe me, kiddo. I'd never do that to anyone, and I hope whoever *is* doing it is caught and pays."

He sounded very sincere, and Mia believed him. "Have you seen anything unusual happening around here?"

"Unusual?" He tilted his head. "Not really." He didn't sound sure.

She had to press him. "Not really? Or no?"

"I mean, Verna's been kind of a bear lately, but she's been dealing with a lot at home with her daughter being sick. Wally told her to take all the time she needs, and he's still paying her full-time. But maybe she's worried about the change with you taking over."

Sounded possible. "You worried about that too?"

He shrugged, his hands going back into those large apron pockets.

She didn't like seeing him uncomfortable. "I should probably get the staff together to tell you all that I don't plan on making any changes this year."

"Yeah, that would be good to know. And I guess if you decide to sell when your year is up, my cabin might not matter."

"I don't know what I plan to do, but I will for sure think about what you told me."

"That's all a fella can ask for. Thank you." A genuine smile spread across his face.

"I'll check in again, once the person issuing these threats is arrested." She started for the door.

"I'll be praying the guy is caught."

"One more thing." She turned back and hated her next

words before they were uttered. "Would you mind turning your rifle over to the forensic team so they can prove you didn't shoot at the lodge?"

"Mind, yeah, I would, but I'll do it." He shook his head. "Was a day when a man's word meant something but now it's all newfangled science stuff. Just tell me who you want me to give the gun to."

"We'll send the tech to your house to collect it from you."

He nodded, but looked disappointed in her. She wasn't disappointed in herself, though. If they were going to find the person threatening her, she had to ask the hard questions.

She exited, and Ryan looked at her expectantly. She didn't want to talk where Nico could overhear them. She took Bandit's lead and started for the lodge. Once a safe distance away, she told Ryan about the conversation.

"Nothing like accusing someone you've always respected of something you should never even think they would do," she said.

"How are you holding up?" he asked.

Holding up? She was even too tired to argue that he thought she needed a babysitter on this walk, but he was just being careful and kind and deserved an answer. "Honestly? Not so good. I just want Russ to figure out who's doing this and make it stop, so I can get on with my year. Honor Uncle Wally's wishes. Help Eddie and maybe other kids if you still need me."

"At least Russ apologized to you."

"Yeah, that was unexpected, but I am thankful for it." She glanced at Ryan. "He reminded me of the Russ I knew from the old days."

Ryan nodded. "The Russ who's not a sheriff doing his

best to do his job. I have to remember that when he makes me mad with the questions he asks you."

She smiled tightly. "Do you think he's right about my father being innocent in all of this? Even after what Colin had to tell us."

"Sorry, but yeah, I do." Ryan held her gaze. "Your father might have hurt you in high school, but I don't think it was intentional. He just didn't know how to recover from his grief. But this?" He waved a hand at the barn as they approached the ruins. "This was done on purpose. The shots fired too. No way that was accidental."

One part of her was relieved that maybe her father hadn't intentionally hurt her, giving her hope for reconciliation. The other part of her was terrified to find out who willingly would do something as harsh as fire bullets into the lodge, risking hitting or killing someone, and burn down the barn.

Bandit suddenly shot off. Ripping his leash from her hand, he raced toward the end of the barn near the only standing wall. The section that hadn't been engulfed in flames before the firefighters put it out.

"No, boy, come back," she called out, going after him and climbing under the yellow crime-scene tape.

Bandit continued running until he reached the far corner of the barn. He stopped and sniffed in the rubble. He yipped in little excited barks, and she started for him.

Ryan reached out to stop her. "Let me go first."

"Here, Bandit," she called in a soothing voice that did nothing to stop Bandit's excited barking.

She picked her way through the muck behind him. The door she'd been trapped in lay in the ruins only ten feet away. As long as she was in the area, she should take a quick peek to confirm it'd been locked.

She took careful steps through the thick gunk to the

door. The handles remained intact, but no chain. No lock. Just like the other end. The lock could only have been removed with a key or bolt cutters. She squatted and picked at the rubble to look for other clues. Nothing but charred wood and muck and maybe some footprints, but they could well belong to the firefighters. Maybe Sierra could locate something Mia was missing.

The charred wall suddenly exploded in an ash-laden cloud and a loud crash of timber.

She jerked back. Landed with a plop, gray particles raining down on her. She coughed out the chest-clogging dust. Just as Ryan predicted. The wall was too unstable to be around.

Ryan. Bandit. Were they hurt?

She pushed to her feet.

"Are you okay?" Ryan yelled from the other end of the barn.

She looked up. He stood, safe and unharmed. Thank goodness.

"Where's Bandit?" She plodded through the murky gunk toward him.

"He's here." Ryan lifted the dirty dog into his arms. As Ryan rose to his full height, he paused and released a shudder. He shook his head then peered at her.

Mia arrived next to him and scanned him for injury. "Are you hurt?"

"No, I'm fine."

"Then why the look?" She scanned his face for a hint.

His expression held something she'd never seen in the brilliant blue before.

Fear. Raw and primal.

Dread settled into her stomach. "What are you not telling me? Is there something in there?"

He grimaced, and looked as if he was waffling between telling her or not telling her he'd discovered something.

She stepped to the side. Peered ahead. Gasped. Sucked in a cleansing breath but pulled in a horrid foul stench that made her eyes tear up. "Oh, no. No. No."

Panicked, she turned to run. Got stuck in the sludge. Lost her balance.

Ryan snagged her hand and drew her into the protective shield of his arms alongside Bandit. She not only let Ryan hold her, she clung to him and laid her head on his solid chest, his heart thumping at a rate matching her accelerated speed.

He was right in not telling her what he discovered.

She didn't need to see the body trapped under the stack of wood.

18

Ryan had been stroking Bandit's soft fur for the past thirty minutes while rocking on the lodge's front porch. Mia had gone in to change her grubby clothes, something Ryan desperately needed to do. He'd cleaned Bandit up with the hose and changed his bandage, but Ryan couldn't leave until Russ took their statements and released them.

Ryan wanted to do that right off the bat, but Russ insisted on evaluating the gruesome scene. He stood by the victim, snapping picture after picture. Ryan was glad to wait here. He didn't need to see the body again. He was fixated on the discovery almost as if his mind had taken pictures he would never be able to erase.

Two legs, calf down, jutted from intact bales lying perpendicular to the body. Wood resembling dropped pixie sticks lay on top. Khaki trousers and expensive leather loafers were the only visible clues to the victim's identity. The fire hadn't reached the body, which should make identification easier. Either the man died before Jessie entered the barn or the body was hidden there after the fire. The ME was working on providing the answer.

The lodge's main door groaned open. Ryan swiveled in

his chair as Mia emerged. She'd changed into blue jeans and an orange T-shirt from Oregon State University. Her wet hair shone in the fading sunlight, but her red-rimmed eyes held a haunted look.

I know You're watching over her and waiting for her to turn to You. I pray she does and You bring her the comfort I can't provide.

Ryan stood, setting Bandit on the floor. The dog slunk under the chair and curled up as best he could with his cone. Ryan would've turned back and held the pup, but Mia needed Ryan more.

He crossed the porch and pulled her into his arms. The fresh scent of her apricot shampoo tugged at his senses and memories assaulted him. Kissing her here on this very porch. Wanting to be with her always. Forever. To take away her pain and anguish over her father. Ryan had failed to do that then, and now she was suffering even more.

Why hadn't he dragged her away before she'd gotten a look at the body? Since she'd arrived back in Shadow Lake, he'd come up short when she needed his help the most.

She eased out of his arms and stared at the barn. Ryan followed her gaze to see Russ headed their way. He had to take their statements, but now that Ryan got a look at Mia's anguish, he wished it could wait. It couldn't though. Good policing meant getting the details from witnesses while the facts were fresh in their minds. And Russ was a great law enforcement officer so he would insist on it. Ryan only hoped they would see the kinder, gentler side of his brother.

At the base of the steps, he swiped his boots covered in muck in the grass before he looked up at the porch. "Let's get those statements over with. I need to hear in your own words what happened."

Hoping Mia wouldn't have to say much, Ryan described

how the wall fell, knocking debris from a pile and revealing the body.

Russ took a few steps toward them. "You concur with that, Mia?"

She seemed to freeze in place, unable to speak.

"Let's sit down." Ryan took her hand and urged her toward the chairs.

She dropped onto the seat as if it was too much effort to stand, but she launched into her story, spilling it along with fresh tears. "I also checked for a padlock and chain on the door where I got stuck during the fire. They were missing."

"We looked at the other door yesterday," Ryan added. "They were missing there too."

Russ trained his gaze on Mia. "You said earlier that this lock and chain trapped you in the barn, but did anyone else see them?"

"I saw the chains on the one door," Ryan said. "So if you're intimating that Mia made it up, you're wrong. But is that really the big thing right now? Isn't it more important that we figure out who the guy is in the barn and why he was killed?"

Russ settled against the porch railing and massaged his forehead. "No 'we' in this, bro. I'll take care of the investigation."

"Then you haven't discovered the man's ID?" Mia asked. "Or how he died?"

Russ turned to her. "The ME's very preliminary finding suggests blunt force trauma to the head. Once he completes his initial exam here, he'll search the body for ID. He'll also do fingerprints at the morgue."

"But this is probably the reason for the fire, right?" Mia's gaze hunted around as if she were trying to come up with a reply. "If I hadn't come along when I did, the fire would likely have burned the entire barn, and we may never have known a body was there at all."

Ryan hated to disagree with Mia when she was in a fragile state, but as a trained firefighter, he knew her interpretation might be wrong. "If the intent of the fire was to do away with the body, it seems likely the arsonist would have started the blaze near the body. And he wouldn't have said he was trying to scare someone off. Plus, if that area *had* burned, our team would've searched it and found the remains. The clean-up crew probably should've inspected that debris pile too, and the chief is going to let them have it for not being thorough."

She narrowed her gaze. "Are you saying the fire and the murder aren't related? That we might be looking for two different suspects."

"Could be," he said. "But it's possible the arsonist just wasn't very good at his job."

Russ pushed off the railing, and the strain of the gruesome discovery hung on his face. "Your theory doesn't take into account the missing locks. The doors could've been locked to conceal the body. If so, our arsonist wouldn't have access without breaking a window like you did. Unless he has a key. Which he would've needed to drive a truck inside as Jessie didn't mention him cutting a chain to open the doors."

"That changes things completely," Ryan said. "Unless the doors weren't locked at that point."

"Since I didn't know about the locks, I didn't ask Jessie how she got in," Russ said. "But I will now. Then once we ID the victim, we should have a better idea on how to proceed."

"I don't suppose anyone in the area has been reported missing?" Ryan asked.

"If only it was that simple." Russ frowned. "Anything else to add to your statements?"

Ryan and Mia shook their heads.

"I'll get back to you if I have additional questions." Russ headed back toward the barn.

Ryan watched Mia as she rocked her chair, and her gaze tracked Russ. She set her jaw. Lifted her chin. *Right.* This was the Mia he knew. She wouldn't sit back and do nothing. She planned to investigate on her own.

Somehow, they found themselves in the middle of a murder investigation, and she was too stubborn to sit on the sidelines. She could be putting her life in danger, and there was nothing he could do to stop her.

Activity at the barn ramped up, and Mia's heart raced. For once she was alone. After a call from Ian at Wilderness Ways, Ryan had reluctantly gone to check in and change clothes. He promised to return as soon as possible. Not only did he want to protect her, he didn't want to miss out on the action. And action it was.

Deputies cordoned off the area around the barn with fresh yellow crime scene tape that fluttered in the breeze as if issuing a warning to anyone who approached. The medical examiner unloaded a gurney from his van and slipped under the tape without a backward glance.

Collecting someone who died was probably second nature to him. Maybe not in a burned building as often as when a person died of natural causes at home, but a deceased person nonetheless.

Mia, on the other hand, couldn't wrap her head around the fact that someone had died in her barn. Was murdered. Not far from her house. On her property. Or what would be her property in a year.

How could that be, and what did it mean?

A white van eased down the drive and parked near the barn. The driver's door held the same black logo that she'd seen on the financial paperwork for the Veritas Center. A guy with thinning dark hair and a slight build slid out from behind the wheel, and a pregnant woman eased down from the passenger side. Had to be Sierra, but she'd never mentioned that she was pregnant.

She stood, hands on her back, surveying the area. Mia jogged down the steps to greet her, and Russ left the medical examiner to head their way.

"You must be Sierra." Mia offered her hand. "I'm Mia Blackburn."

Sierra grasped Mia's hand firmly, pumping it hard. "Nice to meet you. This is my assistant Chad. He'll be working with me on gathering and processing your evidence."

He tipped his head at Mia in greeting and went to the back of the van to open the doors.

Russ marched up to them and gave Chad a clipped nod but extended his hand to Sierra. "Thanks for coming so quickly."

"Good to see you again, Sheriff." Sierra shook his hand. "Where do you want us to start?"

"Russ, please." He frowned. "Before you start, you should know. Each piece of evidence you locate is top priority to process as quickly as possible. We're on day three of the investigation, our leads are thin, and things are escalating."

A tight smile crossed Sierra's face. "We'll do our very best on such short notice."

"That's all I can ask for." Russ closed his eyes for a long moment and inhaled a noisy breath. "As far as starting, we've had a few new developments since I spoke to you."

Sierra peered at the barn. "I'm guessing since the ME's van is here, one of them includes a victim."

Russ's shoulders slumped. "Mia and Ryan found a body in the area of the barn that hadn't burned. The ME's only just gotten here, and his findings suggest blunt-force trauma to the head. We don't yet know if he was killed and then put in the barn or was murdered in the barn. He searched for ID but found nothing. He'll do fingerprints and DNA back at the morgue, but it would be great if you could do a DNA swab in addition to processing the scene."

"Of course," she said. "We can help you determine if it's your murder scene too."

"We'd also like you to investigate the area by each door. We believe the doors were chained and padlocked, but now they're missing. Someone must've taken them."

"Interesting," she said. "We'll look for footprints and anything else unusual."

"Just so you know," Mia said. "Ryan and I went near the doors yesterday. If you need our boots to eliminate our prints from others, we'll be glad to provide them."

"I'll let you know." Sierra paused and frowned. "But you should be aware, fire scenes often produce less evidence than you would like. The water from the hoses is problematic and then the area is pummeled with firefighters' boots too. Still, if any evidence exists, we'll find it."

"I like your confidence." Russ gave a sharp nod of acceptance. "And from what I've seen and heard it's well founded."

"You know it. What's the point in being modest when it's true?" Sierra laughed.

Russ chuckled with her, but it seemed forced. "You'll have to wait for the ME to finish. In the meantime, I can turn over the other evidence I have for fingerprinting and DNA recovery." He jerked a thumb toward his patrol car. "It's all in my vehicle."

"Bring it to the back of the van, and we'll take charge of

it and complete a chain of custody form." She didn't wait for him to agree, but headed toward the rear door of her van.

Mia loved that about this woman. She knew her job and wasn't intimidated by a tough law enforcement officer like Russ. Though, Mia also had to admit, Russ had been firm but friendly, so maybe Sierra had dealt with far worse.

He strode toward his car, but Mia followed Sierra. Mia might not be privy to Sierra's reports, but she didn't think Russ would object to her seeing the items he turned over to her. And if he did, he would have to tell her to leave.

Sierra and Chad slipped on white protective suits that Sierra struggled to zip over her enlarged belly. She chuckled and looked at Chad. "For my last few months, I'll need a larger size when you refill supplies. Make it elephant size."

He nodded, serious and unaffected by Sierra's joke.

She looked at Mia. "Do you have children?"

Mia shook her head. "Not married either."

"This will be our second, and you forget so much about the first pregnancy on what to expect."

"Good or bad?" Mia asked.

"Both. Right now with my ankles reaching elephant proportions, it's not great." She laughed.

Russ marched over to them, evidence bags in his hands. He handed one to Sierra. "The first threatening letter Mia received. I'd like you to do prints and DNA, please."

"You'll find my prints and Ryan's on the letter," Mia said. "We both handled it before it became evidence and Russ touched it too. As did my dad at the post office. But if he sent it, there will likely be more than one set of prints, right?"

"Could be. I'll need prints from everyone you mentioned for elimination purposes." Sierra turned her attention back to the letter. "This isn't standard copy or printer paper. You might also want a paper analysis."

"You can do that?" Russ asked.

"Yes, in the lab. There we can compare it to the paper from any other threats received." She handed the bag to Chad, who wrote on it then recorded it in a logbook before stowing the evidence in the van.

Russ shifted through his bags. "This one accompanied a fake severed hand and bracelet. The box that it arrived in and the hand are still in my vehicle."

Sierra looked up. "How was the box delivered?"

"Someone set it on the table in the lodge," Mia said.

Sierra arched an eyebrow. "So the suspect was in your house?"

"Seems like it."

"Then we need to process that area too."

"You think you'll find anything helpful?" Russ asked.

"Could be." Her eyes suddenly came alive with interest. "We're piloting a new program to isolate DNA in household dust."

"Dust," Russ said, his eyes going wide open. "You're joking, right?"

"I don't joke about my forensics." Sierra grinned. "In our trials we've found DNA from non-occupants in over half of the samples collected from each test site. It's a long shot and might not hold up in court since it's such new technology, but could give you the lead you need to move your investigation forward."

"Then bring on the dust." Mia laughed.

"There's another note from a threat that was made just prior to our discovery of the body too." Russ explained about the bullseye then located the bags with the bullets and two casings. "We got lucky and recovered two casings from what looks to be the shooter's hide. Ditto on prints and DNA for these items."

"We can bring in our weapons expert too. He can perform a trajectory analysis but sounds like you've located the hide and know that. Still, he can evaluate the bullets so if you *do* locate a weapon, he can confirm that gun fired it."

"We actually have a rifle for him to look at." Mia explained about her conversation with Nico. "He agreed to have you all pick it up and test it."

"His cooperation might mean he didn't do it, or he doesn't understand how we can match bullets to rifle barrels and is overly confident," Sierra said.

"My gut says he didn't fire the shots," Mia said. "But it would be good to confirm."

"Absolutely," Sierra said. "Text me the guy's address, and we'll retrieve the gun."

Mia dug her phone from her pocket and sent the info as she didn't want to forget. She looked up in time to see Russ hold out the last bag. Her bracelet. A jolt of fear hit her. Unreasonable for just seeing the bracelet, but the connection to her past couldn't be ignored.

"Mia, I'll definitely need your prints for elimination purposes on this," Sierra said.

Mia hated thinking about being printed, but this was to prove her innocence not her guilt. "We have to get my dad and David to agree to being printed."

Russ ran a hand over his hair. "I can ask for their voluntary cooperation, but I have no reason to insist on it. Have to say, though, if it were me, I would say no, and I suspect your dad at least will do that."

"Likely." She lifted her chin and eyed Russ. "But we should still ask."

Would this finally prove that her father or David were involved in the threats and incidents? Sure, Ryan and Russ both didn't think her family was involved. But they were the only ones who would know such a very personal thing about her like the bracelet and use it to try to scare her away from her rightful inheritance.

19

Mia settled onto the overstuffed sofa in front of the fireplace and set the empty teacup on the table. Ryan had prepared tea when he'd returned after his work check-in. He stood next to the window talking on his cell. His face was illuminated by the fading sun, casting shadows on his cheek. They'd decided dinner with David would go on as scheduled. Ryan had cleaned up and was wearing a lemony-yellow sweater that left him looking darkly handsome and intriguing.

Mia had slipped into black dress pants, a shimmery blouse, and put on her favorite heels. She hoped dressing up might cheer her for the dinner ahead. And it had—a bit. At least it gave her time to think about how supportive Ryan was being again. He might have repeatedly tried to take charge, but knowing about Cara helped Mia understand his motives.

He punched the button on his cell and slid it into his pocket. "That was Russ. He talked to Jessie. She said the barn wasn't locked when she went in, but the man locked the door behind him."

"Not sure why he would take the locks though. Or why lock it to begin with."

Ryan tucked his hands into his pockets. "Good questions."

She would have to give that some thought.

"Russ also said the medical examiner believes the victim has been dead about a week. Means visual identification won't be easy, either."

"But it also means he died *before* the fire," she said. "And that could mean the murder isn't connected to the threats."

"Seems possible, but we can't let our guard down yet." Ryan crossed the room toward her. "The bullets in the door says the person after you is amping up his threats. If the murder is related, our discovery of the body could escalate things further."

She didn't want to admit he was right, but he could be—very right—and her life was still in danger.

As he took a seat next to her on the sofa, a ray of fading sunlight highlighted the crevices of fatigue etched into his bronzed skin. They locked gazes, and the warm intimacy of the moment stole all logical thought.

She wanted to kiss him. Badly.

Could she hold out against these feelings much longer? Did she even want to? How could she think this compassionate man would hurt her?

Without thinking, she smoothed the strand of hair from his forehead and trailed a finger down his cheek.

He leaned his face into her hand. His breath whispered over her skin as he exhaled. "When I think about you stuck in that door with the body so close by, I can hardly breathe." He laced his long fingers with hers and laid their hands on his knee. "What if you'd found the body when Jessie was with you? The trauma could've done serious damage to you both."

Mia shivered, moved closer to Ryan, and concentrated on the musky cologne he'd applied. The scent melded with him and drew her even closer. She looked at their hands, perfectly fitted. Maybe this was how it should be. The two of them together again.

Ryan tugged on her hand, easing her closer. Her resolve melted completely, and she had to fight to think.

No. Stop. His nearness and compassion were drawing her into making a decision she wasn't ready to make. She needed to put distance between them before she did something she regretted. Not move just across the room. The nearness would be too easy to give into. She had to get out of the lodge.

She pulled her hand free and stood, saying the first thing that came to mind. "I asked Verna to file an insurance claim yesterday, but she didn't seem to have a real sense of urgency. I have time to go down to the office to check on it before we have to leave for dinner."

Ryan let out a rasping sigh and came to the edge of the seat. "I'll go with you."

"No. Relax. I'm sure Russ and his men are still at the barn, and I'll be safe." Mia started for the door.

"I really don't want you out there alone," Ryan called after her.

Bandit hopped up, a hopeful gleam in his eyes.

"I'll take Bandit." She grabbed his leash from the table. "You'll guard me, won't you, fella?"

Ryan stood. "Still, I'll come with you."

"Fine," she said though him accompanying her didn't solve her issue. She understood his concern and didn't want to cause him more stress just because she couldn't control her feelings for him.

She snapped the lead onto Bandit's collar. She pulled the door open and rushed out to lean against a post to draw

in the cooling air and clear her head of his scent and intoxi-
cating gaze. She would walk with him, but keep a safe
distance between them.

Because this waffling between wanting to start something with him or not had to stop. She needed to make sure
they weren't alone in a confined and private space again or
she'd find herself running as she'd done since she arrived
here. Running away and maybe running for her life if she
wasn't careful.

~

Ryan waited outside of the office as Mia requested. She
thought Verna would be more forthcoming if he weren't
with them. He agreed and would stand watch outside. And
while he was at it he would try to arrange a protection detail
for her. He pulled out his cell and tapped Russ's icon.

"I don't have any more news, if that's why you're calling,"
his brother said, sounding tired. He might be Mr. Tough
Guy, always acting in charge, but this investigation was
taking a toll on him. He would work even harder not to
show it, but Ryan knew his brother and had seen the impact
finding the body had on him.

"ME hasn't given you the prints on our victim yet?"

"He hasn't taken them." Russ sounded surprisingly
accepting of the delay. "He was pulled away for another call.
Four teens. Two fatalities. Drunk driving incident."

"Oh, man, you have to work that scene?" Ryan asked,
remembering some of the gruesome traffic accidents he'd
responded to as a deputy.

"Next county, but our ME is covering for their guy who's
on vacation."

"That's rough," Ryan said and didn't want to dwell on it.
Instead, he now had to think about protecting Mia for a

longer timeframe. "Can you post someone at the lodge for the night? I'm really worried something will happen to Mia."

Russ let out a long breath. "I'd be glad to, but I don't have enough deputies the way it is. With no actual attempt on her life, I can't justify the cost of overtime."

"Cost?" Ryan shouted, the sound traveling down the hill and halting Mia's steps for a moment. She looked back. He slipped behind a tree and lowered his voice. "Can you put a price on her life?"

"Look. I want to help. I really do, but I have an entire county's safety to think about. Maybe you should stay with her. Or have her come stay at your cabin."

After that little moment between them at the lodge, spending the night under the same roof wasn't a good idea on so many levels.

"Besides, with our presence out here today," Russ continued. "It's not likely the suspect will come back tonight."

"If things change, and you can spare someone let me know." Disappointed, Ryan hung up and watched Mia until she entered the office.

He rushed down the hill and hung outside the door. Russ said it wasn't likely someone would come back here tonight. Well, Ryan wasn't about to risk her life on an assumption, even if he had to dog her every step.

Mia found Verna sitting with slumped shoulders behind her desk. She wore large glasses with thick lenses and fed papers into a shredder. The very shredder she'd purchased the day before. A large garbage bag filled with shreds sat next to the machine. The office smelled like a hot motor as if she'd been running it at maximum capacity.

Just what was she shredding? Mia hadn't thought much about the purchase of a shredder at the time, but now? Now that Verna could be suspect, a red flag flew, bright and bold.

Mia shut the door, and Verna jumped.

She spun her chair. "About scared the living daylights out of me." She slipped a file under a large blotter and glared at Bandit, who lunged at the filing cabinet behind the desk. Nose to the floor as best the cone allowed, he sniffed at the bottom drawer.

Verna watched him, eyes narrowed. "When Wally was alive, that dog wasn't allowed in the office."

Bandit whimpered, and Mia shushed him. He settled on his hind legs, eyeing the cabinet. She needed to get her questioning over before Bandit took aim at Verna and tried to bury her with sloppy kisses that she might not welcome. "I just wanted to find out if you've had a chance to file the insurance claim."

She jutted out her chin. "Didn't have time yet."

Wow. Such a sharp tone as if Mia had asked her to do the impossible. Another red flag, but Mia shrugged as if it didn't matter. "No problem. I'll take the paperwork with me and fill it out tonight."

Verna didn't move, but sat like a queen on her throne, drumming her fingers on her cluttered desk.

"Is there a problem with that?" Mia asked.

"Problem? No. I just don't like you inferring I'm incompetent."

Mia waved a hand. "Nothing like that at all. I want to be sure it's done soon, and I know how busy you are." Bandit slowly eased closer to the cabinet, sniffing the floor on the way. "So is the file in there?"

Verna gave a terse nod.

"The way he's acting you must have food stored in there

too." Mia laughed to try to lighten the mood and deflect Verna's suspicions.

"Not that it's any of your business, but no food." She lifted a key on a chain from around her neck and slid forward to open the top drawer. The metal groaned on the tracks.

Bandit charged ahead on his oversized paws. He rose up on hind legs and sniffed the bottom drawer. *Odd.* If there wasn't any food in the cabinet, why would Bandit be so insistent on getting inside the drawer?

He sensed something Mia didn't, but she aimed to find out what. "Glad to see you're careful with the records and lock them up."

"Never had to do this before, but with all that's been happening since you showed up, I decided it was a good idea to start securing the payroll and tax records."

"Is that all you keep in there?"

Verna eyed Mia. "Why all the questions?"

"Figure I should learn about the business I'll inherit," Mia said, but would let go of questions about the drawer. No point in putting Verna on even higher alert. "Speaking of locking, did you think any more about the barn?"

Verna started thumbing through the files. "Like I said yesterday. There's nothing in there worth locking up, and I didn't give it a second thought."

"Maybe a dead body was reason enough to chain the doors?"

Verna jerked out a folder and slapped it on the desktop. "You won't shock me that easily. Russ Maddox told me all about the body you found." She lifted her chin and pointed it at Mia. "Besides, if the guy was already dead there'd be no need to lock him up."

"You're assuming he was dead and in the barn when the chains were put on. Know something I don't?"

Verna slammed the drawer closed and turned the key. She took a long time to lift her head and fire an angry glare at Mia. "I don't like the tone of your voice, young lady. If you've got something to say, come right out and say it—or leave it alone."

As much as Verna was acting all secretive and weird, Mia really didn't think the woman was a murderer. A control freak, a pain in the rear, but not a murderer. But did she have something to do with the fire? Did she really have a way to steal the insurance money?

"By the way, I'm sorry to hear your daughter's been sick," Mia said, a lump in her throat from bringing up a sick daughter when she wanted to find out if Verna was stealing. How low was that?

Verna's expression softened for a moment. "Yeah."

"Is she doing better now?"

"Yeah," she said.

"I know Uncle Wally let you leave work when needed and still be paid for the time off."

"And?" Her chin went up higher.

"And if you still need time off to look after her, it's fine with me."

"Glad to hear that." Her chin dropped, and her scowl disappeared, but she still fixed a stern look on Mia. "I've given a good chunk of my working life to this place, and it's good to be appreciated this way."

Mia didn't know what else to say except to come right out and ask if she was stealing, and Mia just couldn't do that. Best to leave that to Russ and end the conversation. "I know you're busy. I'll take the paperwork and go."

Verna thrust the folder at Mia then turned her back to resume shredding.

Okay, fine. Mia might've said she was done, but she

couldn't walk out without one more question. "What are you shredding anyway?"

"Old records we don't need anymore," she said without turning back. "Figured you'd want this place shipshape when you took over."

Mia questioned the truth of Verna's answer but couldn't argue with it. Not at all. She tugged on Bandit's leash and stepped outside. A chill settled in. Not from the temperature dropping, but from the vulnerability of being out in the open. She turned and found Ryan leaning against the building.

"Are you okay?" He pushed off the wall and searched her high and low as if looking for injury.

She appreciated his concern, but... "I know you have this innate protector thing that makes you want to make sure I'm safe all the time, but sometimes it feels like you're stalking me."

"I'm sorry. It's just something I have to do. Like breathing." Concern reverberated through his words.

She understood that guilt over losing his fiancée motivated him. She'd rather he could let it go for his own sake, but she couldn't fault him for not dealing with it. Not when she carried so much trauma around from her childhood. She might not be mad at him, but she wouldn't let him pull her into a deep conversation like at the lodge. She would keep things light.

"As stalkers go, you're bearable." She grinned at him.

A broad smile crept across his face, and his shoulders lifted. "Let's get this little guy settled in his crate so we're not late for dinner."

She tugged on Bandit's leash to urge him in the right direction. Ryan fell into step beside her. A ruffling noise sounded ahead on the path. Bandit shot off, dragging Mia behind.

She jogged with him until he reached the porch and paused at the bottom step.

"Wonder what spooked him?" Ryan let his gaze rove over the area.

"Probably some animal."

"Or not." He stopped and let his eyes connect with hers. "In the future, I don't want you out here alone. Especially not at night."

She wanted to argue but she climbed the steps and the bullet holes in the door came into view. She needed to give Ryan's wishes some serious consideration.

Starting with if she would be fine or if the person behind the threats would strike again. Not with a warning the next time, but with a deadly attack.

20

Mia fixed a smile on her face even when nerves stole her enjoyment of spending time with David's family and their good-humored teasing, the tangy scent of enchiladas filling the air of his traditional two-story house. This was the same life she remembered before their mother died. The life she longed for again. The life she could have if she would let go of the pain and demands inflicted by her father. And of course, she also had to find a man she could trust not to take over her life and smother her.

Was Ryan that man? She looked at him, her heart warming over the way he'd jumped in when nerves had her stammering answers to questions. He'd playfully tickled both of the girls, chatted easily with Penny and David while Mia sat frozen on the super comfortable sofa, unable to relax and interact.

How could she with such high stakes? Wally's death left her alone. She didn't want to do anything to jeopardize this potential relationship with her brother and his family.

Ryan crossed the room decorated with traditional furnishings and pale blues and whites to sit next to her.

"Relax," he whispered as the plump sofa adjusted to his

weight. "You're a pretty terrific woman. Just be yourself, and they can't help but love you."

He smiled, an intimate, gentle smile, and a heavy weight lifted from her shoulders. He was the real deal. Everything he professed to be. A strong man, yet one with compassion and kindness. A man who had her best interest at heart. A man she should give in and trust.

"Aunt Mia." Willow, David's six-year-old daughter, came across the room and stood before Mia, ending the moment between her and Ryan.

She wore denim shorts, a T-shirt, white sneakers, and had auburn hair a shade lighter than Mia's natural color pulled back in a ponytail. She fingered Mia's wispy blouse sleeve. "When I grow up, I'm gonna wear pretty clothes like these every day."

Mia offered a genuine smile. "I like to dress up too."

Willow's eyes widened. "Do you want to see my party dresses?"

"Willow," David warned. "Mia's here to visit with all of us."

Willow's lips turned into a pout that rated a full ten on the pouting scale.

Mia couldn't stand to see the precious child's disappointment. "How about we take a quick look?"

"Yay!" Willow shouted and tugged Mia from the couch.

David gave Mia a sweet smile that she remembered from their childhood while their mother was still alive.

Mia smiled back, tentative at best, but a forward step for her, and let Willow lead her up a curved staircase with solid cherry railing to a pink frilly bedroom. Willow jabbered about parties, dresses, and shoes while Mia nodded and offered affirmation when appropriate as she took in the bedroom decorated for a princess. A pink canopy bed and formal white nightstand took up one wall. A matching desk with a pink tufted chair sat on the other wall, and a cushioned seat loaded with purple and pink patterned pillows was built in under the window, books scattered on the seat.

Willow exited her closet and displayed a pair of black patent dress shoes. "Grandpa gave me these for my birthday. They even have heels like yours."

Mia's father. Wow. David was right. Their father did care for these little girls. Mia's stomach ached.

She ignored it and kept a smile fixed in place, but her mind raced over the implications. Would she ever be able to think about her father without this pain or was she deluding herself? Had blaming him for the fire really ruined any chance to repair things with him?

The doorbell chimed, and Willow jumped to her feet.

"Let's go see who's here." She dropped the shoes and raced out of the room, leaving Mia to follow.

Mia dragged her feet as David hadn't said anyone else was expected for dinner, and she had no idea who it could be.

At the landing, she heard Willow shriek, "Grandpa!"

Mia stopped, her nervous butterflies returning, flying around the stress like ground glass in her stomach, and she thought she might be sick.

Male voices she recognized as her father's and David's drifted up the steps.

"Did she come?" her father asked.

"Yes," David said. "But you need to know I didn't tell her you'd be here."

"No, son. Surprising her like this isn't a good idea. Not a good idea at all."

"I didn't think she would come if she knew you'd be here," David said.

"Keeping my visit a secret might not help matters, and this has to stop before it escalates any further. I for one don't want another visit from law enforcement asking me if I'm involved in a crime, do you?"

"No, that was humiliating to say the least." David released a long drawn-out breath.

So this was why her father had come. Not to see her. Not to make amends. But because he'd been embarrassed, and he wanted to ensure Russ didn't bother him again.

Mia's chest tightened, the pain nearly unbearable.

"I can understand her thinking badly of me," her father continued. "I deserve it. People she's run into since she's been back tell me what a fine woman she's turned out to be. I can't reconcile that with her sending Russ to interrogate me."

"She didn't. I did." Ryan's voice, sure and strong floated up to Mia.

Surprised that Ryan joined the other men, she crept closer to get a look at them.

"I don't understand," her father said.

"You never have." Ryan clamped his hands on his waist. "The two of you have the only valid motives to want her gone, but she would never ask Russ to talk to you. Even when Russ blamed her for the terrible things going on around here."

"Are you kidding?" David gaped at her father. "Russ thinks Mia is involved in all this?"

"Not as much now, but he's considering it." Ryan ran a hand over his head. "Look. We're here for a nice dinner. What say, for one night, we forget the past and try to get to know the incredible woman Mia has become? You owe her at least that much."

Tears at Ryan's kindness threatened to break free. True, he was taking charge, making things happen on his time-frame and in his way, but he was doing so with pure compassion and caring for her.

She swiped a thumb under her eyes and headed for the stairs. No matter how her father and David behaved tonight, she wouldn't hide from them anymore. She would do her best to reconcile with them. If they rejected her, it would be the last time she would put herself out there for them to rip the rug from under her feet.

~

After dinner, Ryan held the passenger door for his truck open, and Mia climbed in. He was amazed at how well the evening turned out. He didn't know when Mia had decided to give her father a chance but she had. Sure, their dinner-time conversations were filled with stilted meaningless chitchat and hard to watch, but Ryan saw them both trying to find common ground.

Feeling like whistling over the success of the night, he ran to the other side of the truck and climbed in. He cautioned himself to cool it. To quit pushing as hard as he had in the last few days and let her choose the topic of their conversation.

He slipped the truck into gear and eased onto the highway. They rode in silence for several miles before she started to fiddle with the handle on a camera gadget bag sitting on the seat between them.

"Have you taken up photography?" she asked.

"Me? Nah. Chuck borrowed my truck to get supplies for the documentary crew, and the director called him to do some filming before he could get all of his things."

"Hope he doesn't mind if I snoop." She tugged on the bag's zipper and removed a camera. "Wow. This is top-notch. He must've dropped a bundle on it."

Ryan glanced at her. "I forgot you were once into photography. Are you still?"

"I haven't done much with it since high school, but I still keep up to date on cameras. Would love to have a digital SLR, but this one is around two grand for just the body."

Ryan laughed. "SLR? English, please."

"Oh, sorry. SLR is single lens reflex."

"Right. *Much* better explanation." He laughed again.

"Basically, it means when you look through the lens you see exactly what will be captured." She held the camera up and aimed it through the window. "Maybe when I get back to Atlanta, I should take this up again."

Get back to Atlanta. She said it with such enthusiasm, as if this was the best present she could receive. Not for him. He hated the idea of her leaving. They'd just started to get to know each other again. If the creep threatening her was caught, the two of them could spend time together this next year. As friends. Maybe more. Once all danger had been removed, and he didn't need to worry about losing her.

But what if her heart wasn't free? What if there was a guy in Atlanta and that was really why she wanted to go home? He didn't want to spoil the mood, but he had to ask. "Is there a boyfriend waiting for you there?"

"No one special." Her tone was laced with a hint of melancholy, and she ended with a sigh.

Maybe she *was* free.

He glanced at her. "I'm surprised no guy has snapped you up by now."

She shrugged. "It's not easy finding someone you want to spend the rest of your life with."

"Or keeping them," he said in a whisper that sent all of his pain at losing Cara into the space and filling the cab with tension.

"I'm sorry that you had to go through losing your fiancée." Mia lifted the camera to the window and peered through the viewfinder. "No one should have to experience such a tragedy."

He didn't say anything. He didn't want to talk about it. Especially as the inky darkness broken only by his headlights seemed to shout out to protect her from future danger.

He turned into Evergreen's driveway. No lights from Russ or his deputies or even Sierra. Either they'd finished processing the murder scene or they'd gone home to return in the light of day. In any event, Ryan hoped they'd found a lead to move this investigation forward.

"Did you see that?" Mia leaned forward.

"What?"

She pointed toward the resort office. "Over there. A light flashed in the window." She rubbed her eyes and stared in that direction. "There it is again. Like a flashlight."

He slowed the truck and followed the line of her finger. "There. I see it. You think someone broke in?"

"Verna could be working late."

"With a flashlight? Not likely." He flipped off the headlights and watched the beam cutting through the office. "This could be related to the threats."

Mia sat forward and kept the camera trained on the office. The lens whirred out. "This camera's got a great zoom, but I still can't make out who's in there."

"Let's get closer." He turned off the engine. "I'll coast down the hill. Don't want to draw attention."

With the engine dead, chirping crickets filled the void as did the crunching of tires over gravel. He let inertia pull the truck closer, and near the store, he swung the wheel hard to the left taking them as close to the building as he dared.

He applied the brakes and faced Mia. "See anything?"

"We're not at the right angle." She grabbed the door handle.

"I'll go check." He reached up to flip off the dome light. "You wait here."

"Are you kidding me? I'm coming with you." She eased out of the truck before he could stop her, bringing the camera in case she could capture a photo of the intruder.

Ryan joined her near the front bumper. "I don't want you to get hurt. Can you humor me and at least stay behind me?"

"Yes." She fell into place.

Grateful for her easy acquiescence, he led the way. They crept to the long narrow porch running the length of the office and small convenience store. He signaled for her to stay put while he went to take a closer look. Surprisingly she didn't argue but sat on the porch.

With silent footfalls, he closed the distance to the window and slowly rose up to glance inside. *What in the world?*

Someone was in the office all right, but it wasn't Verna as Mia suggested. A man, flashlight in one gloved hand, pry bar in the other, was trying to break into the file cabinet. Ryan couldn't make out clear details, but he could see enough to determine that the bulky, tall male, didn't appear to be armed.

What should they do? The break-in had to be related to the fire, maybe even Mia's bracelet, and the murder. No way they could let the guy get away.

Ryan eased back from the window and joined Mia, her eyes wide.

"A man's breaking into the file cabinet," he whispered. "We need to call Russ."

"Russ? No. It'll take too long for him to get here. This guy could take off before that."

"We'll sit right here. If he tries to leave before Russ arrives, we'll think of something."

Thankfully, Mia nodded, and Ryan made the call then settled on the bottom porch step next to Mia to wait.

Time ticked by in slow increments, palpable tension enveloping them.

Mia shivered, and he wrapped an arm around her. She looked up at him with a confidence he didn't like glinting in her eyes.

"My turn to go look," she whispered.

He took her hand. "Wait for Russ."

She shook her hand free. "We have to see what this guy's up to so we can act if needed."

"Fine. Then I'll go." Ryan moved before she could stop him. At the window, he raised up like a Peeping Tom. The man had wrenched open a file cabinet and was shoving files into a bulging cloth bag.

How odd. Of all the valuable equipment in the room, why take files?

Mia sneezed, breaking the silence. The man spun and started toward the door.

Ryan dropped down and frantically signaled that the intruder was on his way out and Mia needed to move from the doorway.

Instead of moving away, she stood and planted her legs wide. Ryan heard a whirring sound coming from the camera.

"Close your eyes," she whispered.

The door wrenched open.

Mia fired off picture after picture. The flash's bright light lit the darkness like sharp retorts of gunfire.

"What the—" the man shouted and his hands went to cover his eyes.

She was trying to blind the guy so he couldn't see to leave. Too bad Ryan hadn't taken her advice and closed his eyes. He rubbed them to eliminate the stars and listened. He heard the guy banging around as if he were dazed.

Footfalls traveled past Ryan. The flashes should have rendered this man's eyesight as useless as Ryan's. Hoping to tackle the intruder, he shot from his spot. Missed the man. Banged his shoulder into the porch post.

"Think something that stupid will stop me, girly," the gruff voice came from an area near Mia.

Ryan blinked hard. Through the splotches coloring his vision, he saw the huge male slam into her.

"No!" Ryan leapt to his feet.

Mia went flying and hit the ground hard. Her head snapped back. The camera catapulted into the air.

"Stop!" Ryan bolted toward the man who'd concealed his head with a dark hoodie.

The intruder uttered a foul laugh before charging into the darkness. Ryan wanted to chase after him. Tackle him. But Mia wasn't moving. She needed him.

Please let her be all right.

"Mia." He knelt by her unmoving body. "Are you okay?"

She slowly stirred. "What happened? The camera? Chuck will kill me if I broke it."

Ryan sat back on his haunches and huffed out his worry. Her ability to stay levelheaded when under fire was one of the things he'd always liked about her.

Thank You for protecting her.

"We might be able to catch that guy. Do you think we should go after him?" She'd survived an attack and seemed determined not to run away in fright.

His smile fell away. This was too similar to Cara. She'd said she could handle that creep who'd stabbed her. Said he deserved for her to continue counseling him even when he'd formed an unhealthy affection for her.

Now, Mia, who, God help him, he'd started to care about

more than he should, wanted to chase the man who'd just slammed her onto the concrete. If she tried, Ryan would have to insist she remain put. Even if Ryan accompanied her, his heart just couldn't take the worry of seeing her go after a potential killer.

21

If Mia could believe God looked out for her, she would thank Him for saving her life. More likely, He was watching over Ryan who'd survived the intruder's escape without injury. Sadly, she didn't survive the attack unscathed. The back of her head had hit a parking block and it throbbed. She gingerly touched the area and winced. Her fingers came away sticky. Blood.

No way she would tell Ryan about the blood. He would return to clucking over her like a mother hen. She was beginning to warm to his concern and honestly wouldn't mind if he pulled her into his arms for comfort. But even more, she wanted to get into the office to see the burglar's handiwork before Russ arrived to take over the crime scene. If Ryan knew she was bleeding he would make her sit right here and call paramedics.

She got to her feet. Dizziness enveloped her. She plopped back down.

"Here." Ryan handed her the camera. "Let me help you." He bent low and lifted her by the arm.

She got up, faltering and swaying.

"Whoa." He took hold of her upper arms. "Are you sure you're okay?"

"Fine. Just got the air knocked out of me." Mia pointed down the driveway to divert his attention. "Looks like Russ is here."

She'd expected Russ to come barreling down the drive with lights blaring, but his car crept forward in stealth mode. Made sense. He didn't know the burglar had run off.

"Can you wait here for Russ? I want to take a quick look to see what was stolen?" She didn't wait for an answer, but started moving toward the office as fast as she could before another fresh wave of dizziness took her down.

Inside, she found the tall file cabinet behind Verna's desk tipped on the side. Files splayed across the linoleum like avalanched snow. A white pillowcase stuffed with what looked like file folders sat near the door.

She wanted to peek in the case, but Russ's and Ryan's voices drifted inside stopping her. *Drat.* She was too late. If she took time to look in the bag, Russ would catch her.

Her back to the door, she quickly took in every detail. The computer, other office equipment, and valuables remained untouched. This wasn't some random break-in. The thief wanted information. If they hadn't interrupted him, maybe he would've gone for the computer hard drive as well.

Too bad he'd worn his hood up, shadowing his face. Not to mention in the dark with the flashes of light, she hadn't seen him clearly or she could at least give Russ a description.

"You're hurt," Ryan said from behind.

She jumped and faced him, the room spun and whirled like a carnival ride.

He stood in the doorway, alone. She could hear Russ talking outside. Maybe one of his deputies had also arrived.

Biting his lip, Ryan strode across the room to her. "Why didn't you tell me you were bleeding?"

"I didn't want you to stop me from looking inside before Russ arrived."

"Let me look at it." He turned her around, and she wobbled. "Dizziness isn't a good sign." He softly probed with his fingers. "The wound doesn't look too bad. Are you nauseous?"

She faced him and smiled. "No, I'm fine. It's really just a bump."

His mouth drew up in a pucker. "You might not have a concussion, but I think you should have a doctor look at it anyway."

She waved away his concern. "Really, I'm fine. But thanks."

"If you won't go to the doctor, you'll need someone to check on you tonight. To make sure you really are okay."

"I think you're overreacting."

"And I think you're downplaying how serious this could be." He stroked the side of her face, and paused near the gash, then let his fingers linger long enough to raise her heartbeat.

Even if he was trying to take charge, she enjoyed the feel of his fingers—coarse yet gentle against her skin.

"I hope you haven't touched anything." Russ charged inside, a deputy trailing him.

They split apart.

"Well, except each other." Russ grinned.

"Don't worry. We know the protocol." Ryan dug his cell from his pocket. "I'll just step outside for a minute to update my staff in case the burglar is still on the property. And I'll head up to the lodge to be sure this guy didn't make a stop in there too."

"Take my deputy with you," Russ said. "Report back if you find a problem."

"Will do." Ryan went outside, tapping the screen of his phone as he went.

Now that he was gone, Mia didn't need to keep up the pretense of feeling fine. "Would it be okay if I sat while we talked?"

"Fine by me," Russ said.

She gently lowered her battered body onto the cracked vinyl chair by Verna's desk.

"Tell me what happened," Russ said.

She described coming upon the intruder and her attempt to blind him. Russ interrupted frequently to ask clarifying questions, making the process take forever. His questions went on and on, eating up time Mia could better use to determine who'd broken into the office.

"Can you describe him?" Russ asked.

"Not other than he was big. Over six feet tall. Strong. Bulky, like a football player. He plowed through us both like we were nothing."

Russ gestured at the room. "Can you tell what's missing?"

She started to shake her head, and everything spun. "No, but he dropped the pillowcase by the door and it's filled with files from the cabinet he broke into. Verna told me today that she kept employee files in there."

"That should give Sierra something to go on." Russ pointed at her lap. "Is that the camera?"

She lifted the mangled body. "It is."

"Did our suspect touch it?"

"No," she said. "He wore gloves, but even if he didn't, it flew from my hand when he barreled into me."

Russ scowled. "If I remember right, you're a photography

buff. Any hope we can get a picture of the guy off that camera?"

"Depends. If the flash was bright enough, and if the memory card is still intact then maybe." She tried to open the small compartment housing the memory card. "Card holder is damaged. I can't get it out, but maybe Chuck can remove it without damaging the card."

"Who's Chuck?"

"The camera's owner and a photographer on the documentary crew."

Russ tapped his chin. "He might well be able to do it, but he's a no-go. We need to maintain chain of custody. Sierra can retrieve the card then Chuck can have his camera back."

"I'll let Chuck know in the morning that Sierra has this." Mia handed the camera to Russ.

"Before I let you go, let's take a look in that pillowcase to see if the contents mean anything to you." He set the camera on the desk and then snapped on gloves. He crossed the room and lifted the case onto Verna's desk.

"It's full of files like you said." He removed a stack of manila folders and then handed her a pair of gloves. "Check these out. Anything significant?"

Mia put on the gloves and flipped through the stack. "Looks like personnel files like she said, but it's also financial files for Evergreen." Baffled, she looked at Russ. "I can't see why someone would want to steal only these files, but maybe he was planning to take even more of them if we hadn't interrupted."

Russ gave her a clipped nod. "I'll get Verna's take on them tomorrow."

The idea of Verna looking at these didn't sit well with Mia. "Verna's been acting odd lately. Like she has something to hide. So if she's up to something, there might be evidence in these files to implicate her."

Russ's eyebrow went up. "You think she's cooking the books?"

"I think it would be impossible to do with my brother's firm handling the finances for Evergreen." She reminded him of the separation of duties that Kurt had explained to her. "Keeps things on the up and up."

Russ scowled. "Then I should probably have them evaluate the files before I talk to her."

"Sounds like a good idea." Mia took a breath. "And then talk to Verna not only about the files, but about her debts."

Russ frowned.

Interesting response. "You don't think that's a good idea?"

"Oh, I do, but it's one of the things I hate about small-town policing. You know the people you accuse of all kinds of bad things. Then when they turn out to be innocent, they often hold a grudge and you have to see them again. Frequently. They don't let you forget it."

She hadn't thought of it that way. "Sounds like a tough job, but from what I hear and see, you do it well."

His shoulders went up straighter.

"I'm one of those people, aren't I?" she asked. "I'd actually like to forget about our high school days and our rocky start here and be friends again."

He arched an eyebrow, his inquisitive sheriff stare fixed on her. "You can let everything go including my recent accusations?"

She nodded.

"Then so can I." He held out his hand. "Friends again."

"Friends again." She took his punishing grip and didn't wince.

He released her hand. "Unless you have anything else to add, I need to help my deputy."

"Nothing to add." Mia shed her gloves and exited the building.

Russ clomped behind. Outside, the air had chilled considerably, and Mia wrapped her arms around her stomach to chase away the cold. Sure the temps had dropped, but was her chill from the cold or from the sight of her blood on the parking block?

She could've been seriously hurt. Died even. So could Ryan. She'd been foolish to think she could stop the intruder with a camera flash, but she'd had to try.

Russ came alongside her and made a quick jerk of his head in the lodge's direction. "Looks like Ryan's on his way back."

Ryan clipped along the path with a flashlight illuminating his way, Bandit leashed and tugging him along. When he got nearer, she could see the outline of Bandit's cone as he leapt and snapped at the moving beam of light. He caught her scent and charged. She wanted to bend down and greet him, but that would send her head reeling.

He galloped straight past her, ripping his leash free from Ryan's hand, and racing into the office. Bandit's leash trailed behind him, leaving a path in the dust.

Russ grunted. "Guess you haven't learned to control him, huh?"

Mia didn't bother answering as he was right. She could've been working on training Bandit, if she didn't have so many other things going on.

"I'll get him." Ryan went toward the office.

Before he reached the sagging porch, Bandit charged out. He paused to look up at Mia. She laughed at the crazy expression on his face surrounded by the plastic cone. His mouth was clenched around something thick, small, and brown, and she sobered.

"He has something in his mouth," Russ said. "What is it?"

"Bandit," Mia called. "Come here, boy. Let me see."

So as not to scare him, she eased closer. He wagged his little tail as if he was excited to see her then shot into the darkness.

"You better hope he didn't take anything important," Russ said.

Mia waved off Russ. "Relax. He probably just swiped a treat from the store."

"Like I said, you better hope so," Russ said over his shoulder as he went to the office.

"I need to find Bandit." Mia started up the trail.

"Not alone, you don't." Ryan fell into step at her side.

A car rolled down the drive, the headlights cutting through the dark.

"Who could that be?" Ryan stopped to stare at the vehicle.

Mia watched as the car approached, nerves skittering across her body, until she could make out that the vehicle was a hot-pink Cadillac. Not the kind of car a killer might drive.

The Cadillac stopped, and the driver waved over the roof through the open window. "Yoo-hoo, Mia, hold up."

Her voice was vaguely familiar, but Mia couldn't place her.

The door opened, and a large woman wearing an over-the-top floral dress with lime green terrycloth slippers climbed from the driver's side. Recognition set in.

Mia groaned. Where could she hide?

Mrs. Miller, the town busybody flapped her hands in the air as she jabbered at the scrawny Mr. Miller wearing faded bib overalls and exiting the passenger side of the car.

Despite the woman's reputation, her wild gestures and

animated face piqued Mia's interest. With all of Mrs. Miller's contacts and owning the local gas station, she may have heard gossip about the incidents that could help move this investigation forward.

Mrs. Miller charged Mia, and they met in front of the headlights. "Here you are, you poor dear."

"Hello, Mrs. Mil—"

"Oh, no, no." She waved a plump hand. "You're all grown up. Call us Art and Gladys."

"If that's what you want." Mia watched the pink foam curler perched at the crown of Gladys's head bob up and down.

She swung her body to face Ryan. "Evening, Ryan. Glad to see you here with Mia."

"Glad to be with her." Ryan gave a reserved smile, headlight beams shining on the side of his face.

Gladys stepped closer to Mia and took her hands. "I won't take up much of your time when you should be resting from that dreadful fire, but I wanted to express my condolences for your loss, and I have something that might help find the arsonist."

Just as Mia had hoped. She ignored the condolence comment. "What do you know, Mrs. Mil—Gladys?"

Gladys leaned even closer as if the entire world was listening in. "I was at Reid's place yesterday afternoon checking on little Jessie. Russ showed up and while I played cards with the little sweetie, he and Reid went into the other room. They thought they were out of earshot, but I heard them talking about the man Jessie saw drive into the barn and start the fire." She paused with a beam of satisfaction lighting her face.

Knowing Gladys, she wasn't playing cards but had her ear snugged up to the door to learn all she could.

"I also heard the truck belonged to Orrin Jackson. Probably stolen by the man who started the fire. Now who would go stealing Orrin's truck like that? Not anyone from around here, I tell you. Jessie confirmed that. She can't identify that man as a local, but then at her age, she doesn't know everyone in town."

"So how can you help?" Mia asked, trying to push her along.

"I'm just getting to that. A couple years ago, the hubby and I," she paused to give Art a pointed look, "got tired of city slickers passing bad checks and bogus credit cards at the station. So we started scanning a copy of strangers' licenses and credit cards when they made a purchase. So, if the man who stole the truck and started the fire bought gas with a credit card, I'd have a copy of his license."

Mia tried to keep a straight face when the idea seemed pretty farfetched. "This guy wouldn't be too smart to bring a stolen truck into your station."

"Oh, I know that, but if he's not from around here, he had to get to Shadow Lake to steal the truck. Maybe whatever he was driving needed gas. Or he got hungry and needed a snack." She dug in her bag and withdrew a red case. "Last night I went through all of the files for the last few months and pulled out the pictures of men matching Jessie's description. They're all right here on this DVD." She slipped the case into Mia's hand.

"Sounds like a long shot, but maybe it'll pay off." Mia smiled her thanks. "I'll look at it when I get a chance."

"That's good. Be sure to tell me if I can help with anything else."

"You can," Ryan said. "Right now."

"Tell me how, and it's yours for the asking."

"Mia just hit the back of her head on a concrete block. Broke the skin and she's dizzy, but she doesn't think she needs medical attention."

Gladys snatched the flashlight from Ryan's hand. With her tongue poking from the side of her mouth, she circled Mia and used her finger to probe the bump on Mia's scalp as the flashlight warmed the skin.

"Doesn't appear to need stitches." She gave Ryan his light back. "I can take care of things now. I'll just send my Mister home for some things, and we'll spend the night with Mia so I can check on her."

"That's not necessary," Mia said, her mind imagining an entire night with Gladys Miller. "I'll be fine."

"Someone has to check on you throughout the night." Ryan gave her a pointed look.

Mia flashed him a frustrated look. She didn't know which would be worse. Having Gladys spend the night or Ryan.

"Fine," she said.

Gladys smiled broadly and faced her hubby who looked bored. "Go on home, Art, and bring me things for an overnight stay. Include some antibiotic ointment for this cut."

He took off as if he relished leaving.

Gladys studied Mia. "I just can't believe you're back, and you'll be our neighbor for the next year. I know your father and David are so happy you've come home." She winked. "Why at church last Sunday they were jabbering on about how good it will be to have the family reunited."

Was what Gladys said true? Her father had often gone to church right after one of their big fights with his game face on, making believe their family was coping well with their loss. Was that what he was doing or was he really glad she'd come home?

Gladys slipped her hand through the crook of Mia's arm and started them walking. "Let's get you up to the lodge."

"I need to talk to Russ about something." Ryan gave

Gladys his flashlight and turned on his phone's light. "Then I'll stop in to make sure you're settled, and I'll look for Bandit again."

Mia didn't argue and let Gladys lead her away, following the beam of light dancing over the grass. What was the point of arguing when both of these people had her best interests at heart? Sure, she'd rather be alone to think about what happened and try to figure out who was doing this to her, but maybe it was best not to dwell on it tonight and get a good night's sleep.

Yes, that's what she would do after finding Bandit, but tomorrow she had no intention of simply sitting around and waiting for another attack or incident.

22

Ryan shook his arms to let the worry he'd kept in check in Mia's presence free and started back toward the office. The light beaming from his phone caught the concrete where she'd hit her head. A large splotch darkened one side.

Mia's blood.

His mouth went dry. Like the night he'd found Cara, his emotions ran strong. He needed to face facts. He cared for Mia. How much? He had no idea, but she'd become important to him again. And she could've died tonight.

Without God's protection, she could've suffered permanent damage.

Once again, Ryan had been powerless to help the woman he cared for. It couldn't happen again. He couldn't lose her. He had to protect her. This time he wouldn't let Russ turn down his request.

"Hey, bro," he called out to stop his brother as he stepped out of the office door and marched toward his vehicle. "I need to talk to you about something."

Russ stopped at his trunk and opened it. "Make it fast. I've got a lot of work to do."

"Earlier you said you couldn't put a deputy out here to

watch Mia, but things have changed. You have to admit with what just happened, she's in real danger."

"She wouldn't have gotten hurt if you'd waited for me to arrive." Russ tossed an extension cord to his deputy standing outside the door. "We'll probably be here most of the night, and I doubt anyone will try anything."

Ryan wasn't as confident, and despite Gladys staying at the lodge, he would camp outside in his truck. "And tomorrow?"

"I'll check the duty roster to see if I can do anything." Russ looked at the office. "That all?"

"Yeah, but let me know what you come up with ASAP," Ryan said. "Now go back to tormenting your rookie."

Russ laughed and grabbed a storage bin from the trunk and took off.

Weary, Ryan hopped into his truck and drove the short distance to the lodge. He would check in with Mia and then hunt for Bandit if the dog hadn't come home. He parked out front, glad to see all of the outdoor lights burning brightly to keep intruders away and the blinds closed so no one could look inside. He would stay the night, and if his brother couldn't put a deputy on her tomorrow, he would assign the Shadow Lake Survival team as her protection detail.

He exited his pickup, inhaled the cool air to ease his tiredness, and climbed to the front door to knock. He noted black fingerprint powder on the door. Obviously, Sierra and her assistant had been here to process the place.

Gladys answered the door, flinging it wide. "Good, now you can tell Mia it's foolish to go out looking for that dog after being injured."

"He's not back?" Ryan asked.

"No, and Mia's worried to death over the little thing. I've gotten her wound all cleaned up, and she should rest, not go tromping in the woods at night."

He agreed she should rest, but he also knew no one would convince her not to do it until Bandit was safe. She was a fierce protector of those she loved, and she already loved that little dog.

Since Ryan had already planned to look for Bandit if he wasn't here, he would go along with Mia and keep an eye on her. "Where is she?"

"In the bedroom putting her boots on." Gladys clutched his arm. "You will stop her, won't you?"

Though he doubted he would be able to talk some sense into her for once, that wouldn't stop him from attempting it. "I'll try, but you know how stubborn she can be."

"Don't I ever," Gladys said. "She even tossed aside the DVD I gave her. She thinks it's a real long shot."

Gladys pointed at the laptop sitting on the island. "I put it in her computer and loaded the file. Next time she checks her email it'll be open and waiting. It's for her own good, you know."

"Whose good?" Mia asked as she strolled into the room.

"Never you mind." Gladys toddled over to Mia. "Now why don't you sit down, and I'll make a cup of tea. Ryan can go find the dog."

"I appreciate your concern, but Bandit's my responsibility. He could be in trouble, and I need to look for him."

Gladys jabbed Ryan in the ribs.

He rubbed the ache. "It's not a good idea to go out there alone. What if the burglar is still hanging around?"

"Not likely with Russ, here, right?"

She had a point. One Ryan couldn't dispute. "Still, I'll go with you."

"Great," she said, her easy acquiesce catching him by surprise. "Two people searching for him is better than one."

She went to the door and pulled a jacket down from a

rack shaped like a large fish. She slipped into the light-weight jacket that was three sizes too big for her.

As Mia exited, Ryan turned back to Gladys. "Go ahead and get the water boiling for tea. This shouldn't take long."

At least he hoped it wouldn't because while they were searching, he didn't want to give the intruder a chance to return and exact his revenge.

~

Shining the flashlight, Mia charged down the stairs and toward a stand of pine trees lining the property. Thankfully her dizziness had subsided, and she rushed ahead to the edge of the woods and called Bandit's name. A scurrying sound in the trees caught her attention. She checked it out, but found nothing. These woods were full of small nocturnal animals, and her tromping around had upset their nightly routine.

Ryan gently clasped a hand on her shoulder. "After that head injury, you should take things a little slower."

"I appreciate your concern, I really do, and but I have things under control." Never mind that she hadn't been doing a very good job of taking care of herself lately, she'd survived for ten years without much help and could continue to do so, right?

He frowned. "When are you going to learn accepting help isn't a sign of weakness? Even if the help comes from a guy." He said a *guy* as if it were poison he was spitting out. "Look, I'm sorry. That came out wrong. I know your father did a number on you, and you have every right to be gun-shy. But not all men are like him. Some of us really want to help with no strings attached."

His sincere tone broke through her anger, and she considered his words. He was right. Not that she wanted to admit it, but through the years, she'd honed in on any hint of controlling behavior from every man she'd dated or who'd tried to help her except Wally. One sign of it, she blew it out of proportion, and boom, she ended their relationship. No matter their good qualities. And that's what she'd been doing with Ryan.

She had to get over it. Maybe focus on changing this year of exile and finally let it go. Move on. Be the woman she could be without all the baggage. But that didn't mean she was ready to discuss her newfound revelation with Ryan when she was so very tired and worried about Bandit.

"So, let's find Bandit," she said, ending with a forced laugh to let him know she'd gotten his point without having to discuss it.

They searched for the next hour with no success. Her head pounded, and the cool, damp air settled into her body. She was growing more irritable by the minute and knew it was time to call it a night before she snapped at Ryan again. She told him as much and like the perfect gentleman he was turning out to be, he walked her home.

Wanting to end the night on a good note, she took the front steps but rested against the post on the porch to think of how to thank him for his concern without encouraging him to overreact in the future. Maybe she could start with something neutral and ease her way in.

He waited at the base of the stairs as if unsure if he should stay or go.

"Thank you for coming with me. I appreciate it." She smiled. "Do you think Bandit will be okay?"

"I doubt this is the first time he's spent the night out here alone."

"What if he runs into a bigger and more powerful animal?" A vision of her defenseless little friend at the mercy of wild animals stole her voice.

Ryan climbed the stairs, invading her personal space and coming eye-to-eye with her. "Why, Mia Blackburn, I think you actually care about something of the male persuasion. Maybe there's hope for me in the future."

Picking up on his light mood, she stabbed her finger into his firm chest. "What? A future? For someone who just told me he never wanted a long-term relationship again, this sounds to me like you're hoping to start one."

He latched onto her finger and pulled her against his chest. His eyes were smoky and irresistible in the shadowed light. "Newsflash, Mia. Women aren't the only ones who can change their minds. I may have found a reason to reconsider."

She opened her mouth to issue a snappy comeback, but his lips descended on hers before she could speak. Soft and warm, they melted away the cold that had taken hold of her body. She slid her hands over his shoulders and up his neck, past the rough stubble of his jaw. Just as her fingers tickled the ends of his hair, he set her away.

He traced her face and then leaned close. "I'll see you in the morning," he whispered with his breath tickling her neck.

He jogged down the steps and to his pickup. She touched the spot on her neck and listened to his truck door slam.

Had he just asked to pursue a future with her or was he simply flirting? She shook her head and went inside. Didn't matter what his intentions were. She wouldn't get involved with him for the long run.

Problem was, she'd proven she was barely able to resist his kindhearted nature for a few days. How would she survive unscathed for an entire year?

23

The next morning, dressed in her favorite jeans and equally favorite T-shirt that always brought her comfort, Mia called for Bandit from the porch. No response. Hands cupped around her mouth, she yelled three more times. The only attention she drew was from Sierra and Chad, both clad in their white suits working in the area by the barn.

Nothing for it but to go look for Bandit.

A patrol car pulled down the drive and parked near the barn. Russ. Maybe he had news. Searching for Bandit would wait. She jogged down the steps and across the yard to meet up with Russ. Hopefully, he would let her stay, and she could hear his conversation with Sierra.

The sun beamed from clear skies as usual this time of year, shining down on the rubble and not improving the look of devastation. And no matter how fresh and sweet the breeze usually was around here, it couldn't do anything for the burnt smell that lingered in the air.

She swallowed away her unease and approached the couple.

"Good morning," she said, doing her best to seem

sociable and not like an interloper. "Could I offer anyone breakfast or some tea? Coffee?"

Russ shook his head. "Just here to get an update."

"I'm good for now," Sierra said. "But maybe later if you're around. Seems like I'm always hungry these days."

"You said in the voicemail that you have some results," Russ said to Sierra and didn't tell Mia to take a hike, so she relaxed a notch.

Sierra shifted to face Russ. "We were able to lift two sets of prints from the charms on the bracelet, and a set on the fake hand, but none of the prints returned a match."

"Did you get prints from my father and David?" she asked.

Russ shook his head. "They consulted with your dad's attorney. He told me they'd be glad to comply when we have a court order compelling them to do so."

She gritted her teeth. "What you expected."

"It is." Russ tightened his gaze. "But don't go reading anything into this. It's a common response even for innocent parties."

"And especially for my father."

"If you say so."

"When you get the prints, I'll be glad to run a comparison," Sierra said.

Mia was thankful Sierra was moving them on. "What about the letters or box? Any prints there?"

"Paper is trickier to process and will have to wait until we get back to the lab, but we did get a print from the bullet casing. It matched one of the prints lifted from the bracelet as did the print from the hand."

"So ties our shooter to the bracelet and severed hand," Russ said. "But since you didn't get a hit on the prints from these items, we don't have a hit on the casing."

"Correct," Sierra said. "But it does say that your suspect isn't very careful if he'd leave his prints behind."

"Yeah," Russ said. "Thankfully for detectives, some people don't watch all the forensic TV shows or read murder mysteries and know to glove up."

Mia was one of those people, but not anymore. She now knew more than she wanted to about crimes and crime scenes. Especially when it came to murder.

"I located a single chain link buried in mud by the barn's front door," Sierra said. "Could be from the missing locks you mentioned. Looks to be standard. Someone cut it, and if you find a set of bolt cutters we can match the blade to the link."

Mia looked at Russ. "We should check Nico's shed for that."

"Not we." He eyed Mia. "I'll do it right after we're done."

She had no reason to argue so just nodded.

"We also picked up the rifle from Nico and processed the lodge yesterday," Sierra said. "I took a good sampling of the dust from the table where you found the package and lifted quite a few prints from the target. We'll run all of that when we get back to the office too."

"Were you able to determine if our victim was killed in the barn?" Russ asked.

"The quantity of blood under the body says he didn't die there. I'm sure when your ME does the autopsy, the body's lividity might confirm that he'd been moved."

"Lividity?" Mia asked.

"When a person dies, their blood settles to the lowest area of the body. It remains fluid for a short period of time, but then becomes fixed. If the victim is found in a position contrary to the pooling blood, it can tell you the body has been moved."

"I'll check with the ME," Russ said. "But at least we now know we're looking elsewhere for a murder scene."

Sierra nodded and gestured at Chad. "We're just packing up now to move over to the shooter's hide near your property line and then we'll move on to Orrin Jackson's house. Hopefully, we'll find prints on his gun cabinet. It would be good if you got those bolt cutters to us before we leave."

"Heading out now. Thanks, Sierra." He spun and marched back to his car.

Sierra watched Russ. "He's a serious one. Direct and to the point, like most law enforcement officers I deal with."

"If that's the case, I don't envy you your job." Mia smiled. "I'll take a surly teenager any day."

Sierra shuddered and rested a hand on her belly. "I could never handle that all day long. If this one gets surly as a teen, I'll send it to you."

Mia laughed with the woman, but Mia's phone rang putting an end to her fun. "Excuse me. Gotta take this."

"And I need to get this van loaded." Sierra strode away, a waddle in her step.

Caller ID didn't register, but Mia answered in case the call was related to the incidents.

"Did I catch you at a bad time?" David asked.

"Not at all." Mia headed toward the porch, hoping he was calling to tell her that he enjoyed dinner with her last night and wanted to do it again.

"I'm glad I caught you." His cheerful tone from last night was long gone. "I updated Russ Maddox on Evergreen's files that he dropped off for our review early this morning. I thought you should have a heads-up before the local gossips got wind of this news."

Mia was intrigued more than concerned, but also wished Russ had told her that he'd taken the files to Kurt and David.

"You might not believe this," David continued. "But the folders hold clear evidence of Verna's embezzlement from Evergreen."

Mia stopped dead in her tracks. "Verna stole money?"

"A considerable amount, actually. Not that I had a clue. There was a decline in income, but the records showed higher vacancy rates so it seemed normal." David sighed. "I feel kind of dumb for not seeing the theft, but she hid it well, and Wally didn't seem concerned about income being down. Did he say anything to you?"

"He never talked about business with me." Mia tried to wrap her mind around what this news meant. If Verna was embezzling, she might be trying to get rid of Mia before she discovered the crime. But what did Mia do about it? "Did Russ tell you how he would proceed?"

"No, but as the new owner of the resort, I'd imagine you'll need to press charges against Verna for the theft."

So Verna stole money. Not something Mia would ever expect, but with a sick daughter, Verna had likely done what she thought she had to do to take care of her child. Mia understood that as much as she was disappointed in Verna.

And now, Mia would do what she had to do as well. "Thank you for letting me know, David."

"Of course." His tone held relief, likely from having gotten that off his chest. "I still have files to review, but when I finish, I'll be able to give you the total dollar amount of her theft."

"I appreciate it." Mia ended the call with her brother and raced up the steps to the lodge to decide what to do next. She dropped onto a barstool and stared at the phone, half wondering if she'd imagined that call.

This news certainly explained Verna's odd behavior. She could have somehow gained access to the bracelet and would definitely know it would hurt Mia. She could've locked the barn too. But kill someone? That was too far-fetched. Right? Of course, the murder could be unrelated.

They needed to get her fingerprints. The theft should be enough evidence for Russ to get a court order to print her. Could even be one set of unidentified prints on the bracelet or hand.

Finally! They were getting somewhere.

A knock sounded on the door.

Mia wasn't expecting anyone, so she cautiously crossed the room and peeked out the window.

Ryan. He was back. He'd spent the night in his truck outside her door. She wished he'd come in for a cup of coffee in the morning, but he'd left, and she hadn't known when to expect him. Now he was here.

Overjoyed to see him, she jerked the door open. "Have I got news for you."

She told him about David's call and the information from Sierra, her words tumbling out like the nearby rushing river before Ryan could cross the threshold. "Where do you think Verna is? Do you think Russ will arrest her? Should we go to the office and see?"

Ryan rested his hands on her shoulders, stilling her anxious fidgeting. "Slow down. Let me think."

She didn't want to wait. She wanted Verna in jail and paying for her crimes. "Verna could be getting away."

"That's a little rash. She doesn't even know David reviewed the files." Ryan stroked her arms as if he believed it would appease her, but nothing would stop her now.

"She may not know about David but the break-in to steal files should freak her out. Wait! Would she have paid this guy to break into the office to steal the files?"

He shrugged. "It would get rid of the evidence, I guess."

"But she could just take the files. Or shred them. Like she was doing yesterday." Mia clutched the front of Ryan's denim shirt. "Oh, my gosh! She was probably destroying evidence right in front of me, and I didn't know it. We have to get down there before she shreds even more pages."

Mia rushed out the door without waiting to see if Ryan followed. Sierra and Chad drove off from the barn, and Mia waved as she headed straight for the UTV parked out front. She revved the engine and turned to see if Ryan was coming.

He jogged across the thick grass and climbed in. "I'm surprised you waited."

"Sorry." She shifted into gear and aimed the vehicle down the driveway. "I'm happy we've figured this out, and I can't wait to get it resolved."

"I'm happy too, but I think we should talk to Russ first."

Ryan could be right, but she'd been helpless for days. She had to do something—now.

Ryan leaned forward. "Did you hear that?"

"What?"

"A dog barking." He looked at her. "Did Bandit ever come home?"

She shook her head and slowed the vehicle to listen. An excited yipping echoed from the north end of the barn.

"Sounds like Bandit." She craned her neck to try to see him but he was out of sight. "And it sounds like something's wrong."

"Shut this thing down, and we'll check." He jumped out.

She turned the key and followed him across the lawn into the muck. Still holding moisture from the firefighters' hoses, the ground oozed under foot and water soaked into her shoes. They would be ruined but discovering the reason for Bandit's excited yips trumped destroying a pair of shoes. They climbed under the restrung crime-scene tape and found Bandit very near the victim's location.

Bandit scraped the cone through ashes as he rooted

around like a pig, his cone coated in muck. With each step, visions of finding the gruesome discovery assaulted her. No way she wanted to go closer.

She stopped short. "Come here, boy. You'll get your stitches dirty."

He looked up at her as if he understood, but remained in place to whine and scrounge in the same spot, upping his motions to frantic.

"He's being stubborn," Ryan said.

"Looks more like he's found something and doesn't want to leave it alone." Mia carefully picked her way through the mess.

"I'll get him." Ryan moved past her, plopping his booted feet into the muck and splattering gunk everywhere.

As Ryan lifted Bandit from the debris and held the dirty little fella away from his chest, she searched the dog's body for injury. He aimed his tongue at Ryan, but he couldn't connect. Not with the cone circling his neck.

She turned to the spot where Bandit had cleared the rubbish. The tip of a small brown object poked from the ruins.

"That looks like a wallet," she said.

"Wait. Must belong to the victim." Ryan dug disposable gloves from his pocket. "Russ gave me an extra pair in case we needed them."

Mia put on the gloves, retrieved the item, and held it up to Ryan.

"A man's wallet." Ryan locked eyes with her. "Let's get out of this mess and see if it holds any ID."

They retreated to an area of lush lawn free from standing water.

Mia ignored Bandit's frantic squirming to flip open the wallet and remove the driver's license.

She studied the picture. Her legs turned rubbery and

refused to hold her. She dropped to her knees, sinking into the thick grass.

How could this be? Another person she loved dead. This one murdered and discarded like trash.

She sucked in gulps of air as panic ricocheted through her body.

"What is it?" Ryan squatted next to her.

Bandit wiggled free and yipped at the wallet.

"I know this man." She handed the driver's license to Ryan and rested her chin on her knees.

"Franklin Springer from Dunwoody, Georgia." Ryan looked at Mia. "Isn't that the PI friend that Wally hired?"

"Yes." Heaviness settled into her brain, and her head filled with so much pain it might explode.

"I'm sorry." Ryan wrapped an arm around her shoulders and held her.

She pulled back and peered at him, tears rolling down her cheeks. He wiped her tears with a gentle finger.

He was being kind. Nice. He'd proven himself trustworthy. She could get used to turning to him when life kicked her around.

But then what? Nothing. That's what. She'd already decided she needed to be alone in life. Another death of someone close to her proved her thinking right. That was best. No way she'd open herself up for hurt again.

She eased from under his hand and stood. "I don't know why I'm surprised to learn Fuzzy died. This is the kind of thing I've come to expect in my life. Everyone I care about either dies or turns on me."

Ryan pushed to his feet. "I didn't betray you."

"Guess that means God will have to separate us in another way."

He gaped at her. "Is that what you really think? That

God is causing all of these things to happen to make your life miserable?"

"He could stop them if He wanted, so at the very least He's allowing it." She let her gaze fall away from Ryan's scrutiny. "Right. I forgot. You used to share this opinion with me but that's changed."

"Back then I really didn't know God. Now that I have a relationship with Him, I know He doesn't cause bad things to happen."

"Really? Then why do they happen?" she asked, really wanting to know the answer. To know that God was the loving God Ryan seemed to know, and He really had her best interest at heart. How much easier life would be if she had that kind of God to turn to in times of trouble.

"This is a tough thing to understand. Even those who have a much deeper walk with God than me struggle with it. But here's how I see it." He eased closer and clasped her hands in his. His skin was cool through the gloves, and her hands seemed to be burning in his, maybe reflecting her need to know the answer.

He met her gaze. "Bad things happen for a variety of reasons. For me, it's often a wakeup call. To get my attention and draw me closer to Him."

Not liking the answer, she pulled her hands free. "I did bad things in high school to get my father's attention and that was wrong. So why can God do the same thing and believers think it's a good thing?"

"It's different. God has a perfect understanding of what's good for us. He knows what to allow. But we don't have a clue what's in our best interest. Not a clue. We mostly go with what our feelings tell us we want." He paused as if waiting for her to stop him.

She didn't. She still wanted an answer that she would like. "I'm listening."

"One of my favorite verses in the Bible is in Proverbs. 'Trust in the Lord with all your heart and lean not on your own understanding.' If you can trust that everything will ultimately be good for you and not let your feelings color a situation, life will be a lot simpler. Letting God be in charge of my life makes the living much easier."

"But being in charge stops people from stepping all over me again." The vehemence in her tone shocked her. She knew her past bothered her, but was she *that* bitter about it?

He eyed her. "And how's that working for you? Are you happy? Everything going your way?"

His words were harsh, but his face held a sincerity that ate at her doubt. Maybe he had something here. She'd thought she was happy in Atlanta. Until she'd come back here, but was she really? Didn't worrying about everything and falling to pieces when things went wrong deny the very idea of happiness?

This discussion deserved some legit thought. Which she would do. Later. When she was alone. When she wasn't concerned with finding Fuzzy's killer.

"I hear what you're saying," she said. "I'll think about it, but I'm not ready to accept that God has good things planned for me." She glanced at the wallet still in her hand. "Right now, we need to call Russ."

Ryan pressed his lips together but didn't speak. She hated causing this reaction, but she couldn't flip on a religious switch just because Ryan wanted her to believe the same thing he did. She would think about it. Seriously. That was the best she could do.

"I'll call him." Ryan got his phone from a cargo pocket but didn't make the call. "Seems odd that Sierra missed the wallet when collecting evidence."

Indeed. How could a top forensic expert have missed something so obvious? Maybe she wasn't as good at her job as everyone said. Or maybe when she conducted the search, the wallet wasn't there.

Mia let her gaze rove the area in hopes of finding answers. Bandit lunged at the wallet as if it belonged to him.

"Oh, wait. That's it!" Her heart thumped against her chest. "Sierra didn't miss it—it was Bandit. He knew all the time but couldn't tell us."

Bandit thought she was talking to him and bounded to his feet, dancing with excitement. He jumped and yipped with glee.

"I'm a little lost here." Ryan scratched Bandit's head and quieted him.

"Don't you see? This is what Bandit stole from the office last night. He picked up Fuzzy's scent when he discovered his body. Then he found the same scent in the office, but he couldn't get to the wallet because it was locked in Verna's file cabinet until the break-in."

Ryan blinked at her. "Why would Verna have Fuzzy's wallet?"

"Only one answer." Mia locked gazes with Ryan. "Verna's the killer."

24

Ryan handed the wallet to Sierra, and she laid it on a sheet of clean butcher paper in the back of her van as he, Mia, and Russ looked on.

"Thanks for coming back here to process this for fingerprints right away," Mia said.

"Are you kidding?" Sierra's eyes gleamed. "This lead could outweigh all the others for sure."

She got out a jar of black powder and brush and opened the wallet with her gloved hand. "Leather can be tricky to lift prints from, so I'll need to process the outside in the lab, but if we're lucky we'll get one from the plastic sleeve holding his driver's license."

She dipped her brush in the powder and swirled it over the plastic for several seconds.

"There," she pointed at what looked like a thumbprint now visible in the powder. "Nice and clear. Should be a good one to run through AFIS."

"AFIS?" Mia asked.

"Automated Fingerprint Identification System," Russ answered. "A database of fingerprints for criminals and others that we can submit this print for comparison."

"So it could give us the name of who handled the wallet?"

"Yes, it could." Sierra ripped off a long section of tape. "But it could also just be the owner's print."

"If so," Russ said. "It'll be in AFIS because he's a licensed PI. That means the ME's prints should get a hit too, and we'll have a positive ID of our victim."

Mia winced, and Ryan resisted taking her hand.

"Exactly." Sierra pressed the tape over the print then placed it on a small white card. She looked at Russ. "Where's the nearest AFIS terminal?"

"We have one at lockup," he said. "If you give me the card, I can have someone run it."

"Let me add it to the evidence log for you to sign out and then you're good to go." She got out the log and filled it in.

Russ signed the paperwork and soon had the card in hand. "I'll let you know what I learn."

Ryan nodded. "No point in us standing around here bugging Sierra when she has to get back to Orrin's place."

"Thanks, Sierra," Mia said. "When this is all over, I'd like to come up to Portland and take you out for a nice meal."

"We both would enjoy that." Sierra rested her hands on her belly and chuckled.

Ryan liked seeing her humor, but likely identifying the body in the barn didn't leave him feeling like laughing. He escorted Mia up to the lodge and held the door for her. "I'll give Bandit a quick clean and be right in."

The little fella squirmed under the water, but Ryan made quick work of it so he could get inside to check on Mia. She sat at the counter, looking sad.

"I'll make you some tea." He busied himself with making her favorite Earl Grey tea.

When the water was hot, he put the mug on the counter in front of her then brewed some coffee for himself. When the nutty scent snaked into the air and he'd poured a large mug, he turned to look at her.

She leaned on her elbows and stared ahead, leaving the cup untouched. Maybe she was thinking about what he'd said about God. If only she would come to trust Him with her life. She'd still be in pain, but God would give her the strength to bear it.

Might be good to follow up and see if she had any additional questions.

"Anything you want to talk about?" he asked in a soft tone so he didn't startle her.

She offered a wan smile. "I keep wondering why Fuzzy was up here, and I can't come up with a reason."

Not at all what Ryan was thinking. "Maybe he wanted to visit the place where his friend was always so happy."

"If it was that simple, then why would Verna kill him?"

Ryan didn't like how Mia had jumped to the conclusion of Verna being the killer and stuck with it, but he understood her reasons. The evidence was clear. The wallet pointed to Verna's guilt. But a killer. Nah. That was unlikely. He was all set to tell Mia as much when a car pulled up outside.

Ryan set down his mug and went to the window. Russ climbed from his patrol car.

"Russ is back already. Maybe he'll have some insight on all of this." Ryan crossed the room and opened the door.

Carrying Chuck's damaged camera, Russ took the stairs two at a time. With a grunt as a greeting, he charged past Ryan and over to Mia, where he set the camera on the counter. "Sierra retrieved the card, and she's getting it to their IT expert to review. You can give the camera back to the owner."

"Wait, what about the fingerprint and that AFIS thing?" Mia asked. "Aren't you going to share those results?"

"Gave it to our deputy to run. It's not an instant thing like you see on TV. A person has to run it through the database and then manually review the results before sharing possible matches."

"Too bad it's not instant," Ryan said, wishing that they already knew the killer's identity and he'd been arrested.

Instead of deflating in defeat, Mia sat upright. "Are you going to arrest Verna for killing Fuzzy then?"

His eyes creased. "I'll bring her in for questioning, but I don't like her for the murder. It would take a much larger person than Verna to inflict the trauma that killed Springer."

"So she hired the guy who started the fire to do it." Mia's words shot out, colored with a desperation that Ryan hated seeing. "She could still be guilty of planning the murder."

Russ shrugged. "We'll see. I have a number of loose ends to investigate before bringing any charges."

Mia's mouth dropped open. "Fuzzy's wallet was in her file cabinet. What more do you need?"

"As much as you want to think you've solved this case," Russ paused and Ryan knew they wouldn't like his next statement. "I have no evidence to prove Bandit found the wallet in the file cabinet."

"But we saw—"

Russ thrust up a hand like a stop sign on the side of a bus. "No buts. Charging someone with murder requires real evidence. And we don't have it. Besides, other things don't add up. Like the break-in." He crossed his arms. "Why would Verna hire someone to steal files she could dispose of on her own? And if she did somehow kill Springer or had him killed, why keep the wallet in her file cabinet where someone might find it?"

"Russ is right." Ryan hated to agree with his brother but his facts were solid. Ryan settled on the stool next to Mia and laid a hand on her shoulder. "It doesn't make sense, and Verna doesn't have a good motive for killing Fuzzy, either."

She sighed heavily, but he'd had to speak his mind.

"She could very well have a motive." She turned to Russ. "Fuzzy was a private investigator. Maybe Uncle Wally knew about her embezzlement, and Fuzzy had come here to investigate. She discovered that and killed him to stop him."

Russ arched an eyebrow. "And how would Springer know to investigate her?"

"Maybe Uncle Wally asked him to do it before he died."

"He died over three months ago," Ryan said. "Wouldn't Fuzzy have acted sooner or at least told you about it?"

Mia gave a halfhearted nod. "But how else can you explain it?"

"I can't, but this might help us move forward." Russ reached into his pocket and pulled out a small scrap of paper. "We found a cell phone outside the office last night. It's a prepaid phone, and we can't be sure it's even related to the break-in. There's only one text on the phone, which was sent a little more than a week ago to another prepaid phone. I jotted down the message. Does this make any sense to either of you?"

He slid the paper across the counter to Mia. She pulled it closer.

Ryan leaned over to read. *2533 *5. 36605s*

"That's odd." Mia bit her lip.

Ryan scratched his neck. "My first thought is that it's some kind of new texting slang teens use to baffle their parents."

"More like a code of some sort, but we haven't been able to crack it." Russ looked at Mia. "I want to go through Evergreen's office again. See if it helps. You can agree to the search, or I can get a warrant."

"You have my permission to do whatever you need to

do." She held up the paper. "Can I keep this? In case I can figure out the code."

"Knock yourself out." Russ tipped his head at the counter. "Don't forget to get that camera back to the owner so he doesn't bug me for it."

She nodded. "I'll take it to Chuck when you leave."

"I forgot to mention. Nico handed over his bolt cutters too, and I gave them to Sierra for testing, but they have to take them back to the lab to do it." Russ headed to the door and paused, his hand on the doorframe. "Where can I find you this afternoon if I need you?"

Ryan glanced at the clock. "We have sessions with the students all afternoon."

"Keep your cells on." Russ's voice drifted off as he exited.

Ryan, wracking his brain trying to figure out this new development, listened to his brother's fading footsteps. "This is getting more and more complicated."

Mia fiddled with the scrap of paper. "Part of me says the case is solved, and Russ just has to locate the evidence he needs to arrest Verna. The other part of me can't believe she's actually responsible for killing Fuzzy, or honestly, that she would be behind a code like this. Seems too complicated for her."

Ryan studied Mia for a moment, not sure whether to ask his next question or not. But he had to. "Is it easier to believe your father did it?"

Mia sighed. "No. I don't think he's behind this anymore. I probably accused him for nothing. And like David said, I put a rift between us. One I'll likely never be able to repair." Her voice broke.

Ryan couldn't handle seeing her suffer without being able to help. He had to do something. Even if it was as simple as holding her.

"It'll be all right," he whispered as he pulled her close. "I'm with you, and we can face whatever happens together."

Instead of bursting into tears or even pushing him away, she relaxed and rested her head on his shoulder as if she really believed he would stay by her side through all of this. Had she come to see he would never hurt her on purpose? If so, it was a huge leap from just a few days ago.

He tightened his hold, and the taut muscles in his shoulders relaxed as her soft breath whispered over his neck. A nearly overpowering urge to kiss her came over him.

Not a kiss like the quick peck last night, but a long kiss where he could convey how much she'd come to mean to him again. A kiss like they'd shared years ago when a future together was certain. Before he'd lost her and lost Cara.

And there it was. The truth. Big and bold in front of him. He'd turned into a chicken. Didn't want to feel the pain of loss again. Checked out.

Here he was hoping she could let go of her past when he was hanging onto his just as tightly. She seemed to be making progress, but he was stuck in a quagmire of doubt and fear with no obvious way out.

Mia and the students sat on logs and boulders surrounding a smoldering fire. The team of kids in charge of tonight's meal had centered a cast-iron grate over the glowing and smoking embers. Each frustrated and overwhelmed face around her was like peering into a mirror. The discovery of Fuzzy's identity had left Mia spinning.

As had Ryan's comments about God.

Flashes of attending church as a child came back to her. The preacher standing on a raised platform, declared helping others took the focus off your troubles. He spoke the truth. Her counseling practice confirmed that.

Was a personal relationship with God the answer for her? She would try anything right now to avoid facing the pain of another loss.

What could it hurt to turn to Him? As Ryan said, her life wasn't going so well on her own. Maybe she *should* ask God to help her. Maybe He would listen to her.

Maybe.

She might ask. Later. After she'd had more time to think about such an important step. Now she had to work on the helping others thing.

She clutched Chuck's camera and searched the group until she spotted him on the other side of the snapping fire. His eye was pressed against a video camera. Nikki stood next to him, smiling up at him like an adoring groupie.

Waving wayward smoke from her face, Mia approached the pair. "I've got bad news for you."

"My baby!" Chuck studied his camera and grimaced. "Man. What in the—she's bad off."

Mia explained what happened. "I'm really sorry, Chuck."

He took the camera and gently turned it, studying every angle. "Don't have insurance to pay for a new one, and I need it for work. It's gonna take all of my free time to fix it. Guess that changes my plans for tonight."

"I'm really sorry," she said. "If I'd known it would get damaged, I wouldn't have touched it."

"I get wanting to hold her. She's a beaut and hard to resist." He turned to Nikki. "Hey, kid. Take this to the editing trailer, will ya?"

"Sure, sure," she said, her tone high-pitched and very unique. Her hero worship remaining in her eyes, she took the camera from Chuck and raced away.

"And come right back," Chuck yelled after her. "Gotta

love the enthusiasm of the little newbie." He moved back behind the video camera.

Eddie's furtive movements caught her attention.

He made a thorough check of the nearby area as if looking to see if anyone was watching. He tugged down his T-shirt and sauntered to Chuck in a walk filled with bravado. "Hey, man. Can I look at your camera again?"

Chuck cast furtive glances around. "I told you before— I'm not supposed to do this."

Eddie glowered at Chuck, the strength of his expression giving Mia a moment of discomfort.

"Fine," Chuck said. "I'll give you a few minutes, but this is the last time. Understood?"

Eddie nodded and went straight to another one of Chuck's gadget bags to grab a different 35mm camera, this one an old-school film camera. He touched the camera with reverence. His sullen mouth parted, the corners of his lips quivering. A smile of contentment settled into place. Color came into his cheeks, and he radiated happiness. He jabbered about lenses, F-stops, filters, and lighting. His knowledge of photography techniques spoke to extensive experience.

Oh, how she missed the days Wally spent teaching her how to use a 35mm camera and how to develop pictures in the darkroom. Those were good days. Fun days.

Wait! This was it! The connection she needed. A way to get Eddie to open up. Now all she had to do was find Ryan and convince him to implement her unorthodox idea.

～

Ryan stared across the clearing at Mia, her face suddenly coming alive with excitement. *Oh man. Wow.* She just glowed. He should be concentrating on what Ian was saying to the trio he was talking with. But how could he? Sure, fear kept raising its ugly head, but Ryan couldn't take his eyes from the radiant expression on her face. Even the sight of the raw and red gash on her cheek that reminded him he'd almost lost her couldn't make him look away.

What or who had put her in such a good mood? Why couldn't it have been him?

Imagine if they could learn who was threatening her, arrest him, and she would beam at him the same way. Could he then let go of his fear and explore feelings the mere sight of her raised?

She held a hand above her eyes to block the sun and scanned the crowd. She locked eyes on him and crooked her finger. He needed no more encouragement to leave his group and head her way. When he reached her, she turned him by the shoulders to face Eddie.

"Look at Eddie's face." Her voice squeaked high. "In our session yesterday, I couldn't get him to open up at all. Photography could be the connection I need."

Ryan studied Eddie and Chuck. "Chuck shouldn't be engaging the students in conversation."

"Ignore that for a minute." She gripped Ryan's arm. "Chuck said he would have to work on repairing his camera in his free time. If you'd let Eddie help Chuck, I could hang out with them and see what develops."

Ryan smiled. "No pun intended there."

She laughed. "I could broach the subject of cameras and maybe when he sees we have shared interests he'll open up to me. We could take some pictures together, and I can see if Uncle Wally's darkroom equipment is still around here somewhere."

"Okay, okay, slow down." He faced her and rested his hands on her shoulders. "This sounds like a great idea but we need Chuck to buy into it."

"Do you want to talk to him or should I?"

"I think it'd be best if it came from me. Your enthusiasm might scare him off."

"So when can you do it?"

"After our trust exercises." He glanced at his watch. "We're on schedule and should be done about the same time your sessions end."

"You'll come find me to tell me what Chuck says?"

Was she kidding him? He'd take any excuse to be with her.

"We can meet for coffee after we're done and can catch up on a lot of things." He filled his tone with the promise of something exceptional to come when they met again. A promise he hoped he could fulfill and more.

Mia's last session ended, and she ignored typing up her notes to rush to the lodge to make coffee for her upcoming talk with Ryan. A knock sounded on the door, and she jumped.

Maybe Ryan finished early. She rushed to greet him, but paused to take a quick look through the peephole for safety reasons. Her excitement evaporated. Or more like changed. Nice visitors. Just not Ryan.

She pulled the door open and smiled at Reid and Jessie.

"Hey, you two." She inserted as much enthusiasm into her tone as possible. No way she would let them know she was disappointed in their visit.

Reid offered an apologetic smile. "We were heading home from a follow-up with the doctor, and Jessie hoped she could spend some time with Bandit."

"Sure," Mia said, stepping back. "I just made coffee. Would you like some?"

"Sounds good to me." Reid smiled his thanks, and the pair entered the lodge.

Jessie skipped in. "Bandit."

Still sleepy, he sat up, and looked confused.

Jessie studied him with scrunched eyes then looked at Mia. "He looks like he's pretending to be a lamp."

Mia smiled at the child's imagination and went to the kitchen for the coffee. "He was supposed to be taking it easy, but he stayed out all night. It might be good to keep things kind of calm."

"Aw, no fair. I wanted to be a lamp with him."

"That should be fine," Mia said. "Lamps don't do much moving around."

"That sounds like being in school and it's summertime." Jessie's lower lip protruded.

Mia thought it best to move on and handed a mug to Reid.

"Thanks." He blew on the steaming cup and sat on a counter stool.

"How about some orange juice?" Mia asked Jessie and leaned on the countertop next to Reid.

Shaking her head, she pointed at the island. "I wanna play on your computer."

"You came to play with Bandit," Reid said.

She pouted. "He's too sleepy and has to wake up first."

Reid slid forward. "I'm sure Mia doesn't have any games for you to play."

"Nuh-huh. If she can get the internet, I can play Barbie." Her eyes pleaded up at Mia. "You have the internet? Daddy helps me at home, but he has a big computer and probably doesn't know how to use this kind of computer."

Mia set the sleeping laptop in front of Jessie, and she poised her tiny fingers over the keyboard in anticipation.

"It's not much different than a big computer. It's just all

packed into one little box." Mia pointed at the touchpad. "Here's the mouse." She slipped her finger along the pad, and the computer woke up.

A man's picture filled the screen. Bald-headed, with large dark eyes, he resembled a mean Mr. Clean.

Jessie jerked her face away. "No. Turn it off."

"I don't know where this came from." Mia looked at the file name. *Gladys's Suspects*. "It's okay, kiddo. Gladys loaded these pictures last night. He might look mean, but he's just a guy who bought something at their gas station."

"Nuh-uh!" Jessie started crying, and she tried to push the computer away, but the rubber pads on the bottom held it firmly in place. She pounded on the keys as if she hit the right one it would kill the machine.

"Jessie." Reid grabbed his daughter's hands. "That's no way to treat Mia's computer."

"That's the man," she whispered. She closed her eyes and cried harder.

"Jessie, what is it?" Mia asked.

Eyes still closed, Jessie pointed at the computer.

"He did it." Her voice broke on a sob. "He's the man who started the fire."

25

Even after Jessie departed with Reid, her fear saturated Mia like a sponge soaking up water. The man, identified on his credit card as Lincoln Pope, grinned from the screen as if taunting her. His eyes glinted like hard steel, razor-sharp and deadly.

Ryan had arrived moments after Jessie had opened the photo and called Russ to join them. Russ had gently questioned Jessie then Reid had taken his distraught daughter home.

Poor little thing. Having to see that man once but now a second time? Unfair.

Mia curled her hands into fists to keep from punching her computer screen to erase the snarling man's face. But what good would that do?

She pressed the internet shortcut on the keyboard and sat back to wait for the slower dial-up service to open the home page. She stared over the top of the screen and touch-typed Lincoln Pope in the search box then stretched a kink from her neck.

"Mia, did you hear me?" Russ asked from the other side

of the island where he and Ryan had been discussing this new development.

She looked up. "Sorry, I was typing Pope's name into a search box."

"I just had dispatch run his name. He's clear. No record. No priors at all."

"But he killed Fuzzy."

"No, he allegedly killed Springer," Russ said. "We know he wasn't murdered in the barn and we only have proof that he set the fire. Big difference. I need to get back to the office to direct an all-out search for the guy." Russ pulled a business card from his uniform shirt. "Here's my email address. Send that picture to me. Sooner rather than later."

"Don't worry," Mia said. "I'll send it right now."

Russ left, and she turned back to the computer where the search she'd started on Lincoln Pope remained on the screen. "What on earth?"

"What is it?" Ryan asked.

She pointed at the screen where *35nc63n *6*e* appeared instead of his name. "I typed *Lincoln Pope* in the search engine, and this is what came up."

"That's odd. Maybe you were distracted and mistyped."

"I wasn't looking at the keys or screen so I'll do it again." She studied the keyboard and tapped the right keys for Lincoln Pope.

"Same thing," Ryan said.

She typed different words. "Left-hand keys work fine. Right is screwed up."

Ryan shook his head. "Looks like you're typing in Morse code."

"Morse code?" She peered at the keyboard, then at the text message on the counter. She shot to her feet and ran to the door.

"Russ," she shouted, halting him as he climbed into his car. "Come back. Now. Hurry! I know who killed Fuzzy."

～

Ryan studied the keyboard. What on earth had Mia discovered? He just didn't see anything odd. Nothing at all. His comment about Morse code sparked a fire in her, so it had to be related to a code of some sort, but what?

"C'mon." Mia charged through the front door with Russ and rushed to the computer while he followed. "You're probably familiar with Num Lock on a full-sized keyboard, right?"

Russ rolled his eyes. "I might not be a computer guru, but yeah, I know when it's pushed, the keys on the side of the keyboard work as numbers. If not, they don't."

"Right, but it's different on laptop keyboards without number pads." She pointed at the right side of the keyboard. "See how these letters have small numbers on the keys? If you look at the arrangement, it looks just like the number pad on a full-sized keyboard. When Num Lock is activated on a laptop, these letters form a number keypad, and the computer sees them as numbers."

"So." Russ continued to eye her.

"When Jessie spotted Pope's picture, she tried to push the computer away. But the rubber feet kept it from moving. She got frustrated and pounded on the keys. She must've accidentally turned on Num Lock." Mia slid the paper with the text message toward Russ. "I'll type the code with Num Lock turned off."

She entered, 2533 *5. 36605s and spelled out *Kill PI. Loomis.* She craned her neck to face Russ.

He straightened up. "Kurt Loomis?"

"Yeah," Mia replied. "My brother's partner ordered a hit on Fuzzy."

"Why would Loomis tell Pope to kill Fuzzy?" Ryan asked, catching Mia's excitement.

Russ offered one of his rare smiles. "A good question. What if Verna's not our embezzler and while they tried to steal files, they also planted files to make her look guilty?"

"That makes much more sense," Ryan said.

"So Loomis could be the embezzler."

"Indeed," Russ said. "Something I intend to ask him about when I bring him in for questioning."

"So this is enough to arrest him?" Mia asked.

"Arrest? No. Interrogate? Definitely." Russ jogged to the door. "I'll let you know what I find out."

"You are brilliant." Ryan swept Mia off the stool and swung her around. She giggled like a schoolgirl and wrapped her arms around his shoulders. This was the Mia he remembered. Full of life and excited over new discoveries. The Mia, if he were totally honest, who had found a way to open his heart again.

He set her down, and she peered up at him. He expected to see clear eyes filled with joy, instead, a spark of unease tainted the deep green shade. "What's wrong?"

"We may have figured some of this out, but we still don't know where Pope is—and it looks like he's the guy Loomis hired to kill Fuzzy. Probably do all the other crazy things to try to scare me away too. Even if Russ brings Kurt in, we can't truly rest easy until Pope is arrested too."

Renewed fear over her safety sent Ryan's interest ebbing away. He sucked in air and cleared his head. "Guess you better send that picture to Russ."

She returned to the computer and clicked F11. "That should turn off Num Lock."

"How'd you know about that anyway?" he asked.

"I accidentally turned it on one day and had to get a computer tech to tell me what was wrong." She opened a new email message and attached the photo then looked up. "In all the excitement, I forgot to ask if you had time to talk to Chuck about working with Eddie tonight."

Leave it to Mia to still remember she had a plan for Eddie. "He's cool with it and wants to meet at seven in the production trailer."

"Perfect." Mia started typing again. "I'll mention where I'll be tonight in Russ's email too. If I make a breakthrough with Eddie and we're connecting, I won't want to answer any calls. But this way Russ can find me if something big comes up."

"Sounds like a plan. I'll be in a staff planning meeting and can check my calls." Ryan stood back.

Mia's fingers flew over the keyboard. Her tongue peeked out the side of her mouth as she paid full attention to her work. Hopefully, this picture would result in Pope's arrest, and she would once again be safe. Everyone would be safe.

She clicked the mouse arrow on Send, then peered up at him with a spectacular smile. His pulse quickened. He wanted to let go of his fear of losing her. To hold her close and tell her what she meant to him.

The email finished sending, and the monitor cleared. Pope's hard face returned to the screen.

Ryan swallowed hard. Mia was far from safe until this man was captured.

No way Ryan could relax. He couldn't let go of his fear. Not yet.

Not until the killer was behind bars.

~

Mia sat next to Ryan in the UTV as he drove her toward the film company's production trailer. She focused on the possibilities of her meeting with Eddie and tamped down her fear of Pope. Ryan at her side helped for sure.

His strong profile was lit by the blazing orange ball of a setting sun. Just sitting with him gave her confidence. His presence, hope. His smile, a warm and fuzzy feeling. She'd fallen for him again. Maybe had never stopped caring about him. That was clear now.

She jerked her gaze away to change her focus.

A vehicle came barreling down the drive toward them— Russ's cruiser going top speed.

Ryan hit the brakes hard and shot out a hand in front of Mia, keeping her from slamming into the dash. She clasped his muscled arm, and her body jerked to a stop.

Ryan would always act to protect her.

Always.

She'd not only come to care for him, but she was starting to trust him to know what was good for her. Know when to back off, but be close by if needed. A breakthrough for sure.

Russ fishtailed to a stop by the trailer.

Ryan parked nearby and climbed from the vehicle. Mia joined him and waved away the churned-up dust as they crossed the lot to Russ, who'd already lowered his window.

He leaned out. "Loomis sang like an *American Idol* contestant."

Ryan eyed his brother. "Guess hearing about that is worth having to eat all of the dust you kicked up."

"He actually confessed?" Mia asked, not caring a bit about the dust now.

"I might've led him to believe it would go better for him if he did." Russ smiled. "Not sure it will as he hired someone to commit murder. He'll go away a long time for that."

"What exactly did he admit to doing?" Ryan asked.

Russ turned the volume down on his squawking radio. "Turns out he has a gambling problem. He's been embezzling money from Evergreen almost from the day he and David took over the accounts. He figured David wouldn't touch them due to conflict of interest and was the easiest account to skim from."

"So David didn't know anything about it?"

Russ shook his head. "Not according to Loomis. But Wally found out. Instead of prosecuting Loomis, he gave him a chance to straighten up and repay the money."

Ah, yes. That was exactly something her trusting uncle would do. "Uncle Wally was always more than willing to give people a second chance."

Russ's expression turned skeptical. "Yeah, well I'd never let a guy who stole from me remain in charge of my finances."

"Uncle Wally must've thought of that too," Mia said. "David told me they made some changes in how the books were handled. Maybe Uncle Wally insisted on that to keep Loomis from taking more money."

"So if it started a few years ago, what changed to set Loomis off now?" Ryan asked.

"Wally's death. Loomis knew he'd have to prepare reports for the transition in ownership, and his embezzlement would come out. Then he got the bright idea if he scared you away, David would inherit and not ask for any reports. So he hired Pope."

"Makes sense," Mia said. "But how did he get my bracelet?"

"Accidentally, that's how. He pays Evergreen's bills. That includes one for a large storage unit. Loomis was afraid the unit held files with proof of his embezzlement, so he broke into it." Russ tightly gripped the steering wheel. "Instead, he found items from your house in Atlanta. David told him about how your dad wouldn't let you keep anything, and Loomis figured the bracelet would freak you out."

Her heart sank. "Uncle Wally kept a whole storage unit of our things? Why didn't he tell me?"

Had he deceived me too? The one man I could trust?

A cold wave hit Mia, and she instinctively sought Ryan's gaze for comfort.

He came closer.

"I don't know about that." Russ's voice turned soft. "But at least you now have things to remember your mother by."

He was right—the bracelet was a good thing in disguise. She might have a whole storage unit full of items that could bring nice memories. But why had Wally kept it a secret all of these years? Was he really guilty of betraying her?

No, she would stop with that being her go-to reaction to something like this and she wouldn't believe that he betrayed her. For some reason he'd known she wasn't ready to see them. And he'd been right when he decided she'd want these memories and had kept them. She couldn't wait to get her hands on everything, but first she needed to connect the remaining dots.

"How did Fuzzy get mixed up in this?" Mia asked as Ryan wrapped an arm around her shoulders. She moved into the warmth of his touch.

"Loomis got greedy." Russ's eyebrows lowered and pinched together. "He was confident he'd make you leave, so he not only quit paying back the money, but found a way to steal more. What he didn't count on was that Wally had told Springer about the embezzlement. Springer wasn't so trusting and decided to check up on Loomis. Caught him still stealing, and was going to turn Loomis in, so Loomis ordered Pope to kill Springer."

"So he actually admitted to ordering Pope to kill Fuzzy?" Her tone turned shrill and that's how she felt inside.

"Not only to kill him, but to dispose of the body," Russ said. "Pope must've thought he could take care of the body and start the fire at the same time. Problem was he couldn't know the fire department would arrive before the building was fully engulfed."

"What about the office break-in?" Ryan asked. "Was that Pope too?"

Russ nodded. "Except like we thought he wasn't stealing anything. He made it look like a break-in but he was planting files that Loomis doctored to point at Verna for the embezzlement. Pope put Springer's wallet in the file cabinet a few days earlier, and when he went back to add the files, he made sure we would find the wallet too."

Mia's stomach clenched. "And I fell for it. Thinking Verna was the most likely suspect. We have to find Pope."

Russ lifted a travel cup from a holder and took a long sip. "I've issued an alert, and my team is working full-time on hunting him down. Only problem is, Loomis paid Pope. He could be long gone by now. And if he hasn't split already, when he hears we picked up Loomis, he'll assume Loomis gave him up, and he'll likely take off."

Mia looked up at the trailer. "As much as I want him caught, even if he does get away, at least Kurt isn't ordering him to do anything else. Now we can get on with life and help these kids."

Russ locked gazes for a long moment. "Don't let your guard down. Pope might not be as smart as we think he is and could still be hanging around."

"Don't worry," Ryan said. "I have my eyes wide open."

"Later, then," Russ said.

Ryan stepped back and drew Mia with him to allow Russ to back his vehicle out. She rested her head against Ryan's chest and sighed in contentment. She had no idea what was going on in Ryan's mind, but standing with him covered her with a blanket of peaceful emotions. It felt so right she wanted to turn and kiss him.

"Ready to meet with Eddie?" His breath stirred her hair.

"With all of these terrifying things behind us, I'm more ready than ever." She reluctantly pulled away.

They walked to the makeshift wooden stairs leading to the editing trailer door. The wind pulled a strand of hair free from her clip and whipped it over her face.

Ryan caught the end and tucked it behind her ear. "I'll be in the rec center if you need me." He moved closer, slowly lowering his head.

Was he going to kiss her goodbye? She waited, her emotions on high alert. She forgot about Eddie and the murders, closed her eyes and lifted her arms around his neck.

Nothing. She flashed open her eyes.

With a groan, he slid his hands up her arms and pulled them down. He took a step back, and let a finger trail down her cheek.

"Eddie's waiting." His tone conveyed his reluctance to leave, so why did he set her aside like this?

She drew in a hearty breath to cool her rushing emotions.

How had she so readily responded to him? She didn't know what she was doing anymore. Was she leading Ryan on, or was she ready to commit to a future with him?

A future that meant she would have to remain in Shadow Lake. The love for his job shone on his face every minute he was with the students. The same with his family. She would never ask him to leave his life and family behind to move to Atlanta. He would probably agree to go, but he belonged here.

She had to be careful to keep things less intense when

she saw him later. At least until she discovered what she wanted.

Her cell rang, and she grabbed it. A local number. Maybe David. Good. She wanted to tell him she'd been wrong about their father and admit how much she wanted to mend fences with him.

She quickly answered.

"I read the local newspaper." Her father's commanding voice startled her.

Not David. So what did she say?

"And?" Was all that came to mind.

"The front page was devoted to the many terrible things that have happened since you came back. I knew something like this would happen." Her father's stern tone shot through the phone, dashing her hopes for reconciliation. He was clearly embarrassed over the publicity, and was calling to run damage control. He always had to be in control.

Like her. Keep things within her scope of containment then she didn't get hurt. But that wasn't true. Look at her now. She'd worked diligently to take back her life, but bad things kept coming. She couldn't control anything. Finding the body proved beyond any doubt that she couldn't stop life from unfolding. Her efforts had been futile. Her father's efforts too. No matter his iron will, her mother died, and Mia rebelled.

Oh, my gosh.

She fell back against the railing. She'd been a thorn in his side, making it harder on him. Pushing, testing, trying. Like rough sandpaper, scraping away. Much the same way Ryan had acted with her.

True, her father had been the mature one in the relationship and should have behaved differently, but she was supposedly mature now too, and look at how she was handling things. Making a real mess is what she was doing.

On all fronts. She had to stop. Find another way or she'd end up bitter and angry like her father.

Time to make a change. Extend the verbal hand of compromise. "I'm sorry if this embarrassed you."

"Embarrassed?" His audible frustration that sent her running in the past, swept over her like a tidal wave. "I wasn't embarrassed. I just wanted to see if you were okay."

"You did?" She didn't like hearing her tone resemble that of a little child, uncertain and begging for confirmation from the man who was supposed to love her.

His silence in response sounded as deafening as a rumble of thunder in one of Atlanta's many late afternoon storms. She waited, holding her breath for him to finally make the effort to be her father.

She heard him rummaging around and then he cleared his throat. "I have an emergency page. I have to go."

He ended the call, and she turned toward the door like a wooden soldier. She'd tried to open her heart and let him in, but what did she get?

The same treatment. Maybe she was so unlovable that she was destined to be alone. Maybe God really did want it that way.

If Ryan was right about how God operated, He would have His way, and she had no say in the matter. None at all.

26

Mia entered the trailer where Chuck and Eddie leaned over a table at the far end of the space. She might have struck out again with her father and might even end up alone in life, but Eddie didn't have to suffer the same outcome. She would make certain of that.

Her life was far from what she hoped it might be, but it cheered her to see Eddie bonding with another person. She'd accomplished the best goal of all in coming back to Shadow Lake—getting Eddie involved in something with the hope that he might finally want to talk about his problems and work toward healing.

She paused just inside the door. "Looks like you're both having a good time."

Eddie's head popped up. They made eye contact. He groaned and returned his attention to his work. *Message received.* She was intruding. Still, she wouldn't leave. She had a duty of care to remain with Eddie while he was in the program and working with a non-staff member.

She would try to join in later, but for now she sat at a table by the door to watch, wait for a better time, and hopefully pick up cues on how to better engage him.

The guys continued to work silently. Seated on opposite sides of a workbench, their heads pressed together over the camera. Eddie held the camera body and Chuck a small tool. She enjoyed seeing the contrast of their hair coloring. Eddie's, blond and long, Chuck's, dark and buzzed.

"Now, where were we?" Chuck asked.

Eddie shot a quick glance at her. "Not with her here."

"No sweat," Chuck said. "You don't have to talk about it anymore if you don't want to."

"I just don't need the stuff *she* always gives me about opening up and sharing my *feelings*."

"Like I said. No need."

"Nah, man. I mean, I like talking to you. You're cool." Eddie slipped needle-nose pliers around a small part Chuck held out. "It's just, you know, all these counselors hassling me gets to be too much."

Chuck looked up. "Maybe you should listen to them. Tell them the same things you told me."

"Why?" Eddie's voice held a challenge.

"Because they're trained to help you. I'm just a guy who likes cameras, and they thought working with me would help you feel more comfortable around them."

Eddie dropped the tool on the bench and stared at Chuck until he looked up. "You're saying you're only doing this with me because they made you do it?"

Chuck cast Mia a wary look.

"Don't look at her," Eddie said. "This is between you and me."

Chuck ran a hand around the back of his neck. "Look, man. It doesn't matter. You got the chance to work on the camera instead of doing those sissy group things. Just let it go at that."

Eddie shoved his stool back, toppling it to the floor with

a loud crash. "No way. You tell me why you're doing this, or I'm outta here. Right now. For good."

Chuck planted his palms on the bench. "Fine. I wanted to work on the camera alone, but Ryan convinced me to let you help. All right?"

Eddie looked around, his eyes wild and angry. He let them linger on Mia, burning a hole in her.

She didn't look away, but didn't know what to say. He was really freaked out. Not a surprising reaction for a guy whose emotions simmered just beneath the surface, waiting to erupt with little provocation. And not surprising when he'd expressed frustration over people not having pure motives in helping him.

"Look, man," Chuck said, drawing Eddie's attention. "No biggie. Let's get back to work."

"Dude, I knew she would sell me out. But you? I trusted you." Eddie's last few words came out in a scream as he lunged at Chuck, fists flying.

Mia lurched to her feet and rushed them. "Eddie— please. I know you're hurt but this won't help."

He spun on her. Rage contorted his face, his anger a level she'd never witnessed before.

She took a step back.

"Don't hurt her, man." Chuck got up and reached for Eddie.

The teen charged at Chuck, shoving him to the side. He fell hard. Eddie dropped on top and pummeled Chuck, fist after fist.

"Get help, Mia," Chuck shouted. "I can't fight back. I don't want to hurt him."

Eddie might calm down or this might escalate, but she couldn't take the chance on the teen's emotions intensifying. If he pushed harder, Chuck would have to defend himself and both of them could get hurt.

Ryan. He could help. She dialed his phone. He didn't answer. She bolted through the door and raced for the rec center, pounding over the uneven terrain in the dark, praying she wouldn't fall. She reached the light beaming from the open door as if it welcomed her to a way to save Eddie. Chuck too.

Heart racing, she charged into the room. Ryan sat behind a long table, head bent over a project with paper and scissors.

She charged over to him and gasped for air. "We need you at the trailer."

"Be with you in a sec," he said without looking up. "Almost done here."

She didn't want the others in the room to know what was happening with Eddie, but she needed to get Ryan to move quickly. "Now! It's Eddie!"

"Lead the way." Ryan shot to his feet.

She bolted across the floor, and he fell into step beside her.

"What's going on?" he asked.

"Chuck and Eddie got into it, and Eddie's crazy mad. He attacked Chuck."

Ryan mumbled something under his breath, but Mia couldn't make it out. He upped his pace, taking off, his long legs bringing him to the trailer and inside. Her side ached from the round trip, and she had to stop to recover.

She listened for any sound of a scuffle. Heard nothing except her breathing.

Good. Maybe Chuck and Eddie had stopped fighting while she was gone. Or Ryan had separated them.

She ran to the door to check. Climbed the steps. Looked inside.

Chuck lay on the floor. Blood oozed from his head. Ryan leaned over him. Performed CPR.

He looked up—his gaze anguished. "Call 911. He just stopped breathing."

Mia dug out her phone and searched the room as the call connected. "Eddie. Where is he?"

"Missing. Looks like nearly ended Chuck's life, and if his current condition holds, he could still die."

~

Ryan wanted nothing more than to get away from the lights of the patrol cars strobing through the night outside the trailer. Get away from the ambulance racing down the drive. From Russ's intensity. And even get away from Mia's expression—terror mixed with shock.

She'd barely said a word. After the medics got Chuck's heart going again and loaded him into the ambulance Ryan had tried to comfort her, but she'd shaken off his arm and circled her own arms around her waist. Drawing in. Closing down ranks. Whatever he called it, she was withdrawing from him. Much like when she'd left him behind to go to Atlanta. It cut him to the core to watch her turn inward and shut him out.

She was blaming herself for Chuck barely clinging to life. Ryan got that. Felt the same way, even. After all, Ryan had made the decision to let Eddie work with Chuck. Ryan would like to talk about Chuck's attack with Mia, but she'd fallen back into her old habits of how to deal with being hurt. No matter how much he'd come to care for her, he doubted they could be together until she figured out how to handle emotions like these. The answer was to turn to God. To turn to fellow Christians for support.

Right, like you did that when Cara died. Have done it since then.

Talk about criticizing someone for the same thing he was guilty of doing.

They both had to let go of their past pain.

Russ stormed toward them snapping off disposable gloves as he walked. His face was fixed in a deep scowl, and his sights were set on Mia.

She backed up as if trying to run away before he reached her. Ryan wanted to intervene, but he had to let Russ do his job. Still, Ryan could move closer to help if needed.

Russ stopped in front of Mia. "You're sure the camera was here when you left?"

"Positive," Mia said. "They were working on it before the fight broke out."

He stuffed the gloves into a cargo pocket. "Well, it's missing now. Most logical explanation is that the kid hit Kowalski with the camera then took off with it."

"No." Mia shook her head hard. "Eddie wouldn't try to kill someone. He's a mixed-up kid who got angry, but not a killer."

"For what it's worth, I agree with Mia," Ryan said. "Since Eddie's parents died, he values life too much to kill someone."

Russ narrowed his eyes. "You could be right, but people can snap and do things we don't think they will do. And he took off, casting suspicion his way."

Ryan held up a hand. "Not so fast, bro. Eddie most likely ran because he thought we'd send him back to juvie after going off on Chuck."

Russ rested his hands on his waist. "The kid has to be my number-one suspect, but I'll look at other possibilities."

Mia stepped closer and clutched Russ's jacket sleeve. "What other possibilities?"

"For one, it might have been Pope coming back to get the camera because his picture is on it."

"But Sierra took the card," Mia said.

"He might not know that," Russ said.

"How would he know who had the camera?" Ryan asked.

"Maybe he's kept a better watch on things around here than we thought."

Mia shuddered. "Say it *was* Pope. He took the camera. Why attack Chuck?"

"Could be he's not sure if Kowalski saw his picture and can ID him," Russ said. "Or maybe he didn't think to wear a mask tonight and Kowalski saw him, so he wanted him dead."

"That makes sense, but Chuck survived." Mia's tone had gone higher, bordering on hysterical. "Why didn't Pope check to see if Chuck died?"

Russ looked around the area. "Someone or something could've scared him off, I suppose."

Mia firmed her stance. "Regardless, you should go after Pope and leave Eddie alone."

Russ pulled in a deep breath. "I'd like to do that, but I can't. Until I have anything to point to Pope as our guy for this, Eddie Kramer is wanted for Kowalski's attack and murder if the guy doesn't make it."

"Seems reasonable," Ryan said, but he hated to admit it as he was on Mia's side of the fence here.

"You both can go," Russ said. "I'll call if I need anything else."

"Go? Where can I go to get away from this mess?" Mia burst into tears.

Russ cast Ryan a sympathetic look before heading back to the trailer.

She swiped a hand over her tears. "This is all my fault. If I didn't get the two of them together, Chuck wouldn't be fighting for his life."

"This isn't your fault at all." Ryan ignored her warning look and wrapped his arm around her shoulders. "You know as well as I do Eddie didn't attack Chuck. If Pope wanted to find Chuck, he'd have found him no matter where he was."

"But I took the pictures of Pope, and I gave the camera back to Chuck." Her voice fell off into a silence that hung eerily in the heavy night air.

Her sobbing increased, and Ryan held her tightly against his chest. Her sadness pulled at his heart. He had to find a way to help her through this. He would hold her until she got the initial shock out of her system. Then they could talk, and he'd do his best to help her see she wasn't to blame here.

Mia had been watching everything including when the medics loaded Chuck into the ambulance. The medics didn't hold out hope for him, but they shocked his heart back into rhythm so that was a good sign. The only one, they'd said. Ryan had mothered her, urging her to leave the scene and get some rest, but she remained in place. She couldn't leave. She had to stay there in case word about Eddie or Chuck's condition came in.

She wished she could say she handled the tension radiating around them well. She didn't. She'd snapped, shooing Ryan away. His eyes had creased with the pain of her snub, and she instantly wanted to take it back, but she let him go anyway. In her mood, she was poison to herself and everyone around her. She didn't want to infect him with it too.

She might've hurt him, but she'd kept an eye on him. He currently chatted with his crew, offering them the comfort she'd refused. He'd chosen his profession well. The staff members' gazes held respect and appreciation for his compassion. He would make a fine life companion.

So what?

The earlier call with her father proved she could never let go of her past. And if her past continued to haunt her, she would never be able to move on.

Ryan looked her way and caught her watching him. He excused himself from the group.

"Have you thought of anything I can do for you?" His voice was gentle, caring. Inviting her to let him help.

She couldn't give him the chance to slip into her world. Too much heartache for them both, and she cared too much for him to inflict even more pain. "This is my problem. I caused it. I need to fix it."

She cringed at how harsh her statement sounded. Much harsher than needed. But she couldn't give him even the tiniest of openings to be sucked into her world.

He rested his hands on his waist. "Just like that, huh? I thought we'd reconnected. Now, a little trouble comes and you shove me out of your life."

"I'm sorry, but I've pretty much been on my own for the last ten years, and I like it that way." She sounded so convincing she almost believed it herself. Almost.

"Right, like I buy that." He rested his arm on a fence rail. "If you would talk to me about how you feel, it could only get better."

Ooh, feelings.

Her imitation of Eddie's sarcasm in their counseling session made the tears prick her eyes again. She turned and walked to the end of the fence where she could cry unseen. Out of view. On her own. If Ryan saw her tears, he would only push harder.

She looked at the stars in the vast night sky, her tears sliding freely down her cheeks. She was just like Eddie.

Ryan could no more help her than she could help Eddie. Unless. Unless they chose to let someone into their closed-off world.

Ryan's soft footfalls coming closer sent her into panic mode. She had to either give in to him completely—or send him packing.

She spun and did what she did best. "I need to be alone. I've been feeling vulnerable since I got to town, but I'm better now."

He stared at her long and hard.

She couldn't bear to see the pain she was causing and looked away.

"It's a funny thing, Mia," Ryan said. "When I see someone crying, I don't think the person is okay."

She swiped her sleeve across her face. "Well, I am. Please, just go."

She glanced up to see him turn and take a few steps. He paused and looked back at her. "This time, I'm gone for good. Unless you ask me to come back."

Their eyes locked. Held. His compassion drew her like a magnet. She resisted the force. Stood her ground.

"I won't ask." Her gut aching, she returned her gaze to the sky as if something up there could help her.

Maybe she was searching for God. Ryan said God could fix everything, but death was unfixable. Final. The end here on earth.

The worst thing she could imagine could come to pass— Chuck's death—and it would be her fault. She might as well have attacked Chuck herself for as bad as she was feeling. God hadn't taken her pain or helped with it when her mother died, so what made her think He could make this pain better?

❧

Ryan struggled to breathe evenly and glanced at Mia standing near the trailer. She'd just sent him packing when he wanted to help her so badly. Unbelievable. And unexpected.

Had he misread her actions today? Did she really want to be alone for the rest of her life, or did she just not want to be with him? And he never got a chance to help her see God was still here. He hadn't deserted her no matter their relationship.

A cue Ryan needed to follow right now. God hadn't given up on her and neither could he. She may have put distance between them, but Ryan would do his best to be sure she stayed safe, giving him another chance to help her see her need for God.

But he knew her. Knew her well and she needed time to cool off and process. He would give her that space. Probably should've from the beginning. He needed to talk with Russ about the safety of his staff and students, and now was a good time.

Ryan crossed over to his brother, who leaned against his patrol car.

Russ's cell phone jangled from his belt holder. He snatched it free and looked at the screen then lifted it to his ear. "What's up, bro?" He took his hat off and clapped it against his knee. He shoved it back into place and went still. Perfectly still. "What do you mean she's missing?"

Ryan took a step closer and caught Russ's gaze.

His brother's face paled to a sickly shade of white. "I'm on my way."

Ryan recognized that haunted look. Exactly like Russ's last days as an officer in Portland when a child was murdered, and he blamed himself for the death. Something beyond horrible had gone down.

What now?

Ryan was nearly afraid to ask, but he had to know. "What is it? What's happened?"

"That was Reid." His voice caught. "Jessie's missing."

~

Mia stared at Russ. She couldn't have heard him right. Did he just say Jessie was missing?

She had to know. She raced toward him. "Jessie's missing. Really? How?"

The fear in the strong lawman's eyes upped her anxiety.

He shoved his phone into the holder. "Reid put her to bed about an hour ago. He just checked on her, and she's gone. Pope likely discovered she saw him in the barn, and he's tying up loose ends."

"Pope?" she asked. "But how could he know?"

Russ shook his head. "I don't know, and I don't have time to discuss it." He pivoted like a precision soldier and faced Ryan. "If Pope is still in the area, I need you to get your staff and the kids into the rec center and lock the door. Mia, you go with them. I'll post one of my deputies for everyone's safety." He returned to his men and shouted urgent orders.

Mia couldn't move. Couldn't process. Couldn't fathom what had happened. How could this be? Little Jessie likely in the hands of a killer all because a gambling habit caused Kurt Loomis to embezzle money?

Mia should go to the rec center like Russ said. No. She couldn't. This whole tragedy was brought on because Loomis wanted her gone. If she stayed with the students and staff, she might bring the danger to their doorstep. No way she would do that. She had to think of their safety above all else. And if Pope had Jessie, Mia had to try to find them. To free Jessie.

She turned and rushed to the UTV.

274

"Mia, wait," Ryan called after her, his pleading tone almost stopping her.

Almost.

She turned the key.

Hard to believe it had only been two hours since he'd sat next to her as they'd driven to this end of the property. Life seeming better. Heading toward a possible future together.

Two hours. Only two hours.

One near death and one kidnapping ago.

What would the next hour bring, and could she possibly survive whatever occurred?

27

Too bad the driveway was unpaved or Mia would've burned rubber as she floored the gas in her rental car. She had to find Jessie before Pope did something horrific to the sweet young girl. But where had he taken her? He wasn't from around here. Still, he'd likely been living somewhere close.

The motel. The only motel in town where a stranger like Pope could stay. Mia's best chance to find Jessie was to interrogate the manager. True, Russ had probably already done that, but the manager might remember something helpful since Russ talked to him.

Back tires skidded, and she eased her foot up to safely make her way to the main road. She was about to turn on to the highway when her cell chimed. Caller ID didn't display a name, but she answered using her car's infotainment system in case it was an update on Chuck, Eddie, or Jessie.

"Mia, it's Sydney," her urgent voice came over the car speaker.

Mia sighed. The call had nothing to do with Jessie. Sydney had probably heard about Kurt on the local grapevine and wanted to know if it was true.

"What's up?" Mia asked.

"Is the documentary crew still filming over there?"

Odd question. "Nothing was scheduled tonight, why?"

Sydney exhaled audibly through the phone. "Nikki got a call an hour or so ago. Said they wanted her to help with the filming. But it's getting late, and she's still gone. I'm starting to freak out."

Clearly, Nikki had lied. She wasn't at Evergreen.

"There's no filming going on," Mia said. "Do you know who called her?"

"No. She was acting all secretive." Sydney sighed. "She probably snuck out to meet her friend Emily or even a boy. I'm really gonna let her have it when she gets home."

"I'll keep an eye out for her and call me when she does get there." Mia disconnected, hoping the teen came home on her own.

She turned on the signal, but sat at the end of the driveway trying to decide what to do.

What if Nikki was somehow connected to Jessie's disappearance or Eddie's whereabouts?

She'd flirted with all the boys in the Wilderness Ways group as Sydney had feared, but in particular, Nikki watched Eddie a lot.

Could Eddie have called her? But how? His cell had been confiscated like all program participants at arrival. Still, if Eddie was on the run, a fellow teen and an impressionable girl would be a likely person to call. She knew the area and could make sure he had a safe place to hide.

Where would Nikki think was safe around here?

The cabin. That's it!

She rang Sydney back. In high school Mia had partied with Sydney's cousin and his friends at her uncle's cabin. It was so secluded no one ever caught them. A perfect place for Nikki to hide Eddie.

"Did you find her?" Sydney's hopeful tone cut through Mia.

"Sorry, no, but I have an idea," Mia said. "Does your uncle still have that place on the lake?"

"Yeah, why?" Sydney asked.

"Call 911 and tell them you think Nikki took Eddie Kramer there."

"What? Eddie who?"

"No time to explain. Just do it. The dispatcher will understand." Mia tapped the screen to end the call.

The cabin was less than two miles away. She ignored her blinker still signaling to the right and turned the other direction.

She floored it and took the sharp curves like an Indy driver until she reached the main highway and headed east. She probably should have called Russ, but he still needed to find Jessie, and bringing Eddie in shouldn't be a big deal. Though Mia couldn't handle him earlier, she was sure after she explained what had happened and that Pope might come after Eddie next, he'd be willing to go with her to the sheriff's office for his own protection.

At the cabin driveway, Mia slowed and turned right. She killed the engine and headlights then maneuvered the car as far down the rutted drive as she could without risking Eddie seeing her.

She quickly climbed out, closing the door as fast as she could to douse the dome lights, and made the trip down the steep incline, feeling her way over the uneven ground with only the moon shining above. She would love to use the light on her phone, but she was counting on a surprise visit to keep Eddie from bolting.

A small car was parked in the drive. She didn't know the make of car Nikki drove, but it would be a good choice for a teenager.

Keeping low, Mia made her way to the vehicle and looked inside. A girl's garter, pink fuzzy dice, and a lipstick on a string hung on the rearview mirror. Yeah, could well be Nikki's car.

Mia squatted and watched for signs of life in the cabin.

There. A flash inside. Between the blinds on the front window.

They were smart enough not to turn on any lamps and moved around by flashlight. Just as Mia and her gang had done back in the day.

Mia had to get in there. She remembered the brick path around back well and started that way. Some were loose back then. If not fixed, they could be treacherous in the dark. She slowly picked her way over rough path. Stumbling on a sharp edge then catching herself on a tree that had been much smaller the last time she'd made this trek.

She approached the back door, looking around for another person. Anyone. Friend or foe.

No one. Nothing. No movement. Not even small animals.

She turned the doorknob. Slowly.

The catch clicked open, sounding like an explosion in her ears. She waited. Held her breath. For Eddie or Nikki to come to the door.

Neither did.

She slipped inside. She could easily make her way to the front room where she'd seen the flashlight without turning on a light. As long as they hadn't remodeled the cabin in the past ten years.

She crept along the kitchen cupboards, running her fingers over the worn Formica and along the wall to the narrow hallway.

Soft crying came from the bedroom at the end. A muted conversation drifted from the front room. The entire house remained dark.

What now? Crying or conversation?

Conversation. She could eavesdrop and learn something to help, like maybe who was crying and why.

She turned toward the family room and stopped just shy of the doorway.

"Who's gonna believe me?" A male voice asked.

Eddie! It was Eddie.

"I can tell them what happened." Nikki's unique high-pitched voice gave her identity away. "I've never been in real trouble. They'll believe me."

"I can't risk it. If they think I had something to do with this, I'll go away for a long time. You need to take the kid to the cops and tell them what happened."

Kid? What kid?

"And what about you? You gonna hoof it all the way back to Portland?"

"I don't know, but I'm not turning myself in."

Before either of them decided to make a move, it was time for Mia to announce her presence. She spun around the corner and felt along the wall where she remembered a light switch was located and flicked it up.

A bright glow flooded the room, blinding her. She counted on Eddie having the same reaction and wouldn't jump her or run. She blinked away the spots, and her eyes adjusted.

"Mia," Nikki shouted. "I'm so glad you're here."

"What's going on?" Mia asked. "Who's in the bedroom?"

Nikki's gaze flitted to the doorway. "This isn't what it looks like."

"Shut up, Nikki. Don't tell her anything." Eddie crossed his arms, but thankfully he remained seated on the worn plaid sofa.

"No, you shut up, Eddie." Nikki locked gazes with the boy. "You didn't do anything wrong. Mia will help us."

"Oh, yeah, she's *all* about helping." Sarcasm liberally flowed through his tone.

Mia ignored him. "I asked who's in the bedroom."

"Jessie Maddox," Nikki said.

"Jessie? Seriously? Is she okay?"

"Fine," Nikki said. "No one hurt her. She's just down there so we could talk without her hearing us."

Mia turned toward the hallway. "Jessie! It's Mia. Are you all right?"

The door creaked open, and the slide of small feet sounded on the wood floor. Dressed in teddy bear pj's, Jessie turned the corner, spotted Mia, and raced ahead. Jessie slammed into Mia and wrapped her arms around her waist as if she'd never let go again.

"You okay?" Mia clutched the little girl, ignoring the residual pain from the gashes in her side, and bent her head to lay it on Jessie's soft curls.

She nodded. "Eddie saved me."

Mia looked at Eddie. "If ever there was a time for you to talk to me, it's now."

Nikki nudged him. "Do it. You can trust her."

His gaze raced around the room as if he were looking for any way out other than placing his trust in her. Oh, yeah. Mia knew the feeling. She'd just been in the same spot with Ryan. She hoped Eddie was smarter than she was and made the right decision.

He slapped his palms on his knees just below the hem of his baggy shorts and stared at Mia as if daring her to question him. "I was fighting with Chuck. You saw that. But then when you left, Chuck pinned me down. I calmed down. Got my stuff together and was worried I would get into trouble and get sent back to juvie."

"So what did you do?" she asked while still holding Jessie close.

He scrubbed his palms down the fabric of his shorts. "I convinced Chuck to let me up. Then I bolted outside. I was gonna take off. Not sure where, but I wasn't going back to juvie." He shook his head. "That place is the pits. I'd go anywhere but there. I was about to leave when I saw this dude sneaking up in the dark. I figured it was one of the guys playing a joke. So I kept going until I spotted a car. I thought about stealing it or hiding in the back to get out of there. I opened the front door and found a phone on the seat."

He stopped to glance at Nikki, who returned his gaze with a nod of encouragement.

Eddie sat up taller. "Nikki gave me her number to use after this program ended. So I called her. She said she'd come talk to me. We decided to meet at the place in the woods where we did the trust exercises. Then I heard this noise in the backseat. Jessie was on the floor. Tied up with tape over her mouth. When she saw me, she started crying."

Jessie let go of Mia and ran to Eddie. She wrapped her arms around his neck. "I was scared. But Eddie said he would help me."

Eddie didn't push her away but nodded. "So I picked her up and ran into the woods. We waited for Nikki to get there. Then we came here."

"You're a hero, Eddie." Mia's voice rang with conviction.

He blinked at her. "You believe me?"

"Of course, and so will the sheriff." Mia crossed the room and patted him on the back. Then it dawned on her. He probably didn't have any idea what happened to Chuck. "Did you see the guy who went into the trailer?"

Eddie nodded. "And I saw him come out and drive away too. I don't think he knew Jessie was gone when he left."

"Well, he knows now." A crusty male voice came from the hallway as a gun-toting hand shot around the corner.

Lincoln Pope's hand.

~

Ryan left Ian in charge at the rec center and headed for the lodge. Ryan had wanted to go after Mia when she'd taken off. He couldn't. He had no choice but to join his staff and students first and let Mia fend for herself. The lives of teens and his staff were in his hands. He had to be sure they were safe and hope Mia didn't do anything rash other than foolishly flee into the night instead of coming with them.

The students and staff were now in the care of a deputy, freeing Ryan up to help Mia.

She was alone and needed him.

But what about poor little Jessie? Who was with her? Did Pope really take her?

It really was the only likely scenario. She wouldn't wander off in the night. Reid had taught her about the dangers in the area. The river. The lake. Dark woods with wild animals where she could get lost.

Ryan offered another prayer for his niece. One for Chuck too. Ryan had been offering them every moment he could, flooding God on their behalf.

Ryan reached the lodge, hightailed it up the steps, and turned the door knob. Unlocked.

No! No!

Had Pope gotten to Mia too?

Please, no. Don't let anything happen to her or Jessie. Help me help them both. Please. I can't lose either of them.

He entered. Turned on a light and cleared all the rooms. No sign of Mia. No sign of a struggle. Bandit whimpered from his crate but Ryan had to ignore the dog to focus on Mia.

"Where are you?" He had to find her, but how?

Searching for anything that might help, his gaze landed on Wally's gun safe. He didn't know where Mia or Jessie were, but at least he could be fully armed as he went in search. He carried whenever he could in an ankle holster but couldn't carry around the teens in the program. He was off duty now and would arm himself to the teeth.

He raced to the kitchen for the key and got the safe open. He chose Wally's favorite revolver. A Smith & Wesson Model M&P R8. Ryan kept the same model in his personal arsenal and was familiar with it. More firepower than other revolvers with a never-say-die reliability.

Something Ryan might need tonight.

Why hadn't Mia thought to take a gun? Wally had taught her to shoot. Had Pope grabbed her before she could or did she not think of it?

Ryan snatched a box of ammo and loaded the cylinder. He shoved the gun into the holster, locked the safe, then ran outside, and pointed his truck toward the trailer where he would check with Russ before going off half-cocked. He floored the gas, spitting gravel. He eased up a bit and rounded the first curve.

Russ's patrol car raced toward him. He slammed on his brakes, nearly sideswiping Ryan's truck and fishtailing the squad car to a stop.

Ryan stopped and lowered his window.

Russ backed up, and his window came down. "Mia thinks she found Eddie. He's at Nate Tucker's cabin and went to see if she was right. I'm headed there now and will call if I hear anything else."

"Are you kidding me?" Ryan slammed the truck into park and turned off the engine. "I'm coming with you." He shot around the front of his brother's car before he could take off. He jerked open the passenger door and got in.

"This is official business." Russ glared at him across the front seat. "You need to wait here."

Ryan buckled his belt. "Then you'll have to waste time dragging me out. I'm responsible for Eddie, and I'm not moving."

Russ upped the intensity of his gaze, but Ryan fired back a more lethal glare.

"Fine." Russ shifted into gear. "I don't have time to waste arguing, but when we get to the cabin, you stay in the car." He flipped on the lights and siren, and they merged onto the highway, leaving a wailing trail in their wake.

Russ brought the vehicle to top speed, careening around curves, the headlights cutting into the inky dark night. Ryan mounted the gun holster on his belt then held onto the door handle and decided to keep quiet for the ride to let his brother concentrate. They would only argue about what would happen when they got to the cabin anyway. Not that Ryan had a question in his mind about what he would do. He would be out of the car, revolver in hand, before Russ could stop him.

As they approached the intersection nearest to the cabin, Russ flipped off the sirens and strobing lights. "Don't want to alert him that we're coming."

A few miles further down the road, he slowed and navigated the turn, leaning the car so precariously Ryan had to hang on with both hands to keep from sliding into the center console holding Russ's computer and other equipment.

The car righted itself in waves. The radio squawked, begging for Russ's already divided attention. Ryan issued a prayer for safety then listened in to see what he could pick up from the initial law enforcement speak Russ traded with his dispatcher.

"I have a call to patch through the 911 operator from a

Mia Blackburn," the female dispatcher said dispassionately. "She says it's regarding your missing niece."

Ryan sat forward and shared a worried look with Russ.

"Russ, are you there?" Mia's shaky voice came through the radio loud and clear, Ryan's heart creasing at the stress in her tone.

"Go ahead, Mia," Russ said calmly.

"I have Jessie at the cabin with me."

"Is she okay?" Russ shouted as if yelling would make the answer what he wanted to hear.

"She's fine. A little scared, but fine."

Russ fired a quick look at Ryan, their eyes connecting in shared gratitude.

A scuffling noise and arguing voices came over the radio. Russ slowed the car, his hands grasping the wheel tightly.

"Maddox, this is Lincoln Pope. Since you know all about me, I won't bother introducing myself." Pope gave a disembodied laugh.

"He has Mia and Jessie," Ryan whispered and clenched his fist to keep from smashing it into the dashboard. "We need to get there. Like yesterday. Speed up."

Russ made a slashing motion across his throat and pointed at the next driveway on their right. The cabin. It was just ahead. Good. Great even.

"What do you want, Pope?" Russ asked as he maneuvered the vehicle around a squad car sitting in the dark at the mouth of the driveway and turned onto the unpaved drive.

"To get out of here alive, and you're gonna help me do it."

"Not a chance." Russ sent the car down the steep drive, the vehicle bottoming out then bumping over humps and ruts.

"You forget. I have your niece here, and I'm not opposed

to hurting her." Pope paused. "Hold that thought." The phone fell silent.

"What's he up to?" Russ brought the car nearer the house and stopped behind three other vehicles in the driveway.

Ryan scanned the cabin and spotted light seeping through slats in the blinds. "They're in the family room. Someone's looking through the blinds."

"That you in the driveway?" Pope's irritation came over the radio. "'Cause if it is, I suggest you back on out of here if you want to help your niece."

"Let's cut to the chase, Pope," Russ said. "What do you want?"

"Listen up and listen good. I'll only say this once. I want a clear path to my car. Get all your men off the property and make sure there aren't any roadblocks. If I see one person or one roadblock, your pretty little niece is history."

"How do I know you won't hurt her anyway?" Russ asked.

"Guess you'll just have to trust me." Pope laughed again, this one low and ugly. "Call me back when you and your deputies have cleared out. Oh, and Maddox, I'll be watching your car leave so don't try anything funny." The call went dead.

Ryan drew the handgun he'd taken from the lodge. "I'm going in there."

Russ grabbed Ryan's arm. "No way, bro. It's been a while since your deputy days and you're rusty."

"So what do you suggest? That we sit around and wait for Pope to hurt someone else? Maybe kill them this time?" Ryan shook off his brother's hand. "One of us has to go in. You never came to the parties here and don't know your way around. I did. There's a cellar entrance we used sometimes, and I know the interior layout of the cabin. I can get in without Pope knowing."

Russ continued to eye him. "You've never had to shoot a person."

"Then I'll have to man up. It's their only chance. You know as well as I do that Pope will kill them once he doesn't need them anymore. They've got a better chance with me."

"I don't know." Russ ran a hand around the back of his neck. "Pope might see you exit the car."

"Not from this distance if we turn off the dome light. He doesn't know I'm with you. When you drive off, he won't be looking for me." Ryan grabbed Russ's arm. "C'mon, man. I trained for situations like this as a deputy, and now we teach people how to survive a home invasion every week. I know what to do, and I have a vested interest in succeeding."

Russ stared ahead. "You won't take any chances? Put them in more danger?"

He held up his first two fingers. "Scout's honor."

"Don't make me regret doing this." Russ flipped off the dome light. "Now, get going, but be careful."

Ryan slipped silently from the car and duckwalked into the cover of the woods bordering the drive. He held in place, waiting for Russ to depart. The moon cast a bright light over the house but the trees blocked it in the woods. The wind blew softly over his face and moved the bushes and grasses in the undergrowth in gentle waves of greenery.

He listened for any sound coming from inside the cabin.

What would he find in there? Would Pope hurt Mia now that he thought Russ would get him what he wanted?

Please don't make this a repeat of Cara!

His old friend—panic—tried to take his breath. *No. No.* He was capable. He could save them. Had to save them. He could do this. But not alone.

His words to Mia, *trust in the Lord with all your heart and lean not on your own understanding*, reverberated through his brain.

He was something else. Telling Mia to live by these words, but not following them himself.

Russ's car retreated up the drive. Ryan lifted his head.

I don't know why this is happening. Keep Mia and Jessie safe. Help me to trust that You will keep them alive.

Confident now, Ryan eased out of his space. He came to a running crouch and headed for whatever danger he would face in the cabin.

28

Mia slid down the wall next to Jessie at Pope's order. He'd lined the four of them up like sitting ducks against the living room wall, and that's just what she felt like. He stood at the window, his body odor from half-moons of perspiration under his arms fouling the air. He lifted the slats on the window blinds and took a long look. He glanced back at them, his eyes wild and rimmed in red.

He was losing control. Mia had to come up with a plan on how to get these kids out of there safely. But how? She was in over her head. Only an act of God could save them. If Ryan were here, he'd pray. Maybe it was time she tried it too. What could it hurt if she did?

Okay, God. We haven't talked in a long time. Things have been going kind of badly lately, but You know that. I was wondering if You might help me here. I know I don't deserve anything with how I've acted toward You, but Jessie, Eddie, and Nikki need You. Please show us a safe way to escape. And please, please don't let Chuck die.

A loud peal of laughter snapped her eyes open. Pope stared at her, his mouth cracked in a sneer above a nonexistent chin covered with gray whiskers. His glazed eyes held what she thought was the joy of inflicting terror on the innocent. He was going to hurt them for sure and enjoy every second of it.

A car's engine rumbled in the distance. Help?

No. The sound receded. It was Russ leaving just as Pope had commanded.

The lunatic had won.

He whipped his face toward the window. "That's better. The sheriff has turned tail and run." He cackled as he crossed the room and sat facing them in an easy chair, his handgun on his knee. "Thanks for leading me here, Mia. Looks like things might work out just fine. I knew if I watched you, you'd bring me straight to little Jessie."

His sickly fond tone when he said Jessie's name crept along Mia's nerves and rage blossomed in her chest. Rage at a level she'd never known. It urged her to move. To lunge for his throat. It ate at her whole being.

She couldn't take action. Not now. Not with the gun on his lap. That would be foolhardy.

She planted her feet hard on the floor. She had to keep calm. Play his game. Find a way to manipulate him exactly as he thought he was doing to her. She could get him talking about what he'd done, and he'd get cocky. Relax. Give her an opening.

She swallowed her anger. Put on a neutral face. "Why are you doing this, Pope?"

He arched an eyebrow sending wrinkles over his shaved scalp. "Thought a smart girl like you would have it all figured out by now."

"You're too good, I guess." She lightened her tone to keep him talking. "I owe you big time for that smash on my head when you plowed into me while I was holding the camera."

He smirked. "You thought you were so smart. Didn't

count on me outwitting you, did ya? All I had to do was close my eyes like you were doing."

His confidence sent a flare of anger blazing inside her. She wanted to leap across the room and claw at his smug smile.

Count to ten. Blow off his snide comments. Refocus.

"Why did you lock up the barn and then come back to take the locks?"

"Loomis had me lock it after I set the fire. He didn't want anyone to wander in and get killed in the fire or the fire department to get inside before the body burned up. But I didn't want the fire department to know about the locks or they might think the fire wasn't an accident."

Mia didn't point out that they would've known it was arson, but she supposed a small town fire department might not have dug deeper. "So you were in the clear, but why didn't you just take off when you had a chance?"

His narrowed eyes turned mean. "That's for me to know and you to find out. We'll have lots of time for talking since you'll be driving me out of here."

He thought this would scare her, but she'd willingly go with him to protect Jessie and the others, maybe get a chance to free them.

"So tell me," she said. "How'd you hear about Jessie in the first place?"

He grinned wide, revealing a missing tooth on the right side. "Not that you'll make it out of this alive, but if you did, I'd suggest upping the security on your wireless network. I hacked into your email to the good sheriff."

Oh, no! She'd brought this on them. If she hadn't emailed Russ, Pope would never have known Jessie identified him or even where the camera would be. Still, there was nothing Mia could do about it now. She just had to keep trying things until God provided the help she'd asked for.

Surprisingly, she believed He would come through for them. Maybe not her, but for the others.

She took a quick breath and tried not to let Pope see how upset she was over his news. "You didn't say exactly what will happen now?"

He scrubbed his hand over tired eyes. "Shut up. I've got some thinking to do."

Mia leaned back. She wouldn't push it. If there was any good news in all of this, it was that Pope didn't appear to be mentally impaired in any way. Mean, ornery, and a murderer, but not impaired. She could work with that. Someone who'd gone over the edge was another story.

Time ticked by. Slowly. Maybe fast. She didn't know, but it felt like an eternity as they sat silently and awaited their fate. How must sweet little Jessie be feeling?

Mia leaned forward and tried to get the child's attention to give her a thumbs-up, but her head was hanging as she sobbed quietly.

Grr. This man would pay for what he'd done to her.

Mia shifted her focus to Eddie to take a visual measurement of how he was coping and if he was going to try to be a hero. His arm was slung around Nikki, who trembled and nibbled on her lip. Mia motioned with her hands to stay calm and keep his anger in check.

He gave a nod of acknowledgment.

Good. He didn't seem like a loose cannon.

Mia's phone rang. She looked at the caller ID. "It's the sheriff."

Pope stood up and crossed the window and cracked the blinds. "Answer it."

"Russ."

"Is Pope listening?" Russ's voice was low and urgent.

"No."

"Ryan entered the house through the cellar. He should

be nearby. He has a gun. Stay as far away from Pope as possible. Now tell him we've done as he asked, and the road is clear."

"Okay, let me tell him." Mia looked at Pope. "The sheriff has left, and the road is clear. We can go now."

"Tell him I have my gun in the kid's neck. Anyone takes a shot at me, she gets it. And tell him you're driving." Pope's face took on a hard determination.

He wasn't impaired, but he was still a killer.

She relayed the message to Russ, though he'd likely heard Pope say it.

"End the call and give me the phone," Pope demanded.

She did and handed it over.

He tossed the device to the wood floor and stomped on it, then ground the heel of his boot on the screen until it shattered. Her phone lay in pieces.

He went back to the window. "Okay, people. On your feet."

With Pope distracted, Mia quickly signaled with her hand for the others to stay put and jumped up. "How about leaving the others here and just taking me?"

Pope spun around. "The brat is my insurance policy. Nobody likes it when a kid gets killed."

Jessie's cries grew louder.

Mia faced Jessie. "Don't worry, honey. He's not going to hurt you."

"Says you." Pope snorted and waved his gun at Jessie then locked his stance on her. "You'll be okay, kid, if everyone does exactly what I tell them."

Mia had wanted to comfort the child and failed, but Nikki took Jessie into her arms and stroked her hair. Jessie's heart-wrenching sobs subsided a fraction.

Mia scanned the room for a way to stop their captor. Ryan was nowhere in sight. She couldn't let Pope get them in a car. She had to act now. It was up to her to disarm the man.

"I said for you all to get up." Pope waved the gun over the group, ending with it pointed above them.

Mia seized the moment. She launched into Pope, chopping up with her arms locked together to force his gun free.

He held tight and tumbled backward. His free hand caught her hair. Jerked her down on top of him.

The gun discharged.

The bullet pierced the ceiling. Showered debris down on Mia. She flung her arm out. Knocked the gun from Pope's hand. The weapon slid across the floor above his head. She broke free and lunged for it. Her fingers touched the handle.

Pope clamped a hand on her leg and jerked her backward.

She stabbed a toe into the wood and held her ground. She reached harder. Slapped her hand at the gun to send it skittering across the floor into the corner. Out of reach.

Pope growled and pulled hard, flipping her over. He rose up, glaring at her with fiery eyes. Veins in his neck surged to the surface, flushing his face to a raging red.

Hoping to poke him in the eye, she shot out a hand.

Pope leaned on an elbow and clamped his other hand on her arm.

Everything moved so fast. Seconds, really, and he'd taken control again.

"Get off, Pope!" Ryan yelled from above. "Or so help me, I'll empty this gun on you."

Pope's eyes narrowed. He rolled to the side, releasing Mia and blinking up at Ryan.

Breathing deeply, Mia peered at Ryan too. His eyes burned with the same revulsion that coursed through her veins.

But under it all, she found thankfulness and gratitude

burning bright. Ryan had saved the day. They were safe. Thanks to him. To God. Her anger dissolved so rapidly she could hardly believe the rapid change.

She'd asked God to help them. He had. Sent His hands in the flesh. Right beside her. The rescuer she'd asked for. Not just any rescuer, but Ryan. The man who could help her let go of all the anger and hurt from past betrayals. The man who could walk beside her and lead her in a God-filled life.

If only she would give in and let him. Let God. And she would. Starting now. Trusting Him with her life. With her problems and her fears. Let Him take charge and give her the peace she'd sought for ten long years.

"We need to call Russ and get him down here," Ryan said.

"He smashed my phone, but I can use yours."

Not taking his eyes from Pope, he dug it from his cargo pocket and handed it to her. She found Russ's icon and tapped it.

"Ryan has Pope under guard. You can come down here."

"Hang tight. I'm on my way." Russ ended the call.

"He's on his way." She gave Ryan a big smile then looked at the others. "Everything is over, and we're all safe."

Nikki still held Jessie, her hand over her ear to keep her from hearing anything. Nikki exhaled deeply, and Jessie pushed free to run to Mia. The child flung herself into Mia's arms, and she clutched her tight.

"Ouch," Jessie said. "You don't have to squish me so hard."

"Sorry." Mia loosened her arms. "I'm just so glad you're all right."

Mia's heart swelled. This resilient child would be okay.

So would Mia. *If* she trusted and let God and Ryan into her life.

Ryan nodded at his brother as he barreled into the room with a deputy. Cuffs in hand, the deputy took charge of Pope and dragged the scowling man through the door. Ryan wanted to shout a hallelujah that the killer was on his way to jail, but there were other issues to handle here first.

Russ turned to look at Nikki and Eddie. "We called your sister, Nikki. She's on her way to pick you up. Eddie, I need you to come with me."

Mia looked at Russ from the spot near the wall where she'd dropped after the altercation. "I'd like to be with him when you question him."

Russ shook his head. "Sorry. No can do, but I *will* have a social services rep present."

"He didn't do anything wrong." Mia lifted her chin and relayed that Eddie had played a big part in saving Jessie.

"We'll expect him back at Wilderness Ways after your questioning." Ryan planted his feet to let his big brother know he meant business.

"That will be up to social services, but if what Mia says is true, I can't see why they wouldn't allow it." Russ helped a reluctant Eddie to his feet.

"Especially now that Pope's in custody, and the danger is eliminated," Mia added. "And he saved your niece from that creep, so you should do everything you can to make sure he's not in any trouble."

"I'll do my best." Russ locked gazes. "But at this point, it's Eddie's word against Pope's on the murder. If Pope confesses, we can resolve it right away. If not, the kid will likely have to stay in custody until Sierra finishes processing forensics. Of course, we'll now have Pope's prints and can compare them to the ones she's already lifted."

Mia came to her feet. "Don't worry, Eddie. I'll make sure you're released as soon as possible. You can count on me."

"I'll be right beside her," Ryan said.

Eddie cocked his head, studying them like a high school biology experiment. "I actually believe both of you."

A big, huge leap in Eddie's progress, and Mia's face blossomed. Maybe she was seeing that God had made good from a bad situation. Just as Ryan told her. If only Russ could find a way to get the teen back to the program as soon as possible, Ryan had hopes that they could turn this kid's life around for good.

Eddie looked at Nikki. "I hope you don't get into too much trouble."

"Are you kidding?" Nikki said, tears in her eyes. "My sister's a real softie."

Ryan thought she was being overly optimistic, but she could simply be trying to make Eddie feel better. "Any word on Chuck?"

"He's in surgery to relieve swelling on his brain. It's still touch and go."

Mia cringed and clapped a hand over her mouth.

"Keep us updated, okay?"

"Of course." Russ took Eddie's elbow. "Come on, kid, let's get you out of here."

Jessie bolted across the room and hugged the young man's waist. "I'll come see you as soon as you're back."

Eddie gave her a fond look. "Thanks, kid."

"We have to go now, squirt." Russ waited for Jessie to let go then led Eddie out the door.

"We'll both be glad when Eddie is back." Nikki knelt and took Jessie into her arms.

"Thanks for your help, Nikki," Ryan said, "Mind taking Jessie out on the porch to wait for her dad?"

"Will do." She took Jessie's hand and led her outside.

Ryan remained in place, taking in the cool air that had followed Russ inside. God had come through for all of them. Big time. Saving lives and detaining Pope. But Ryan received a bonus. Freedom from his fear.

The pain of losing Cara would forever be with him. There was no way it could ever be erased from his life without erasing her, and he would never do that. But tonight told him to put aside his fear of losing someone else. Trust God again to control his life—to allow whatever was good for him.

Right now, he was sure that was Mia, and despite this traumatic situation, he had to tell her he was letting his fear go and wanted to pursue a relationship again.

He crossed the room to her. Their eyes met. Held. He opened his mouth to speak, but she launched herself into his arms.

"I prayed for God to send help," she whispered through fresh tears. "And He sent you. My miracle. I want to trust Him with my life again. Just like I did as a kid, but I'll need help. Your help."

Ryan loosened his hold and searched her face. A radiant glow beamed back at him. A glow of contentment he'd never seen before but was certain came from letting go of her life and fully trusting God. That peace knew no bounds.

He didn't want to scare her, so he smiled, keeping it lighthearted. "You think I'm a miracle, huh?"

"I do. If it wasn't for you, I wouldn't have even thought to pray." She touched the side of his cheek.

He willed his mind from her gentle touch. "I have a confession to make. I haven't been as trusting as I should've been."

An encouraging smile followed, urging him to go on while she softly traced his jaw, driving him mad.

He captured her hand and held it tight to his chest. "You

mean a lot to me. I was afraid to admit it and then lose you like I lost Cara. Tonight I came to grips with that."

She wove her fingers with his and rested her head against his chest.

Why wasn't she saying anything? Had he jumped the gun and scared her by his admission? Or worse yet, misread the signs that she might be feeling the same way?

He had to find out. "This is right. Like we've never been apart. We're good together."

"You think so?" She leaned back, a playful grin on her face. "Even when I try to take over and do things my way?"

"Even then." He tweaked her nose. "But as you learn to trust God more that'll change."

"Trying to change me already, are you?" She jabbed him with a playful punch.

"Me?" He chuckled. "Seriously, no. You're the perfect woman for me. Always have been. Always will be." He clamped his arms around her. "*This* is perfect."

A contented sigh slipped from her lips as she snuggled closer. Perfect?

Almost. She hadn't actually admitted how she felt about him.

So what? Her body language told him everything he needed to know for now. He had plenty of time to convince her they belonged together. She wasn't going anywhere for the next year. He was a very persuasive man when he set his mind to it, and his mind was set on making her his wife.

29

A week later, Mia stood next to Ryan for the worship service's closing song. The service was so different from the ones she attended growing up. When her mom was alive, church had held a place of significance in their lives. When she died, Mia's dad went through the motions of raising them in the church, but she saw the emptiness of his plan and that's when her rebellion against her faith set in.

The song ended. More hope for the future than she'd experienced since her mom died rained down on her. Incorporating her newfound faith in her everyday life for just a few days had given her this peace. Would give her this peace on a regular basis. As long as she embraced it and didn't revert back to her natural tendencies to run from and ignore her problems. Or to always insist on being in control of every little thing.

And on top of that, God heard their prayers for Chuck, and he would fully recover.

Ryan turned to her, a timid look on his face. "So how was it?"

She smiled with joy. "Wonderful. Not anything like I

expected. Who knew church had changed so much since I was a kid?"

"Glad to hear you liked it." Ryan squeezed her hand.

Mia spotted Verna exiting the worship center. Mia had talked to Verna only once since Pope's arrest when she'd asked Verna to stay on as Evergreen's manager, but Verna hadn't yet responded.

She hesitantly approached Mia. "You sure you want me working at Evergreen after thinking I did all those things?"

The heat of a blush crept over Mia's face. "I'm sorry about that. I really am. You were so testy and seemed like you were trying to hide something. I didn't know what to make of it."

Verna planted her hands on her hips. "Can't a body be worried about keeping her job? I figured you would take over and send an old lady like me packing, and then how was I going to support my daughter."

"Why would I do that? I wouldn't know how to run the place without you."

Verna sniffed, but a tight smile slipped out. "That's fine, then. I'll see you first thing in the morning."

"And we can talk about finding the money to build Nico his cabin."

"Now that's downright good of you." Verna squeezed Mia's arm and then departed.

"C'mon." Ryan clasped her hand. "There's something I want you to see."

He led her to the door near the kitchen. He pushed it open. She stepped in, and a loud chorus of voices shouted, "Surprise."

Mia took a step back, inhaling the aroma of bacon, onions, and tangy spices. She took the time to look at the festive tablecloth, balloons, and flowers covering a long table where church members sat looking expectantly at her. The décor was loud and boisterous, colors clashing, and shouting that Gladys's flamboyant style was behind it all.

"Relax," Ryan whispered near her ear. "I know you don't like public demonstrations, but this is different. These people all love you and want to let you know how proud they are of what you did to save Jessie and take a murderer off their streets. They're our friends."

Memories of being publicly grilled for her poor decisions in high school rushed to the surface. The urge to flee as she had in the past clung to her like fabric sheets in the laundry.

Ryan squeezed her shoulder. "Think of this as a start to building a life here."

She offered a prayer. She could do this. With Ryan or without. God was here. Among His people. And she was strong. She would be the person God wanted her to be.

She put on a smile.

Gladys rushed forward. "About time you got here."

She entwined her arm in Mia's and ushered her to a chair at the end of the table.

Gladys lifted a glass of sparkling cider to the group. "To Mia. Thank you for returning our community to the calm place we know and love. And of course, for taking care of our little Jessie and Nikki."

Glasses raised all around to calls of, "To Mia."

Gone were the frowns of disapproval from her teen years to be replaced by thankfulness and gratitude.

Acceptance.

She could now walk down Main Street without dreading it. She could greet her neighbors and make a life for herself here. A real life with relationships and neighbors helping neighbors. A deep solid life with God at the center.

She searched the tables for two familiar faces. No. No. Her dad and David hadn't come.

The old pain rose up and tried to swamp her.

"Now, let's eat." Gladys clapped her hands. As if she were conducting an orchestra, the others started passing dishes. The potluck offerings were scooped onto plates until they were heaped full.

Mia wiped moist palms on her knees, dug into a hash brown breakfast casserole, and caught a smile from Jessie. The little girl wore a pink party dress and sat at the far end of the table with Reid and Russ flanking her. Sydney, Nikki, and Eddie took up the seats on one side, Sydney watching the pair as if uncertain about them sitting together.

Mia connected gazes with Eddie. He gave her a thumbs-up. She smiled at him, and he returned it with a beaming smile she'd not seen before. *Oh, man.* What a rush of emotions. The good feeling from helping to change a life erased the last of her unease, and she fully relaxed to gobble down the spectacular food.

Ryan was right. These were her friends now. Well, maybe Eddie wasn't a friend as he was a client, but they'd formed a special bond. He was far from a docile teen, but after forensics pointed to Pope, he confessed, and Eddie was released. He'd opened up and was working to change.

Just like she was.

Mia leaned closer to Ryan and tipped her head at Eddie. "We did good with that one."

"We did, didn't we?" He winked at her. "And this is just the beginning. There'll be a lot more success stories in the year to come." He met and held her gaze. "And longer if I have my way."

Her heart rate kicked up. She loved this man. She hadn't admitted that to him, but she would soon find the courage to tell him he was the perfect man for her. He'd proven she could trust him.

Not only that, but his compassion and skills as a counselor translated into his relationships. He didn't let her get away with hiding from things she feared. And his smile, the one causing her stomach to flip-flop right now, was oh so sweet. She tuned everyone else out and returned a smile that she hoped conveyed her heart's desire.

"Mia." Gladys tugged on her arm and bent down to whisper, "I think it's time you went somewhere private and told him how you feel."

Instead of irritating Mia, Gladys had read her mind. Eyes locked on a flushed Ryan, Mia hastily made their excuses, and they ran to his truck together. Not wanting to talk and break the mood, Mia clutched his hand for the ride to the lodge.

As they approached the building, her heart fell. "Someone's here."

Ryan pulled the truck to a stop next to a large black SUV and turned to face her. His adoring eyes locked with hers. "I didn't want to tell you about this surprise earlier because I thought it would keep you from enjoying the party."

What in the world did he have planned?

"That sounds ominous," she said, staring at the vehicle.

He laughed. "Not at all. When I heard your dad and David turned down the invitation to come to the party, I went to see them."

"But you had—"

He held up his hand. "Wait before you say anything else. You know I want you to be happy living here. I don't think you could ever really settle down here unless you reconciled with your family. So I talked to them. They didn't come to the party because they wanted to meet with you in private."

She looked through the window and contemplated an escape. What if she went inside and they turned away from her again? What if nothing had changed? For the second time that afternoon, she wanted to run. But what good would that do?

Her throat dry, she swallowed hard and opened her door. "Will you go in with me?"

"You know I will." He got out and escorted her up the steps and to the large porch.

She prayed for strength until she stepped across the threshold and stopped. Perched on the long mantel was a large portrait of her mother that used to hang above their fireplace at home. As if in a dream, Mia entered the family room and searched the space, taking in her mother's special items scattered throughout the room.

David stepped forward. "We thought you'd like to have these things from Wally's storage unit."

Tears threatened. "Thank you."

"Mia." Her father crossed the room and stood in front of her. He clutched his hands together. "I was wrong to try to erase the memory of your mother. The pain of her loss was," his voice caught, "*is* still almost too much to bear. I pushed you away when I should have reached out. Can you forgive me and give me another chance?"

Wow. The moment she'd waited years for had come. What did she do? She stared into the warm, loving eyes of a father whose gaze had only registered coldness for sixteen years. Sixteen long years of pain.

She couldn't fall into his arms as if nothing happened. No way. But her renewed faith allowed her to forgive him and give him another chance. "You're forgiven, and I'd like it if we got to know each other."

His shoulders sagged, and he held out his hand. "How about we start by looking at your mom's things together?"

Mia accepted her father's hand. David joined them at the counter where her mother's jewelry box sat open. Treasures Mia had played with as a child lay in the blue velvet-lined box, and her heart creased at the pain of loss.

She picked up the first item and fingered it. "Her pearls. She let me wear them for dress up."

"She inherited them from her mother. They were her favorite thing to wear." Her dad took the strand from her hand and put them around her neck. "She wore them for every special occasion, and this is a very special occasion."

She looked up at him. At his happiness. Felt it in her heart, with just a hint of reserve lingering.

Help me let the last of my pain go.

"I'm sorry, Mia," David said. "I had no idea what Kurt was doing. That he would go to such an extreme is just shocking. If I'd known, I sure wouldn't have given him charge of Evergreen's finances."

"It's not your fault." She waved a hand. "Money makes people do crazy things."

"But murder?" David shook his head. "Here in our little town. And to think I was partners with the guy who facilitated it. Crazy. Just plain crazy."

She agreed but didn't want to ever think of it again. "Let's put all of that behind us and start fresh from now on."

"Sounds like a plan," Ryan said. "But if you need help, be sure to find a counselor."

"I will. Trust me." David shuddered.

"Counseling helped me for sure," her dad said. "I'm only sorry I was too proud to get help sooner."

Oh, wow! Her dad had gone to counseling. Not anything she would ever expect from him.

"I know today has been an emotional one so we'll leave you alone to enjoy your mom's things," her father said.

"But we want to have dinner with you tonight." David

shoved his hands into his pockets. "At my place. Can you come?"

"Yes," she said without reservation.

"Good," David smiled. "Because we already invited Ryan and his family, and they all said they would come if you did."

Ryan took Mia's hand. "Just try to stop us."

David laughed. "We'll eat at six, but please come earlier. The weather is great today, and we're going to grill."

Her dad smiled at her. "I'm making burgers just the way you once liked them."

Her hope for a nice night grew inside, but she tamped it down. She may have given God charge of her life, but she would still take things one at a time and be cautiously optimistic.

"Just one thing before you go," Mia said. "Why have you been buying land? Like the property next door?"

Her dad arched a brow. "Nothing more than an investment."

"Real estate is always a solid investment," David added. "We bought in a down market, and will be selling some of the properties soon."

"If that includes the lot next door, our family might be interested," Ryan said. "Our business is really taking off, and we could use more space."

"Call me and we can talk," David said.

With a promise to see her tonight, her father and David left.

Fingers on the pearls, she collapsed on the sofa and stared up at her mother's portrait. How she missed her and was so very glad to be able to see her face again. "This has been a very good day."

"I agree." Ryan sat next to her and circled his arm around her shoulders.

She slid closer settling into the curve and lay her head on his chest.

"Even better now," she whispered.

She reveled in the warmth of their connection and the beating of his heart, strong and solid beneath her ear. He loved her. At least she thought he did.

He'd intimated after he'd come to the rescue with Pope that he loved her and wanted to spend the rest of his life with her. Problem was, he hadn't said another word since then. He hadn't officially declared his love. Or asked her to stay in Shadow Lake. Or even tried to hold her or kiss her.

Looking up at him, she relived the days since she'd been back in Shadow Lake. His strong arms as he carried her from the fire, the concern in his voice each time he tried to warn her to be careful, and his joyful face when she revealed her renewed faith. And now, his captivating blue eyes telegraphing a message she hoped was love.

But maybe he didn't love her.

Maybe he regretted what he'd said at the cabin. When people survived an intense incident, they often said things they didn't mean in the heat of the moment. Her counseling experience and training told her that.

Maybe Ryan had simply felt relief that he could save her life, and in that moment, he'd confused his feelings with love. Or maybe he was waiting for her to go first. To tell him how she felt.

Could she do it?

Could she let down every single wall she'd erected for years and say those three words that were so foreign to her? *I love you.* Was that so hard? Because she did love him. More than she ever could have imagined she would love a man.

What should she do? She sighed.

"What?" he asked. "What's wrong?"

Here was her opening.

He fixed a tender gaze on her face. Warmth radiated to her very soul. She opened her mouth to speak. The words didn't come.

"You look terrified of something," he said.

"I am."

His eyebrows drew together, and he leaned back. "Is it about your father?"

She shook her head.

He loosened his hold on her and took her hands. "About us? Together, like this?"

"Yes," she whispered and waited for him to acknowledge his mistake in admitting he cared for her.

"This isn't something to be afraid of. It's something to celebrate." He caressed her cheek. "After you left, I didn't think I'd find you again. Ten years since we saw each other and it feels like we've never been apart."

Ten years. Such a long time to spend searching for what she'd already had.

"We wasted so much time," she said.

"Don't think that way. God used that time to mold us into the people we are today. We both needed to grow up to recognize what we have together is special." He cupped her face and held her in a trance. "I love you, Mia. More than I can say."

Tears wet her lashes, and her heart exploded with joy. She should say it back, but before she could respond, he withdrew his hands and crossed the room.

What?

He lifted his jacket from the back of a chair.

"Wait!" She jumped up and raced toward him. "Don't go, Ryan. I love you too. Please don't leave."

"I'm not leaving." He dug into his jacket. "I've been trying to be patient for the past few days and not scare you off, but I can't wait anymore." He pulled out a blue velvet box and knelt in front of her. "I love you, Mia, and I don't want you to leave Shadow Lake again. Will you stay and be my wife?"

"Is this for real?" Her face burned, and she waved her hand to cool her skin.

He opened the box and held it out. "You didn't answer."

Emotions overwhelmed her, closing her throat and she couldn't get any words out. She dropped to the floor next to him and drew his head close to kiss him. The kiss would answer his question.

His lips were warm and insistent. He slid his hand into her hair, cupping her head to pull her closer and deepen the kiss. She gave in, her heart thumping wildly in her chest. Feeling like it might stop, but she'd never felt more alive.

The ring box dropped to the floor, and he circled her body with his strong arms, holding her as if his life depended on it. She threw her arms around his neck. Held on. Returned the kiss ounce for ounce. Let the feelings swamp her.

He finally reached up for her arms and pulled back. He retrieved the ring and held it out again. "That felt like yes, but I need to hear the word."

"Yes. Yes. Yes." She stopped at three, but the way his eyes met hers in a loving caress, she wanted to shout the word a thousand times.

He slid the ring onto her finger, the cool metal brushing her skin as the solitaire diamond in white gold setting slid into place. The past ten years of heartache slipped from her mind.

Never had she felt more at home, more at peace. She'd risked everything in coming back to Evergreen to inherit the place. But instead of a place, she'd inherited a family who would see her through good times and bad. Found her faith again. And Ryan had proven he'd always be there for her.

No matter what the future brought, they would face it together.

NIGHTHAWK SECURITY SERIES
Protecting others when unspeakable danger lurks.

A woman being stalked. A mother and child being hunted. And more. All in danger. Needing protection from the men of Nighthawk Security.

Book 1 – Night Fall
Book 2 – Night Vision
Book 3 – Night Hawk
Book 4 – Night Moves
Book 5 – Night Watch
Book 6 – Night Prey

For More Details Visit -
www.susansleeman.com/books/nighthawk-security/

THE TRUTH SEEKERS

People are rarely who they seem

A twin who didn't know she had a sister. A mother whose child isn't her own. A woman whose parents lied to her. All needing help from The Truth Seekers forensic team.

Book 1 - Dead Ringer
Book 2 - Dead Silence
Book 3 - Dead End
Book 4 - Dead Heat
Book 5 - Dead Center
Book 6 - Dead Even

For More Details Visit -
www.susansleeman.com/books/truth-seekers/

The COLD HARBOR SERIES

Meet Blackwell Tactical- former military and law enforcement heroes who will give everything to protect innocents... even their own lives.

Book 1 - Cold Terror
Book 2 - Cold Truth
Book 3 - Cold Fury
Book 4 - Cold Case
Book 5 - Cold Fear
Book 6 - Cold Pursuit
Book 7 - Cold Dawn

For More Details Visit -
www.susansleeman.com/books/cold-harbor/

ABOUT SUSAN

SUSAN SLEEMAN is a bestselling and award-winning author of more than 50 inspirational/Christian and clean read romantic suspense books. In addition to writing, Susan also hosts the website, TheSuspenseZone.com.

Susan currently lives in Oregon, but has had the pleasure of living in nine states. Her husband is a retired church music director and they have two beautiful daughters, two very special sons-in-law, and three amazing grandsons.

For more information visit:
www.susansleeman.com

Made in United States
Orlando, FL
07 September 2023

36797907R00193